Also by Rob Edwards

Holiday Novellas:
The Friendship Effect - A Thanksgiving Novella
Seven Tails of Christmas - A Christmas Novella
Life at 24 Frames Per Second - A New Year's Novella

Threads of Life:
Prisons - A Novel

I Do or
I Don't

A Novel

Threads of Life: Book Two

Rob Edwards

For Morgan and Amanda,
my daughter and bonus daughter.
And for Dayna Marie.

The front page article from "The Hollywood Ledger - The Top Source for Entertainment Industry News!"

The Queen Bs! Television's Hot New Dynamic Duo!!

By Graham Lacey

The way things have shaped up so far, this fall season has been a surprise to many. Shows that were a slam-dunk didn't see their fair share of the ratings. And shows that were considered get-bys until the more popular mid-season replacements came along, seem to have grown legs.

But no show has been more surprising than *I Do or I Don't*, the reality-based dating show that takes couples on a whirlwind dating/engagement scenario that ends at the altar. That's where the two must make the decision that will shape the rest of their lives, no less, in front of a live studio audience, and (by the way) the largest home-viewing audience of any show on any channel! Talk about cold feet!

I Do or I Don't has become a ratings leviathan, averaging nearly 4.2 each week. No other show comes close to numbers like that, aside from football, of course.

The bright, shiny face of the show is the former darling of the Global Info Network, Brooke Winthrop. Her platinum locks and million-dollar smile greet the couples each week, and she guides them through the wild world of speed courting, hoping for a happily-ever-after. But in all honesty, aren't we all truly watching for the disaster?

When asked about her jump from the world of news to reality television, and why her new show is such a hit, she gave an incredibly "Brook-ish" answer.

"I think people get tired of the constant negativity that the news tends to feed them. I find it sad that if it isn't someone killing each other or stabbing someone in the back, then it isn't news worth talking about. I think people are ready to watch more than suffering and anger day after day. They want to truly believe there is love and happiness in the world. So, our show offers them hope. And I'm happy to be a part of something that's healing."

The other half of this super team is the show's producer, Becca Dodge, daughter of the late television exec., William "Billy" Dodge, who committed suicide when Becca was just a teen. Becca is the sharp-tongued, steely-eyed side of the team. She is all business and has astutely made all the right decisions and deals, from getting the best studio to produce the show, right down to snagging the best time slot—Tuesday nights at nine. When asked about their overnight success, Becca laughed out loud.

"Nothing is an overnight success in this business. Brooke and I have been working on this concept for years, honing it, finding the right people to be involved, and making all the right deals to see it succeed. The success of the show is a testimony to all the hours of sweat we put into the pre-production process."

Together these two women, affectionately dubbed "The Queen Bs," seem to have become an unstoppable force in Hollywood. It's exciting for this writer to see where they take us next, but until then, I'll remain one of the millions of faithful glued to my TV Tuesday nights to see if the couples say, *I Do or I Don't.*"

Chapter One

"Two minutes!" said the floor director, shooting two fingers in the air.

The "Stand By" sign glowed bright white over the stage. The audience in the studio, chattering loudly just seconds ago, was now quiet and still, excited for the chance to watch a popular nationally televised show live.

Brooke Winthrop sat in her chair, her last name emblazoned in bright white capital letters across the back. Her hair and make-up person, Fiona, was at work on her platinum blond locks, intent on smoothing all the fly-aways. Armed with a can of hairspray in her left hand, and the fingers of her right, she followed an endless routine of spraying and patting at Brooke's head, never seemingly satisfied.

"Okay, Fee," Brooke said. "I've got to get on stage."

Fiona did what she always did when Brooke said that was enough. "Okay, just one more pop," she said in her British accent. Then she would spray, pat, and step back. "Perfect."

Standing, Brooke smiled at her assistant. Fiona was one of those anomalous individuals. She had bright-red hair that she kept in a long ponytail down her back. With both nostrils pierced, two piercings on her lower lip, and tattoos up both arms and down both legs, Fiona looked street tough. When she opened

9

her mouth, you expected to hear a thick Jersey accent. Instead, something musical came out sounding like a proper Briton. And her demeanor was not that of a hardened street urchin, but of a kind, caring, mothering type. Brooke had never met Fee outside of the studio, but in the short time they had been together, a tight bond had developed between them.

"Break a leg...gently," Fee said.

Brooke walked calmly to her predetermined spot on the floor. Though she was about to go live on one of the top-rated shows on television, she was calm, composed, and in control. In all her years in broadcasting, this was by far the biggest gig she'd had, but it was also the easiest. The previous eight years were spent as a reporter for Global Information Network, a.k.a. GInfo, the twenty-four-hour news station with offices and studios around the world.

"Stand by in the studio!" floor director Randal shouted to an absolutely quiet studio. "Oh, sorry," he said more quietly and reached up and moved his headset microphone away from his mouth.

Brooke's GInfo years were exciting but tough. She recalled the hurricane in South Carolina where, while on camera in the storm, she lost her footing and was literally blown over and tumbled down a muddy street. Of course, the cameraman did his job dutifully and followed her squirming and sloshing around. When she finally managed to get up and out of the wind, she looked like she had just stepped out of a mud-wrestling ring. That one was hard to forget because it went viral on YouTube. And since she'd reached a new level of fame on this show, it was once again making the rounds.

There was also the clash in Richmond, Virginia between a large group of "Black Lives Matter" protesters and a gang of skinheads. That was scary because it grew violent quickly. Within minutes of both sides arriving, fists began to swing and the police, expecting trouble, gassed the area immediately and without warning. Brooke and her crew ran from the mess, choking, gasping, and trying not to get crushed in the exodus. She ended up bruised and cut, needing four stitches on her left calf.

"Okay Brooke, we're going in...," Randal said, sticking his

right hand back in the air and splaying his fingers. He brought a finger down with each number. "Five...four...three..." The last two fingers were brought down silently. The bright red "on-air" sign gleamed brightly and the audio speakers blared the intro, "Tonight on, *I Do or I Don't*." Several tease shots were seen on the monitors in the studio, the same time they were broadcast to the rest of the nation.

While the intro played, Brooke looked out across the people in the seats, eyes staring up at the screens above them. Even though her audience tonight was ten times larger than anything she'd ever had in news, nobody was going to gas her on the set. Brooke made a last-minute inspection of her black, cold-shoulder top, making sure no bright specs were shining under the studio lights. She glanced over quickly at her production partner and producer, Rebecca "Becca" Dodge, who just walked in. Becca smiled at her and pumped a fist.

The intro finished and the "Applause" light blinked in the studio. Randall ran to the edge of the audience clapping over his head. The audience followed along and clapped, happy to do their part. Sammy, the camera-girl on the large jib, swung into action. The arm extended out and slowly swung over the audience's heads. The lens locked in on Brooke and smoothly maneuvered in her direction. Randal spun around and pointed at Brooke, cueing her.

Brooke's smile shined brighter than the lights, and she introduced the show.

"Hello, America, and welcome to *I Do or I Don't*, the show where we help loving couples find their happily-ever-after. We have one such couple ready to step up to the alter today and we'll find out at the end of the show if they will look each other in the eye and say either 'I do,' or 'I don't.'"

Brooke turned to Camera 3 at that point, knowing that it was framed up to show the floor-to-ceiling video wall behind her in the back of the studio. On the screen was a graphic with the words, "Selection Stress," framed over her left shoulder.

Brooke looked into the teleprompter and read the scrolling words.

"For those of you who've seen the show before, you know that probably the most stressful part of the process is selecting that special someone. After answering the grueling questionnaire required to be a part of the show, experts, backed up by computer AI, pick ten individuals for each person whom they find is best suited for them. It is then the responsibility of each person to pick out their potential husband or wife from those ten. Of the hundreds who enter this selection process, the only ones who make it onto the show are those fortunate few who have selected each other. Let's take a look at the process in action."

The screens above the audience changed from the studio shots to a pre-produced video piece.

"Clear!" Randal shouted, and the lights in the studio dimmed.

The video featured shots of the contestants in cushy rooms, pouring over pages of questionnaires and video files. The audience was also privy to see many of the supplied photo album pictures and a few of the submitted video introductions. Interviews with the contestants clued the viewers into their mindset as they're going through the process. In the end, the fun of the segment was whether the contestant chose the same person for themselves that the audience chose. Also, did their chosen one select him or her as well?

While the video rolled, Brooke walked over to Becca who was smiling from ear-to-ear. "Hey there fellow queen," Becca said.

She pulled out a copy of the Hollywood Ledger and let it unfold in front of her. On the front page, the headline read, "The Queen Bs! Meet Television's Hot New Dynamic Duo!!" Under that were pictures of Brooke and Becca, with the words, "Brooke Winthrop and Becca Dodge, A.K.A. the Queen Bs"

Brooke took the paper from her and stared at it disbelievingly. This is the moment she had only dreamed of as a girl growing up in Pennsylvania. She'd always wanted to be in front of the camera in some capacity, but her family always made fun of her. They would laugh when she pranced around, acting as if she were presenting something important.

"Turn the next letter, Vanna," became her dad's favorite saying, and everybody would laugh.

Brooke had always wanted to be well known, but it had to be for something worthwhile. Though she'd been homecoming queen in high school, and then Walkerville's Harvest Festival Queen, Brooke did not want to be known as the pretty girl. She wanted to be the smart girl. The girl who made a difference. And now, plastered across the front page of the Hollywood Reporter, Brooke had realized her dream. She was a Queen B on the biggest stage in the world. And Brooke was proud.

"Brooke," Randal said. "We're ready."

Handing the paper back to Becca, Brooke scurried to her spot just as the lights in the studio came up and the segment ended. The light on Camera 2 glowed red, and Randal pointed to her.

"So many people try to find that one person to walk with them, side-by-side through life. And as you can plainly see, it's not as easy as it seems. Out of the thirty men, and thirty women, only Christopher and Kristine saw something in each other that they agreed upon. We'll see if their connection continues when they finally get a chance to meet, face-to-face right after this."

The applause sign flashed, and the audience clapped wildly, as the jib swung back for a wide shot.

"Clear," Randal said, and the lights dimmed once more.

Brooke took the chance to walk into the audience and thank them for their participation. She shook several hands and received two marriage proposals, which she politely turned down saying, "It's not you, it's me." Everybody laughed, but somehow she felt they understood she was actually not lying. Brooke's marriage to NFL quarterback, Jake May was tabloid fodder for the two short, tumultuous years they were together. He married Brooke after his first season with the Cleveland Browns. Then he was injured in his second season, became addicted to pain killers, and was suspended from the league. His opioid addiction devolved into an experiment with heroin, and Jake was thrown out of the NFL for life.

It was obviously tough on him, and he took it out on her, becoming emotionally and then at one point, physically abusive before she walked away for good. After several stints in and out of rehab facilities, Jake had finally beaten his demons. But their relationship was damaged beyond repair, and their divorce was on every rag in every grocery store stand in the country. What didn't appear in the articles was the damage he'd really done. It looked as though he'd given her a black eye. But what she didn't tell anyone was the fact that her eye socket had been fractured, and she'd almost lost sight in her left eye. Brooke didn't know why she'd kept that secret, but somehow, she still felt she needed to protect him...even from himself.

Randal caught her attention and Brooke stepped on her spot on the center steps. When the lights came up, the audience around her clapped, and the jib camera swung into motion. Brooke took a couple of steps down and addressed the camera.

"Chris and Kris have seen something in each other that they feel comfortable with, something worth pursuing. So now it's time to sit across from each other, look each other in the eye and see if what they instinctively felt now holds up to scrutiny. Let's watch what happens when I introduce them."

The monitors switched over to the pre-produced introduction segment, where the camera zoomed in on Kristine sitting alone in a cabana by a pool, dressed in shorts and a t-shirt. Brooke walked in with Chris and introduced them. It appeared awkward at first, but as the two began asking each other questions from pre-written cards, it was easy to see a connection quickly forming. They laughed and joked and generally felt at ease together.

As she watched the exchange with the audience, Brooke understood the irony of it all. Here she was, facilitating the marriages of others when hers ended up in a very visible flaming wreck. If long successful marriages were a requirement for her job, she would probably only be able to sell popcorn in the gift shop. Thankfully, the country seemed to be giving her a pass on that little issue. And now she was in the papers for something wholly different than being a failure.

The introduction segment concluded and the couple had decided to continue with their grand date weekend. Brooke introduced that segment as well. The audience watched the couple learn how to sail and work their way out of an escape room without the slightest irritation with each other. The couple had a grand dinner in a vineyard and sipped wine afterward by a fire, where they shared their heavily edited innermost fears, wishes, and dreams for the future.

The following segment was live in-studio. Brooke interviewed two couples previously on the show, and another woman who, at the crucial moment, had said "I don't." This was the segment where Brooke felt the most comfortable. With her years of experience doing live interviews for news cameras, often in the worst possible circumstances, this was a cakewalk for her.

Then came the moment, when the set changed to the "Chapel Set." The video wall displayed a shot of beautiful white roses swaying back and forth in a gentle breeze. A large white arch was rolled out onto the stage with vines of red roses and white twinkly lights wound through it. Justice of the Peace Warren B. Cummings, a short, gray-haired man, with thick-framed glasses, sauntered onto the stage and dutifully took his place under the arch.

One of the production assistants escorted Chris Haddock onto stage. Brooke walked over and shook his hand. "Are you ready?"

Chris looked a little frazzled but pulled himself together enough for a shrug and a quiet, "Guess so."

"Great," Brooke said. She had a good feeling about him. With such a lackluster response, she was sure he was going to be an "I don't," which would mean this episode would be talked about for the next week solid.

Another PA escorted in both sets of parents. Brooke quickly rushed over and welcomed them as well. She had met them previously but wanted them to feel at ease on the stage and ready for when the lights brightened and the cameras came on again. Mr. And Mrs. Brent and Ellen Haddock were pleasant people, excited to be there and obviously proud of their son. Brooke wondered how they would feel by the end of the segment when he walked away without a wife.

Corrine Bullock appeared giddy at all that was happening, but her husband, Duncan Bullock III, looking positively official in his Marine Dress Uniform, was far from excited about being there. He'd expressed his misgivings about the whole idea before they even shot the introduction segment, and the fact that his daughter felt inclined to continue with it all was sincerely aggravating to him.

"I'm glad you're both here," Brooke said to the Bullocks, and she meant it. She hadn't been sure Mr. Bullock would even show.

"Well, whatever makes our daughter happy," Mrs. Bullock

said with an awkward chuckle. Mr. Bullock forced a smile.

"Thirty seconds, Brooke," Randal called over to her.

"Okay, let's take our seats then," Brooke said. The PA escorted the families to seats on the stage, except for Mr. Bullock who was taken away to be with his daughter.

Brooke rushed over and stood with Chris at their spots on stage.

When the lights came up and she received her cue, Brooke turned to Chris. "So now comes the big moment, Chris. Without divulging too much, how are the butterflies?"

Chris Haddock had a charming smile. Even now, while he was clean-shaven, no longer sporting his sexy stubble, he looked killer. He shrugged, "I feel good. I'm pretty confident with my decision, so I'm not looking back."

"All right. That's good to hear," Brooke said. She gestured to the wedding arch. "Then go ahead and take the groom's position over by Justice of the Peace Warren Cummings, and we'll get the nuptials underway."

Chris left the shot and Brooke turned to the camera. "Well, Chris Haddock's and Kristine Bullock's whirlwind courtship has officially ended. Their short journey has taken them to this moment where they are going to make a very important decision. I will now step aside and let The Honorable Warren B. Cummings take over."

As Brooke stepped down, the speakers blared the opening sequence of the "Wedding March" and the audience stood. The jib swooped high over the crowd, and at the top of the stairs, the doors flung open. Kristine Bullock walked into the studio in a flowing wedding gown with white flowers in her hair. Arm-in-arm with her proud father, she proceeded down the steps and up onto the stage, stopping just before an awestruck Chris Haddock.

Justice Cummings never broke his formality. As soon as the music stopped, he welcomed everyone to the event and asked who was giving the bride to be wed.

Duncan Bullock muttered something barely audible, quickly kissed his daughter's cheek, and took his seat next to his crying wife.

Justice Cummings went on to discuss the worthiness of marriage with an emphasis on possible struggles married couples face.

"This is not a covenant to be entered into lightly, but one of thoughtfulness, love, empathy, compassion, and above all, kindness."

He then reached over, grabbed a ring off a pillow and handed it to Chris.

"Chris Haddock, do you take Kristine Bullock to be your wedded wife..." The camera slowly zoomed tight on Chris's face, as if being closer would give the audience a better chance to read his mind.

"...as long as you both shall live?"

As instructed before the show, it didn't matter which way he decided, Chris waited the seven dramatic seconds before giving his answer. "I do."

A small murmur of approval and anticipation rumbled through the studio audience, and even though the cameras took shots of several people in attendance, Randal waved them all silent.

Justice Cummings handed the second ring to Kristine. "Kristine Bullock, do you take..."

Again, the camera zoomed in closely on Kristine's face. A soft diffusion effect was applied to her shot, allowing her to glow slightly.

"...as long as you both shall live?"

Kristine had been instructed to wait ten seconds before giving her answer. She seemed exceptional at this, not even smiling, giving the impression she was not ready to get married. Then her eyelids drooped, she grew wobbly and began to stumble to her right.

The audience gasped, and both Justice Cummings and Chris reached out and grabbed her before she fell.

Brooke ran over, but Duncan Bullock reached Kristine first, put his arm around her shoulders, and steadied her. "Come on, honey," He whispered in her ear. "Let's get out of here."

Kristine rubbed her face, shook her head, and waved him off. "No, I just got a little light-headed. I'm okay now."

"No. Come on, kiddo," Duncan said, continuing to try to guide her off-stage. "You don't have to do this. We can go."

"No, Dad. I'm good now."

"It's okay, sweetie." Duncan pushed her a little more forcefully toward the side of the stage. "You don't owe anything to anybody here."

Kristine stamped her foot. "No, Dad. Stop it!" She scowled at her father.

Duncan stepped back and stood straight, almost at attention.

"I'm doing this whether you like it or not!" Kristine said, wagged her finger in her father's face. "This is my life."

Duncan nodded, spun on his heels as if he'd just received orders from a commanding officer, marched back over, and took his place next to his wife once again.

The audience was silent after witnessing the awkward exchange between father and daughter. Brooke backed away and returned to her designated spot on the stage once again.

Kristine gave her father one more angry glare, then turned, took a deep breath, and stepped back up in front of Chris.

Justice Cummings put a gentle hand on her shoulder. "Are you sure you're all right?"

She nodded at him. "Yes, your honor. I'm fine now."

"Then the question still needs an answer. Do you take this man to be your husband?"

Kristine's face lit up with a bright smile, and she exclaimed loudly, "I do."

"Then by the power..." That was all that was heard from Justice Cummings. The ear-splitting screaming, crying, and clapping from the audience drowned out everything else. When his lips stopped moving, Chris and Kristine embraced and kissed, and confetti fell in a torrent from above.

Brooke turned and directed her attention to the jib camera that swooped down in on her. With the delay caused by Kristine's drama, there wasn't much time left in the show. She glanced over at Randal and saw the ten-second cue. The network would cut away whether she was done talking or not. "Another happy ending. We wish Chris and Kristine all the best on their honeymoon and beyond. Thank you for joining us and we'll see you next week on *I Do or I Don't*."

The red light on the jib camera went dark.

"Clear!" Randal shouted. "That's a wrap."

Edwards

Chapter Two

Becca arrived at her office early the next morning. She'd had the usual bottle of champagne on ice and a half-gallon of orange juice delivered and began to get the mimosas ready. It had become the custom, ever since the first episode, for her and Brooke to follow each broadcast with a mimosa. It was good to toast to another successful week and get the next one started off right. But this morning it was different. Now they were acknowledged as the toast of Hollywood, so that called for a bottle of Dom Perignon, along with a large tray of chocolate-covered strawberries. Today was special, and no calories would be counted.

She closed her office door and checked her reflection in the full-length mirror on the wall behind it. She was happy with her hair, cut into a shaggy crew cut and shaved up the back. Becca felt it made her look no-nonsense. Her white slacks, a red blazer with a matching red cami underneath, and strappy Jimmy Choos let everyone know in the day's meetings that she was on top of the hill now and intended to stay there. Motion in the reflection from behind her gave her a start, and she spun around.

"Imagine my surprise when I found you were already expecting me."

It was William Tully, a studio lawyer wanna-be and last evening's brief companion. He was lying on her couch naked with a copy of the *Hollywood Ledger* over his privates. Holding a chocolate-covered strawberry up over his head, he winked at her. "Let's pretend this is mistletoe, shall we?"

"What the hell are you doing with my strawberries?" Becca shouted. " And get your sweaty ass off my leather couch!"

William dropped the strawberry and it rolled under the table. He sat up, his face now as bright red as the berries. "But last night..."

"Was just that," Becca shouted. "Last night. That's what you are to me. Why do you think I kicked your butt out when we were done? If I wanted to see you in the morning, I would have let you stay. This is today and you're back to being a flunky in the law office. Now get the hell out, and don't let me catch you in here again, unless I call you in here." She pointed to the door. "And *never* again without pants."

William scooped up his pile of clothes. "Okay, I'm sorry. I just thought..."

"I wasn't interested in your thoughts last night, and I'm not interested in them now."

"Okay. My bad." He dropped the paper and turned around slightly. "I'll just get dressed...."

"No." Becca ran over and yanked his clothes from him. "Not here." She opened the office door and threw his clothes into the hall. "Find somewhere else to do that."

Brooke walked in. "What's going on...oh my." She turned to leave.

"No, girlfriend. You stay," Becca said. "*He's* leaving."

William's face had now turned a ghostly white. He grabbed the *Hollywood Ledger*, opened it up, and wrapped it around his waist. "Sorry for the interruption, ladies." He sidled all the way to the office door with his back against the wall. Giving an awkward smile to both of them, he dashed out into the hallway, grabbed his clothes off the hallway floor—mooning them—and raced off.

Becca slammed the door, and a woman screamed in the distance.

"What the hell was that?" Brooke asked.

"Last night," Becca said, unwinding the wire on the champagne. "Apparently he got the wrong impression of me. He thought I gave a shit about him."

Brooke walked over to the couch. "You have to be more careful, Becca."

"Don't sit there, Sweetie!" The cork popped from the champagne bottle. "His bare ass was all over that thing. I'll have Physical Plant get it cleaned later." A small wire waste can sat on the tall cherry-wood shelving unit behind Becca's desk, the bottom covered with champagne corks. Becca threw the new cork in with the collection. She poured two glasses, then added a shot of orange juice and brought one over to Brooke, who was now sitting in one of the tall white leather chairs.

Brooke took the glass with a disapproving glance. "You're going to get yourself in real trouble one day."

Becca giggled. "Until then, I'm going to enjoy all of this as much as I can." She held up her glass to Brooke. "Here's to the Queen Bs."

Brooke smiled and clinked glasses. After she sipped, Brooke peered into her glass. "Hey, this is great."

Becca sat in the chair across from her. "A $400 bottle of Dom better taste great." She reached down and held the platter of strawberries up for Brooke, who took one and pointed it at her.

"Remember the old saying, 'pride comes just before the fall.'" She bit into the strawberry slowly and followed it with a sip from the mimosa.

Becca swirled her mimosa around in the glass. "I have no idea what you're talking about. I have worked my ass off, earned my place at this studio, and now I'm just living the dream."

"I'm not talking about champagne for breakfast," Brooke said. "In fact, *never* stop this. I'm talking about your little one-night stands."

Becca reached down and snatched a strawberry off the tray. "I'm not doing anything any red-blooded American male producer isn't doing."

"Ahhh, but there's the point isn't it. You're not male. And females who screw around aren't referred to as studs, though the word does start with an 's'."

Becca chewed her strawberry and followed it with a swig of mimosa. "You don't get it. You have to think and act like a man in this position to be taken seriously. My hair is cut like theirs, and I always wear slacks instead of skirts. In fact, I'm thinking of even shortening my name. What would you think if I just went with "Beck."

"Please don't," Brooke said. "I think there's already rumors starting that you and I are lovers. If you go with Beck, that will seal the deal."

"But 'Beck' sounds like 'Buck.' I could be a real stud."

"Like I said..." Both girls laughed.

The door opened, and Marilyn, the middle-aged, chubby office manager stepped in. "Miss Dodge, Mr. McGregor is here to see you."

Becca felt her stomach lurch.

"McGregor?" Brooke said. "Head of the network, McGregor?"

Derek McGregor popped his head in around the door jamb. "How is Hollywood's newest dream team today?"

Brooke jumped up from her seat and scurried to the door. "Good morning, Mr. McGregor. It's nice to finally meet you."

Becca sat her glass down on the table, but her hands were trembling so bad it tipped over and broke. "Shit. Clumsy of me."

McGregor stepped in all the way into the office and shook Brooke's hand. Marilyn walked out, closing the door behind her.

"Marilyn," Becca called to her.

Marilyn stopped and turned her hair-dyed head to Becca.

"You can leave the door open," Becca said with a nervous smile.

Marilyn nodded and pushed the door back open.

Becca stood, her leaden legs felt like they were dragging behind her as she went over and greeted one of the most powerful men in the industry. "What brings you in today?"

"Are you kidding me?" he said, reaching over to pat her on the shoulder. Becca tried not to flinch when he touched her. "With that article in the *Hollywood Reporter,* I had to stop by and congratulate you two personally. Everybody at the network is over the moon at the success of the show. We are kicking everyone else's ass on Tuesday nights because of you two."

"Wow, that's such a nice thing to say," Brooke said. She

gave Becca an awkward glance as if picking up on her friend's uneasiness.

Becca took a breath and put her power-player mask back on. "That is much appreciated, Mr. McGregor. We are all pretty excited about it here, too. It's nice when your hard work can pay off so well."

"Yes, it is," McGregor said.

"Did you want a celebratory mimosa?" Brooke asked.

Becca could see, in her mind's eye, slapping Brooke.

"That's a kind offer," McGregor said. "I have a few other folks to see here today before I go off to work. But I wanted to make sure this was my first stop."

"Well, maybe next time then," Becca said.

"Sure." McGregor stepped to the doorway and stopped. "I'm sure your father would be very proud of you, Becca."

It felt like a rock formed in Becca's throat.

"I know I am." McGregor smiled and winked at Brooke. "And I'm proud of you too, young lady."

Brooke chuckled. "Thanks." When McGregor was gone, Brooke whirled on her. "What does he have on you?"

"How's that?" Becca asked, rounding her desk with wobbly legs and sitting in her chair before she completely collapsed.

"Something's going on here." Brooke leaned on the desk. "Becca, 'Fearless and Tearless' Dodge looks a little rattled. Does that man have some dirt on you that I don't know about?"

Becca remembered when she'd received that nickname. It was back in her college days at the University of Pennsylvania. One Friday night, She and Brooke were headed to the bar with some friends, when a dude stepped out of an alley, acting all scary-like, and clicked open a switchblade. "I'll let you keep your purses and your faces," he said to them, trying to make his voice low and intimidating. "I just want your cash and your credit cards."

The other girls, including Brooke, started whimpering and rummaging through their purses. But Becca stepped forward and looked him in the eye. "Big mistake, loser."

"Listen bitch, you ain't got a choice." He waved the knife menacingly around her left cheek. "Unless you want me to carve my initials into that pretty little face of yours so you'll remember me forever, you'd best be getting that cash out."

Becca didn't flinch. Nor did she take her eyes off the assailant. "I have a better idea, girls," she said. "Instead of money, get your phones out of your purses and take a picture of this asshole. That way if he tries to do anything to me or anyone else, we have several angles of him for the police."

Brooke was the first to comply. Her phone flashed, and the man stepped back. "What the fuck!" More phones flashed and he put his arm up over his face. "Bitches, cut that shit out!" He ran back down the alley and all of the girls laughed and bought Becca's drinks all night long.

"So, what is it?" Brooke asked again.

Becca snapped back into the present. "What is what?"

"What is the shit he's got on you? Why are you keeping secrets from me?"

Becca shook her head and opened her laptop. "No secrets, sweetie. Network heads just give me the willies." She clicked her email open. "Now you have to run. You have two 'meet-and-greets' to shoot today."

"Don't tell me then." Brooke said crisply. She turned and finished her mimosa with one gulp. "Catch you later." She sat the glass on the table and scooted out of the room.

Becca tried to respond to an email but found her hands were still trembling too much to type. She grabbed the bottle of champagne and chugged from it.

CHAPTER THREE

When Brooke walked into the make-up room, George Crone, one of the segment producers on the show, jumped up from the chair, waving a clipboard in the air. "Girl, we have got the best problem ever," he squealed with delight.

Brooke couldn't help but chuckle at his exuberance. "Is there really such a thing as a good problem?" She hugged Fiona and sat in her chair.

"You be the judge," said George, putting a hand on his hip and pointing the clipboard at her. "We have three connections this week."

"Are you serious? That's wonderful." This had never happened before. There had been a couple of weeks that nobody had selected matches. "Are we saving one couple to shoot next week?"

George raked his hand through his bright blue hair. "Becca said no. We have applications coming in now at nearly a hundred a day. She's expecting this to become the norm rather than the exception."

"But..." Brooke began. Fiona stopped dabbing on the foundation so she could speak. "...how are we supposed to shoot all three couples. Don't we still have two escape room segments to shoot this afternoon?"

"Not to worry, sister. I have it all worked out." George looked down at his clipboard. "At nine, you will start with Debra and Tony at the pool set. You get an hour to get them going and then at ten, you will head over to the fireplace set and meet Doug and

27

Anne. Once your segment is shot there, we'll put you in a cart and whisk you over to the east lot. The soap opera "Winds of Change" has a sports bar set they can loan us for the morning. They are even 'lending' us their crew," said George, his fingers making an air quote," for gobs of money. But Becca says it's no problem to pay. So there you'll introduce Chad and Kristen. But we can't start any later than 11:30, because they have a production in there that starts at two, and they'll need to set up some lights beforehand."

"Becca knew about this?" Brooke asked, eyes closed while Fiona was applying liner.

"She helped me swing the deal," George said.

Brooke was surprised she didn't mention it during their mimosas. They usually brought up things like that heading into the next week's cycle. But McGregor had arrived and blew up the whole morning.

"So, Fee," George said, swirling his hand in the air, "a big pronto on the make-up. And then Brookey, you need to get your skinny butt to the pool, stat, so we can get the day started. Got it?"

"Yes sir, General." Brooke saluted.

George smirked. "At ease, sister." Then he scurried out the door.

Both women chuckled. "This is really starting to get exciting," Fiona said.

"And a little bit intimidating," Brooke added.

"Bullocks," Fiona countered.

She stood back and smiled down at her. "Once those cameras are live there isn't anything that intimidates you. You're the reason this whole thing is taking off."

Brooke smiled up at her friend. "You're so nice."

"Nice has nothing to do with facts," Fiona said and grabbed the lipstick.

Rushing to the pool set, Brooke thought about Fiona's kind words. She had to admit, Fee had her figured out. Brooke only felt truly comfortable and alive when the cameras were on and she was interacting with others. Where she fell flat was when she was alone or had to deal with real feelings, especially those between two people.

Opening the gate to the pool, she could see that all three of the camera people were busy setting up. George stood to the side cradling his clipboard. He glanced up when she walked in and pointed a pen at a side door to her right. "The girl first. And hurry."

He was not messing around. He really was in General George mode today. Entering the small green room off to the side of the pool, designated for the females, Brooke found the girl sitting on the couch, crumpled over, practically in a fetal position, crying. "Oh my goodness," Brooke sat next to her and gently rubbed her back. "Are you Debra?"

The girl nodded, not looking up.

"Debra, what's going on?"

Debra put her arms across her knees and rested her forehead on them. "I don't know," her voice quivered when she spoke. "I was fine until I got in here. Then I got scared."

"Oh, honey," Brooke said, rubbing her back a little harder. "There's absolutely nothing to be scared about. I'm here for you, and I'm not going to let anything happen to you."

"You don't have any control over the fact that this guy may hate me, and I could make a complete fool of myself on national TV."

"I want you to sit up and look at me." Brooke touched her shoulders and guided her up. "You don't want to rest your forehead on your arm anyway. It will make it all red."

Debra sat up, and Brooke brushed her auburn hair out of her face. "I just didn't want to get tears on my shirt," Debra said.

Brooke smiled at her. "Good move." She grabbed tissues out of a box next to her and handed them to Debra. "Wipe those beautiful eyes and blow that pretty nose."

With trembling hands, Debra took the tissue and did as she asked.

"Now listen to me." She pointed toward the door. "That man out there chose you out of a slew of other women. He is excited, and probably just as nervous to meet you. But I know he'll spend three minutes with you and realize he's made the best choice of his life."

Debra smiled.

"Oh my gosh, when you smile, you light up the whole room. I would go with that look over tears any day. It really works for you."

"Stop," Debra said, with an embarrassed giggle.

"And let me ask you a question," Brooke said. "When it comes to making a fool of yourself in front of the nation, can you think of anybody who did it bigger than me?"

Debra's eyes widened. "Oh, you didn't make a fool of yourself. Things just happened to you, that's all."

"Thank you for saying that," Brooke said. "Point being, you will have to work very hard at outdoing those who have come before you. So please don't stress about things like that."

"Thank you, Miss Winthrop. You're so nice." Debra leaned in and gave her a big hug.

"You're welcome," Brooke said, pulling back. "And call me Brooke." She took Debra's shaky hands. "Now, I'm going to go talk to this Tony fella. But first, I'm going to send in my own personal make-up artist to fix you all up before you two meet."

After a look of surprise, exclamations of thanks, and another big hug, Brooke was able to exit the room. Passing George, she pointed her thumb back. "Could you call Fee? She's needed in there."

"On it." George pulled his cell out of his pocket and hit speed dial.

Brooke headed on into the men's green room. A guy sat on the couch with a mop of black hair on his head, stubble on his cheeks, staring at his phone. He looked up when she entered.

"Hey, Brooke," he said with a charming smile.

"Hey, Tony,"

Tony went back to his phone. "Are we ready?"

"In just a few," Brooke said. "I just thought I'd come in to see if you had any questions before we go out there."

Tony shook his head. "Nah. I'm good."

Brooke stared at him. Somehow, she felt they were perfect for each other. "Okay then. I'll be back in just a few moments to get you."

"Great," Tony said, not looking up from his phone.

Brooke closed the door, walked out, and said hello to the cameramen. Then she stood in place and shot the introduction of the segment. When Fee left Debra's green room, Tony was brought out to the pool. She fetched Debra and introduced the two while the cameras rolled. Then she stepped aside and let them get acquainted and ask their questions. Once each of them had asked and answered five questions, Brooke stepped back in and asked each of them if they wanted to continue on to the next step. Both Debra and Tony answered yes.

"What is it you see in her?" she asked Tony.

"Well obviously, she's beautiful," The same thing every guy has ever said. "But she's so chill. I feel very relaxed around her."

"Interesting," Brooke said, then turned to Debra. "And just what is it about Tony that makes you want to continue?"

Debra had a big smile and she never took her eyes off Tony. "Just from his answers. He seems adventurous. And it sounds like he wants kids someday, and I definitely want a family."

"Okay, well this was a success," Brooke said. "You two will separate now. Next you will see how you work together as a team at the Escape Room before the big date day. Thank you,"

Debra and Tony hugged and then walked back to their rooms.

"Annnnnnd, stop recording," George said. "Brooke, you've got five minutes to change and get to the fireplace set."

Brooke flew back to her dressing room, and then on to the next two shoots. Though the morning was hectic, she felt invigorated. Days like this didn't wear her out until she got home and fell into her bed, her energy zapped. Until then she was wide awake and rolling with it all.

After a quick lunch back in her dressing room, she ran to the weekly production meeting to work on putting together the next show. This part of the job was Becca's since she was the senior producer, but Brooke was required to be there to give input and keep up to date on what was happening throughout the week. All of the producers and casting directors were waiting when she arrived. "Sorry I'm late," she said, taking her usual seat between George and co-producer Rosalie York, at the opposite end of the table from Becca.

"Not a problem," said Darrel Shrewsberry, the casting

director for the men. "Everybody knows about the three shoots you've already had this morning." He turned and fist bumped Amantha James, the women's casting director.

"Well then, it seems everybody knew but me," Brooke said.

Becca, who had been typing in her laptop up to that point, looked up. "Sorry, that was on me. I meant to let you know this morning."

Brooke smiled and shrugged at her. "It's all good."

"Okay, with the extra couple on board, this week is going to look a little more hectic," Becca said, sliding her laptop to the side. "Do we think there's any way we could shoot two escape rooms and two dates in one day?"

"Not without paying some serious overtime or hiring a whole other crew," Rosalie said.

"I think we need to consider the idea that this could be the way it is from now on," Amantha said. She looked at Darrell. "We are now getting close to a hundred applications every day."

Darrell nodded his agreement. "Yeah, easily a hundred."

Gunther Pindal, the producer for the studio portion of the segment, spoke up in his thick Norwegian accent. "If you need help getting through this week, I'd be willing to go out with one of the crews to shoot a dating segment." It was hard to believe he would even volunteer to go in the sun with his extremely fair complexion.

"Thanks, Gunth," Becca said. "Just so you all know, with the good press we're getting and the increase in applications, I'm contemplating pushing the network to give us either Sunday night or Thursday night, too."

"Are you serious?" Brooke said.

Becca looked up. "It's either that or two hours on Tuesdays. We need to make hay here. With our numbers the way they are, sponsor rates are at a premium. That gives us leverage for a mid-season renegotiation. I say we go for it."

"Hell, yeah," Amantha said and others at the table chuckled.

The door opened, and a young girl walked in and rushed over to whisper to Amantha. Brooke had seen her before but didn't know her name. She just knew she was Amantha's casting associate.

Amantha listened and turned to Becca. "So, apparently we have a woman who's not comfortable with any of the ten individuals we've supplied her with. She's in tears and is begging RuLanne for a few more applications."

Becca shook her head. "No way. That's part of it. You may get lucky or you may not. Tell her that we're sorry it didn't work out for her and send her on her way."

"Hold on," Brooke said. "Becca, can't we give her another five or so? We're supposed to be helping people find love."

"No, we can't," Becca leaned forward. "And don't think for a minute that it's our job to help people find love. We're here to put on a show. If suddenly we start giving extra applications for people to go over until they find someone, they'll never make a decision and we'll never have a show."

"Oh," George said. "You mean that show we have about helping people find love?"

Becca glared at him and then turned to RuLanne. "Do this. Go tell her we're sorry but we can't give her more applications to go through. But promise her ten seconds on the next broadcast so she can tell all her family and friends. Then get her name to the editors and tell them I said to put her in, or I'll have their ass. Clear?"

RuLanne nodded and rushed back out.

As soon as the door closed Becca slammed her hands on the table and stood. "The name of this show is not called 'Finding Love.' It's called *I Do or I Don't* and don't think for a minute that anybody watching this show is hoping for the former. There's a huge segment that is hoping to see someone say 'I don't.' Because watching a train wreck is a *shitload* more entertaining than watching someone else's happiness." She pointed at George, glaring. "And, George Crone, if you argue with me one more time in front of the crew, your fucking ass will hit the pavement so fast you won't know what happened. And you can just keep on bouncing because you aren't getting back in. Got it?"

George closed his laptop quietly and rested his hands on top of it. "Got it."

The door burst open, and Alanna Gates, Fiona's little sister and Becca's personal assistant rushed in. "Miss Dodge,"

"What?" Becca shouted, impatiently.

"Ehhh..." Alanna paused briefly at the harshness of her boss. "I think you all should come see this right away."

"See what?" Becca asked. "We need to finish this meeting."

"Kristine Haddock, the bride from the show the other night." Alanna looked around the room. "She's dead."

Chapter Four

"She was just standing there, and then she was gone." The Global Info Network played Chris Haddock's short interview relentlessly. He was standing in front of a rush of reporters doing his best to speak without breaking down. "I went over to the edge of the cliff...she slipped..." He shook his head and buried his face in his hands. Someone put their arm around him and waved the cameras away. As they turned him around to walk into a building, the picture dissolved to the reporter back in the studio in New York.

"And again, if you're just joining us, that was Chris Haddock who was on his honeymoon in Costa Rica. He was talking about the tragic and sudden death of his wife. They had just married two nights ago on the popular new show, *I Do or I Don't* which is hosted by our own former journalist Brooke Winthrop."

"That poor man," Brooke said. "What do we do now?"

"We have to make a statement," Rosalie said.

"Brooke and I should both make one," Becca said.

"What's that going to do to the show?" Darrell asked.

"It's probably going to double the ratings," Becca said.

Everyone looked at her, and she shrugged. "I told you, people love their train wrecks. We have a bona-fide train wreck right here."

The next two days were taken up with handling the fallout, as it were, with Kristine Haddock's death. Brooke and Becca both put out statements saying they were sorry to Chris and Kristine's family for the loss. Legal got involved to make sure there was no culpability on the part of the show or the producers. That bullet was dodged simply by the fact that Chris picked the location of the honeymoon. The couple received $7,000 from the show to go wherever they wanted. The show did not choose Costa Rica, nor did they have any stipulations on how the money should be used.

Brooke and the crew worked through the weekend, finishing the segments and preparing scripts for the next show. It had been decided, with all the extra distractions, to put off the third couple until the following week. Both Brooke and Becca had multiple interviews with entertainment news magazines, both in front of the camera and on the phone. It put the whole production behind. They wouldn't have had time to shoot anything extra if they'd wanted to. Brooke had to put off an interview with GInfo until the day after the next show was to air.

The night of the broadcast, when Brooke went out beforehand to meet the audience, there was a distinct cloud over the festivities. It was as if nobody was ready to get excited about the show until last week's tragedy had been addressed. Brooke tried discussing it with the audience, to help them move past it. But it didn't help. In fact, it made them even more subdued. She needed to discuss it with the whole nation before it could be put to rest.

The studio remained silent when the lights went up. There was no musical intro, only a single voice and graphic stating, "A special message from Brooke Winthrop and the crew of *I Do or I Don't*." When the floor director pointed at her, Brooke looked into the camera and delivered the speech she and Becca had worked on together that was now rolling on the teleprompter.

"Good evening. I'm Brooke Winthrop and I want to thank you for joining us. We were all saddened at the news of the sudden passing of Kristine Haddock. It was one week ago tonight when Kristine stood in this very studio, and married Chris Haddock in front of the whole nation. That was supposed to be the start of a new and beautiful life for the two of them. Instead, it was just the prelude to a nightmare for Chris and Kristine's families. I speak for the producers and the crew of this show as I give our deepest condolences to you all. We share in your sorrow and pray for your comfort at such a difficult time."

The video monitors in the studio faded to black and then segued to a fabric softener commercial.

The rest of the show went on unabated. No more was said about the tragedy and the studio crowd grew livelier. It was as if, once the incident was addressed, the audience was given permission to enjoy themselves.

The show followed one couple through all their segments and ended, once again, in front of Judge Cummings. This time, it was the groom who said, I don't. Once this happens, it is Brooke's responsibility to pull them aside separately and ask: "What was the deal-breaker?"

"I guess after everything that happened this week," the groom said. "I just thought it might be a good idea to take it a little slower. This is all very serious, you know. Like, for the rest of your life, however long that may be."

When Brooke spoke to the bride, she concurred. "Actually, I'm glad he said that. Because I would have, had he not. What happened this week really put things in perspective for me and let me know I have to make big decisions very carefully."

Once the show had wrapped and the audience was gone, Brooke slumped into her chair while the crew struck the equipment.

Becca came back into the studio after leaving about halfway

through. "Hey girl, you could look a little happier. You just hosted a hit show."

"Is it?" Brooke said. "After what happened, it feels like the magic is gone."

"Ahhhh, no magic is gone." Becca stood in front of her and bent down to look her in the eye. "I have been in my office trolling ratings data, and it looks like we were close to a share of 51. Do you know what that means?"

Brooke shook her head.

Becca stood tall and proud. "It means, BFF, that not only were we the highest-rated show of the evening, but we were also the highest-rated show of the week, and of the month. We're approaching Super Bowl numbers." Becca threw her hands in the air and cheered.

Brooke smiled and picked at a fleck of polish chipping off her fingernail. "But it's like you said, they're watching to see a train wreck."

"Honey, I don't care why they're watching, just so long as they are. It means you and I get to write our own checks for the next project we take on."

Gunther ran into the studio calling to them. "Brooke, Becca, watch the screens." He powered on the confidence monitor next to them, turned, and screamed back to the booth. "Volume!"

There was jerky vertical phone camera footage of a woman and two kids on the beach, in the shade of a rocky outcrop. A male news reporter's voice spoke up. "Here's another look at it. This is the Juarez family of Costa Rica getting some footage before they head out to the beach for the day."

A faint scream is heard in the distance, and Mrs. Juarez turned to look around the rocks. Her husband's voice speaks up. "Hay alguien en problemas?"

"You just heard the scream of Kristine Haddock," The anchor said. "And now Mr. Juarez will locate the source of that scream."

The image swished around. "Oh, alli arriba!" Mrs. Juarez

said. The camera swished again and pointed upward, toward the top of a cliff. The picture zoomed in to show a distant figure at the top, clinging to rocks, her feet dangling below her. "There is Kristine Haddock hanging on for her life off the cliffs at Peñón de Guacalillo. Now as the camera zooms in you can see Chris Haddock get down on the ground, appearing as if he is going to try and help her."

The footage slowed down as the anchor narrated. The image was jerky and fuzzy at points, but it was clear that a figure was there on the ground, reaching down for Kristine's hand. Then it froze. "I want to advise the viewers before we go forward that the rest of this is hard to watch. If you get queasy at all, you may want to look away."

Becca and Brooke looked at each other sharing the same horrified expression. Brooke knew she should look away but couldn't. As she watched the news report, all she could think was that this was not the story that Chris had given on camera earlier.

The footage moved again. Chris clenched a fist and pounded on one of Kristine's hands. You could hear her scream and she released her grip dangling precariously with one hand. Chris smacked at her other hand and Kristine fell out of frame. The image froze and the shot cut back to the anchor. "This is terribly distressing and shows clearly that Chris Haddock lied about the death of his wife. If the figure in the footage is Chris Haddock, and we have no reason to believe it isn't, then he has murdered his wife, Kristine Haddock, and it was recorded on video."

Edwards

CHAPTER FIVE

The next morning was no big surprise for Becca Dodge. She received a text from Allen Morrall, the head of the studio, to meet as soon as she got in to the office, to discuss the fallout from the previous evening's bombshell—and there was sure to be plenty.

Becca had a great deal of confidence in her abilities as a producer and was usually ready to handle any curve ball thrown her. But she had never expected anything like this to happen. She had to admit she was out of her depth and welcomed input from Allen.

She had to spend a little more time on her make-up, due to the live interview later that day with GInfo, which Brooke had scheduled. After doing her best to hide her obvious strain, she quickly toasted an English muffin, poured coffee in a travel mug, and ran to her car, eating and drinking on the way.

Of course, every morning radio show was talking about Kristine's murder, blaming the producers for not screening Chris well enough and letting a murderer get married to an unsuspecting, innocent woman. Becca knew there were going to be inquiries, and processes were going to be scrutinized to the nth degree. She had to just put on her big girl panties and deal with it. She couldn't say it out loud to anyone else, but she understood the business well enough to realize there truly wasn't such a thing as "bad publicity." As tragic as this was, the show would be on everyone's lips for the next several months. And she, Brooke, and the show would be the better for it.

Arriving at the studio, she rushed into her office to grab her laptop. The champagne was already there on ice. With the tragic news on her mind the previous night, she hadn't had time to consider canceling the order. She knew she had to do something with it now. If anybody saw this in her office the day after it was discovered Kristine was murdered, it would be an optics nightmare.

Grabbing a couple of tissues, she pulled the bottle out of the ice, wiped it down, and hid it in her bottom desk drawer. She picked up the ice bucket, ran down to the lady's room, and dumped the ice in the sink. Then she set it down on the floor next to Allana's desk for her assistant to take care of discreetly.

She snagged her laptop from its dock on her desk and ran down the hall to the conference room. When she opened the door, Allen was already seated with three men she recognized from legal, including William Tully, who looked up at her uneasily.

"She just walked in now," Allen said to the phone speaker in the middle of the table. He gestured her to a chair.

Becca took her seat as instructed and opened her laptop. All the men at the table had their ties loose and their sleeves rolled up, looking as if they had been at this all night.

"Derek McGregor from the network is on the other end," Allen said.

Becca froze, and her stomach pitted again.

"Good morning, Rebecca," McGregor's voice said over the tinny speaker.

"Oh, good morning, Mr. McGregor," Becca said.

"So, your situation has put us all here at the network in a bit of a whirlwind."

"I'm so sorry about that," Becca said.

"The network feels they need to suspend the show for the rest of the season," Allen blurted out.

Becca always related well with Allen because he was a no-nonsense guy. If he could get something accomplished with four words instead of forty, he would say those four words and move on to the next thing. There was no wasted talk or time with the guy. But this morning, these were not the words she expected, nor wanted to hear. "You've got to be shitting me," she said.

McGregor spoke up. "I know that's a punch in the gut, Becky, but..."

"It's Becca," she said, cutting him off. "Sir, with all due respect, that is probably the worst thing you can do right now."

"Becca," Allen said, putting up a hand, signaling her to quiet down. "They have a lot they have to take into consideration."

"That is true, Becca," McGregor said. He emphasized her name, reminding her who was in charge. "We have had armies of lawyers in here, analyzing this every way from Sunday. They are all in agreement that our butts are hanging out on this one, as are all of yours. The Bullock family is going to get a payday that will make lottery winners jealous, and we have to stay ahead of that. Public opinion is a huge part of the equation, and if we keep throwing a love party on national television every week, what is that going to say about us?"

Becca was silent while everyone in the room stared at her. She said nothing.

"Not to mention," McGregor continued. "That we've already had seven sponsors pull out. It's very hard to produce a show when you have no sponsor money to pay for it."

"Mr. McGregor, can I just point out our ratings numbers from last night's show," Becca said.

"I know," McGregor said. "They were over-the-moon good. And that just makes this whole thing hurt that much more. Trust me, I'm hurting right with you, darling."

Did he really say darling? Becca cringed.

Allen tapped his pen on the table. "Let's talk about next steps. Brooke and Becca already had a big interview scheduled with GInfo this afternoon to discuss the show. Do you folks think they should cancel that?"

"That depends on the girls," McGregor said. Again, with the demeaning talk. "If they think they can keep it together and show true remorse over the situation, then I say go ahead. It can only help us."

"What do you think?" Allen said to Becca. "Can you pull that off?"

Becca tried not to narrow her eyes at him. She had just produced the highest-rated show this studio had ever seen, and now they were speaking to her like a college intern and asking her if she can hold her shit together.

"I can." She closed her laptop and stood. "I'll let Brooke know." Then she walked out the door.

"Becca, hold up," Allen said. But she didn't slow. She walked back into her office, slammed the door, and threw her laptop on her desk, a little too hard. Dropping into her chair, she looked at the bottom desk drawer. It took everything she had not to pull out the champagne and chug from the bottle.

Brooke was already in the studio when she arrived. "Are we ready for this?" Becca said, taking her seat. The sound guy walked over and positioned a boom mic on an arm, just above her head, out of the shot.

"I'm ready," Brooke said. "I'm just so sad about how all of this is playing out."

"Sad is good," Becca said. "Just don't give the impression that we've done anything wrong. We haven't. We've put on a show with the best of intentions and followed all the rules for something like this, to the letter."

"No, I get that." Brooke made a last check of her make-up in the mirror that Fiona held. "But Kristine would still be alive today were she not a part of our show. Just thinking about that makes me want to cry."

"Let me put it in perspective for you." Becca leaned over and did her best to look consoling. "Every time somebody gets up from bed and begins their day, risks begin. You could eat something that doesn't agree with you, you could trip on a curb, fall and break something. You could be standing in the wrong spot during a mass shooting, or you could have the proverbial bus run you over. Each decision you make can increase or decrease your risk factor. Involving yourself with anyone else during your day increases your risk factor. So entering into a show where you could end up marrying someone you've never met before makes the risk needle jump into the red."

"How is that helping?" Brooke said.

"What I'm saying is that Kristine made this decision. You did not bend her arm behind her back and push her into anything. The show is designed for people to back out at any point along the way. Kristine didn't. There had to be warning signals, and she chose to ignore them. I'm sitting here with a much different attitude than you. Now our show has been mothballed because of the bad decisions that Kristine made. I'm a little pissed off."

"Becca, you can't seriously be pissed."

"Okay," Randal said, walking onto the set. "We have the uplink set and we're ready to start the interview."

The crew had accepted the invitation from GInfo, to handle the production work from the L.A. studio. They would uplink their feed to New York so it could be broadcast from the GInfo studios. Plus, they were getting paid for the gig. Since the show was suspended, it was a last chance to earn a little bit as well.

"We're going in five, four, three..." Randal silently dropped his last two fingers and then pointed at the camera that sat right in front of them. The teleprompter screen now showed the live feed from GInfo, instead of scrolling text.

A graphic behind the anchor's back showed the *I Do or I Don't* logo along with the fuzzy image of Kristine hanging from the cliff, and Chris ready to hit her. Becca felt her teeth grind. The anchor, looked into the camera and began, "By now you've heard that the death of Kristine Haddock, the bride from the popular TV show, *I Do or I Don't*, was murdered, and that Chris Haddock, the groom, is the alleged killer. Chris Haddock has been taken into custody by Costa Rican authorities, and the FBI, operating out of the U.S. Embassy, is investigating. The producers of the show have decided to let the studio go dark until investigations are completed." The image of the anchor slid over into a box, and another box opened with the shot of Brooke and Becca in it. "With us today are the two individuals who brought the show to the screen. First is GInfo's own former journalist and host of 'Deep Dive,' Brooke Winthrop. How are you Brooke, it's good to see you again."

Brooke smiled shyly. "Hi Adam. It's good to see you too. I miss you guys."

Adam chuckled. "We miss you too. And we have her impressive producer partner, Ms. Becca Dodge. How are you today, Becca?"

"I'm good," Becca said with a smile. "Thanks for having us."

"Well, thanks for joining us from the *I Do or I Don't* studio in Los Angeles. Now, before we start with talk of Kristine and Chris Haddock, I think it's fair to let our viewers know that this interview was scheduled before any of that ever happened. We were bringing you on to discuss the stunning success of your show."

Both Brooke and Becca nodded in agreement. "Yes," Becca said. "It has been a week of real highs and lows."

"That is an incredibly true statement," Adam said. "Especially where you two ladies are concerned. Your show has achieved extremely high ratings, meaning that it has struck a chord with the American people. In fact, you two were dubbed the Queen Bs for your unusually fast success."

Brooke and Becca looked at each other and smirked.

"I take it you disagree with that statement," Adam said.

"Well, it wasn't overnight," Becca said.

"Not at all," Brooke added. "We have been working on this together for several years. Long before I ever left GInfo."

"Oh sure," Adam said. "I think we all know there is no such thing as an overnight success, but you have done remarkably well on your very first attempt. You have to be proud of that."

"We are proud," Brooke said. "But then when things happen, as they did with Kristine, you realize that success isn't everything that's important."

Becca said. "Yes. It's hard to bask in the glow of your accomplishments when someone has lost their life, and families are in pain."

"Okay, then," Adam said. "Since you brought it up, let's talk about what happened to Kristine Haddock. Do you feel it was due to any sort of flaw in your process?"

"Honestly, I don't," Becca said. "We have a solid casting department who go over each application rigorously, and then, before an offer is extended to any of the individuals who have their profiles viewed on the show, we have each person run through an extensive background check. So by the time they get to air, they have been vetted several times."

"So how do you explain Chris Haddock's behavior?"

Becca and Brooke looked at each other. "I think to explain Chris Haddock's behavior," Brooke said. "We have to understand the mind of a killer. And our minds don't work that way."

Adam nodded. "Fair enough. That is a hard one to understand."

"I can tell you it had nothing to do with any breakdown of information on our end," Becca said. "Chris was vetted as well as anyone else." Becca wanted all the studio and network heads to see she had their backs on national television.

"Yes, that's good to know," Adam said. "I guess my question isn't necessarily directed at your specific culpabilities, but I think, more to the process of the show itself."

"I don't follow," Becca said.

"Well, do you think this kind of a 'dating format,' for lack of a better term, can lead to worthwhile and long-lasting relationships?"

"I believe that," Brooke said. "Or I wouldn't be involved with it. I generally want people to be happy."

"Let me also add," Becca cut in. "Not only *can* it lead to such relationships, but it also *has*. Those that have been married, have since returned to the show and are doing very well."

"Yes, but in all fairness, they've only been married a few weeks."

"We could easily be doing a show about arranged marriages," Becca said. "The success rate of marriages where someone else picks a partner for an individual is remarkable. So what we're doing is not entirely out of the norm or crazy for long-term happiness."

"You are aware that there are those who would disagree with you," Adam said.

"I am," Becca said.

"Well let's hear from one of them right now, shall we?" Another box opened on the screen and the other two boxes grew smaller to accommodate it. Inside the box was an older man with thinning dark hair, black-rimmed glasses, and a mustache.

"I have Dr. Emery Mackley, from Barsaw University in Connecticut. He is a strong advocate against programs, like yours, saying they are responsible for a great deal of relationship issues and not just with those who appear on your show. Thank you for being with us Dr. Mackley."

Without smiling, Dr. Mackley spoke. "Thank you for having me, Adam."

"So, Dr. Mackley, you have been very vocal in the past, on your blog, and other talk shows, saying that these shows are not only harmful to the people on them, but to the society as a whole. Can you explain such a bold statement?"

Dr. Mackley nodded. "I can, Adam. It's important to realize that relationships are extremely hard work. And the best relationships are not just the result of lucky pairing, but the result of two people who are very committed to each other and to making the relationship work. To send a message that true love is something that can be won on a game show is a very dangerous message to send, and as we saw with the death of Kristine Haddock, it can end tragically."

Becca leaned forward. "I just want to stress that *I Do or I Don't* was not in the game show category. It is categorized as a reality show. And we have taken the responsibility of finding such individuals who were willing to work on a relationship very seriously."

"That's a good..." Adam was cut-off by Dr. Mackley.

"Except there is nothing even close to reality on those shows. It's true, they are given an option to walk away, but everyone knows that's discouraged. The individuals are chastised in magazines and on radio and television shows as not being serious if they back out. So there is a certain amount of pressure to move forward. All of these are bad messages to send to men and women who are trying to navigate the insane world of dating today. All the rules are getting confused, not just with social media and all of the pressure imposed there, but because of shows like this and the new rules that go along with them."

"I have to interject here, doctor," Brooke said. Becca was thinking it was about time. "On the contrary. I make the greatest effort possible to respect our bride's and groom's feelings. If they are in any way unsure about continuing, I pull them aside and tell them it would be better for them to walk away than enter into something they truly aren't sure about."

The doctor pointed at the camera. "There. You just said it. You called them brides and grooms. They haven't even had a real date and yet you refer to them as brides and grooms. Just by doing that you are putting undue pressure on them."

"But Doctor," Adam cut in, "in any culture, there are labels and rules. I think Brooke was just speaking in the vernacular of her show."

"And you just said the keyword, Adam. Culture. The problem is that the culture doesn't stop at the door of the studio, it bleeds out into the world and affects the culture of everyone who watches. But in changing the culture, it doesn't change reality."

"And just what is reality?" Becca asked.

"Reality is that there are specific things that relationships need to truly be successful." Dr. Mackley started counting on his fingers. "First, you need time. Your show provides very little time for two people to get acquainted before they make a decision that will affect the rest of their lives. Second, they need trust and transparency. We won't even get into that, because your show doesn't either. Next, there needs to be affection and intimacy. That does not equate to sex. I know that many of your contestants have had sex, which is a completely separate thing and unfortunate for those involved because there is little caring for the other person with sex. Sex, by its very nature is a selfish act. Which leads me to the next point, which is that you have to think of the partner first and foremost. There are no opportunities for that. And how about strong communication? Many would think that is the most important part of a relationship. And part of that is arguing. There are studies that show that couples who argue are often more connected than those who don't. It's because they communicate. You can't have a difference of opinion if you don't communicate. When people argue on your show, they take it as a bad sign. It's actually a very good sign and quite frankly one that is completely necessary. How many of the couples that you have married on your show have had really important arguments before they tied the knot?"

Brooke and Becca looked at each other uneasily. "I can't speak to that," Becca said.

"I can," Dr. Mackley said. "Zero. They haven't had the time to. And if they did, it would be considered a red flag instead of a real opportunity to understand the wants and needs of the other person, discover boundaries, and really be able to support their partner. Respectful arguments in a relationship are a binding agent, not a chink in the armor. But shows like yours make them out to be bad. These are all terrible messages to send, and the current dating generation is more impressionable to outside agents than any generation before them. And I believe that shows like yours are destroying the very fabric of our culture and could even lead to the downfall of marriage as an institution."

Adam spoke up. "I have to say, doctor, your arguments come across as very valid, but that is a heavy accusation to put on two women who fill a time slot on Tuesday nights from nine to ten p.m."

"Well, it's not just them," Dr. Mackley said. "There are more shows like theirs out there. These two have just been the most successful at it. So now they take the blame for everyone else, I guess." Dr. Mackley smiled for the first time since his box opened on the screen.

"Well, thank you for your time, Dr. Mackley," Adam said.

"Thank you, Adam, and ladies," Dr. Mackley replied.

Brooke and Becca both forced smiles as the doctor's box shrunk away and their box grew larger once again to fill the space on the screen. "Well, before we let you two go," Adam said. "I just wanted to ask you a few more questions regarding the Kristine Haddock situation. Have either of you been contacted by the police, and how will it affect the production of your show going forward?"

Becca glanced over at Brooke, who glanced back. Becca could see the lost look in her eye. She had always been the prominent, strong journalist but had never been on this end of the investigations or accusations and was less prepared for it than she thought. Becca spoke up. "We haven't heard from the police, nor do I expect we will. This happened in Costa Rica, and as far as I know, will be taken care of by their own law enforcement. As far as the production of our show goes, once we get back to the grind of producing, we are going to have to reassess how our candidates are vetted, and perhaps add another layer in there somewhere. Right now, I don't see how we could. The process is extensive and thorough already, but it's always worth a look."

"And do you have a message for the family and friends of Kristine Haddock?"

"The message hasn't changed from last night," Brooke said, apparently regaining her swagger. "In the short time she was with us, I got to know Kristine, and could tell she had a sweet soul. This loss hit us all very hard but certainly not as hard as those who have known her all her life. We send our sincerest condolences to the family and friends at this tragedy. Our hopes and prayers are with them."

"That's all anyone can ask for in times like this," Adam said. "Thank you, ladies, for joining us."

Becca nodded. Brooke said, "Thank you, Adam."

Becca watched as their box shrunk away.

"Clear," Randy said.

Becca stormed out of the studio.

"Becca, wait!"

Becca heard her but didn't slow down. She stormed into her office, pulled out the now-warm bottle of champagne and began unwinding the wire.

Brooke followed her in. When Becca saw her, she screamed. "Are you fucking kidding me?"

Brooke stopped and closed the door. "I know that was a bit

brutal but...."

"A bit?" Becca stood. "Those assholes set us up and hung us out to dry." She gnashed her teeth. "And that Adam just loved watching us get our comeuppance, didn't he?"

Brooke shook her head. "No. Adam is not like that. In fact, he was trying to defend us..."

"Bull-shit!" The cork popped on the champagne and Becca took a swig from the bottle.

"Becca, I want to talk about what the doctor said."

Becca swallowed and wiped her mouth with the back of her hand. "That doctor can kiss my ass. Not only are we responsible for breaking down society, but we're the reason Iraq had weapons of mass destruction and the Titanic sunk. It's all shit."

She held up the bottle for Brooke to take a drink, but she waved it off.

"The problem with being really successful at something is that then you create a target on your back," Becca said, taking another swig from the bottle.

"But perhaps we change the format of the show to account for some of his points," Brooke said.

Becca waved her hand and shook her head. "No. Absolutely not. When you have something that works you don't screw with it. What the doctor needs to understand is that cultures have changed since the dawn of time. And the current culture of America is unrecognizable to the culture of America from 200 years ago when he was born. It's not bad. It's evolution. He's a Darwin specimen. He will piss and moan until he's extinct."

A knock came at the door.

"What!" Becca screamed.

The door opened slowly and William Tully, her recent one-night stand, sheepishly pushed his head in.

Becca rolled her eyes. "Tully, what the hell do you want."

"Well, ahhhh, we've been looking through the contracts that

the candidates signed when they agreed to participate in the program and we have a problem."

"What's the problem?" Brooke and Becca asked at the same time.

William stepped in slightly and held on to the doorknob. "It seems that if they signed a contract, we are required to put them in episodes. If we don't, the studio is in breach of contract and they can sue us."

"So, what does that mean?" Brooke asked.

"It means we have to continue recording episodes until we've blown through everyone who has signed."

"So, we're back on the air?" Becca asked.

"Not necessarily," William took another step back out of the office. "The contract says we have to shoot the episodes. It says nothing about having to air them."

"So, we're going to do all of this work for nothing?" Becca asked.

"Nope. You're going to do it for a paycheck," William said, and then closed the door quickly.

CHAPTER SIX

Work on the show commenced but at a much slower pace. Since there was no air date, there was no sense of urgency. Brooke and the crews didn't break their backs trying to get in three or four shoots a day. They now had the luxury to take their time. Since they were being paid per episode, they weren't worried about the hourly rate either. Lunch hours were taking longer and there was no rush to eat and get back to the set.

Brooke ate alone in her dressing room, watching the news. There was so much out there about Kristine and Chris Haddock. At one point she switched between three different news stations and found differing reports about the situation—and her show.

GInfo had a reporter in Costa Rica. "....and though extradition has been officially filed by the United States claiming it was a U.S. citizen attack on a U.S. citizen, Costa Rica is still considering it their jurisdiction. They will not hand over Chris Haddock and have begun the process of trying him locally."

Entertainment news had a story about the show going ahead with production, "even after a formal statement earlier this week that they had suspended production pending further investigation into the death of one of their contestants. Here with more on the story is correspondent Arturo McNeil."

Scenes showing Brooke within different segments of the show were edited together with Arturo's voice over. "The producers and studio heads of *I Do or I Don't* are trying to keep their legal difficulties at bay as much as possible. Though they felt that suspending production was their most sensitive route, they've discovered that it's legally not an option. The contestants waiting in the wings could sue them for breach of contract, so the show must go on, as they say."

Local news at noon had a report from Sacramento. "Mr. Bullock has not been seen since the night the family learned that their daughter was murdered. Mrs. Bullock is extremely worried about her husband's whereabouts, though she has not commented yet on her concerns over his mental status. It has just been learned that Kristine was the second and their last child to lose her life. The couple had a son, Daniel, who died of leukemia, at the age of thirteen." The scene cut to a shot of a tombstone engraved with the name of Daniel Duncan Bullock.

Becca walked in and plopped down into Brooke's make-up chair. "It's insufferable, isn't it? Like nothing else in the world is happening but our stupid show. Don't you wish a war could start right about now?"

"Did you hear this?" Brooke pointed at the TV. "Kristine was the *second* child they lost. They had a son who died five years ago."

"No, I hadn't heard that," Becca said. "All I'd heard was that the father split the night they reported she was killed and hasn't been heard from since."

"Oh, those poor people." Brooke grabbed the remote and clicked off the TV. "Becca, I feel awful about this."

"You're allowed to feel bad for them, but don't start thinking that you are in any way responsible for this, because you're not."

Brooke scraped at her cottage cheese bowl, spooning out the last little curds.

"But if she hadn't been on our show, she'd be alive today." She popped the spoon into her mouth.

"Her choice. Not yours or mine. And you aren't the one who married her off to a crazed murdering asshole either. She made that choice as well."

"I don't think dodging responsibility is as easy as you make it sound." Brooke stood up, brushing a few crumbs off her suit. "If we weren't in any way responsible, we would still be on the air, and this wouldn't be the story it is."

Becca leaned forward in the chair, resting her arms on her knees. "Listen Brooke. You can't say anything like that outside this room, and to nobody else but me."

Brooke frowned. "I know that. I'm not an idiot. I just feel badly about the whole thing and I'm sharing it with you."

Becca slid out of the chair and walked to the door. "I had a feeling you might be thinking like that so I wanted to come talk to you." She opened the door. "Also, I wanted to let you know there is no hurry for the pool shoot this afternoon. Ben Hufnagel, one of the cameramen, is still AWOL, and everyone else is down in Anaheim at the Disneyland shoot. So, you've got nothing to do until he shows up. Relax and watch some uplifting TV—if you can find anything." Becca smiled and walked out.

Brooke grabbed a bottled water, sat back down on the couch, and clicked the TV on again.

Ben still didn't show up the next day. And what's more, Fiona didn't show up either. Brooke sat in the make-up chair and called her for thirty minutes, before getting up and heading down to Becca's office.

When she entered, Becca was on the phone, wrapping up a conversation.

"Okay....yeah....uh huh...Okay, I'll make sure it gets taken care of." Becca pushed a button and said. "Thank you for holding.

No, Alanna isn't here yet. I'll make sure she gets you all of that information as soon as she arrives. Uh-huh. Thanks for calling."

Becca slammed down the phone.

"Alanna isn't here either?" Brooke asked.

"Hell no, and I'm pissed." The phone rang again. "That girl is in trouble." Becca went to answer the phone and then stopped. "Wait a minute, what do you mean, either?"

Brooke shrugged. "I haven't seen Fiona yet. Which makes it the first time she's ever been late or missed a day, period. I've tried calling her for the last half hour and it just goes to voice mail."

Becca picked up her cell phone and hit Alanna's number. She waited while it rang and then hung up. "Nothing. But they usually come in together. Maybe they're having car trouble in a spot where there's no signal." She tossed her phone on the desk. "Or maybe they got fed up and decided to quit with all that's going on."

Brooke sat down slowly. "Becca, what if something has happened to them?"

"Like what?"

"I don't know. But Ben hasn't been seen or heard from in two days, and now Fiona and Alanna are missing too. Doesn't that sound a little suspicious?"

"I don't think we can jump to conclusions," Becca said. "Ben was an alcoholic before he got this gig. I know he's been on the wagon for four years now but still, with all that's happened around here, I wouldn't blame him for falling off. And Fiona and Alanna could just be stuck somewhere."

"You don't think we should call the police just to be sure?"

Becca chuckled and picked up her coffee cup. "I don't think they'll give it a second thought. I think you have to be gone for like a month before they'll call you a missing person. They have too much else to do."

There was a knock on the open door and Gunther walked in. "Are we still planning on shooting the studio segments tomorrow?"

Becca looked up. "Yeah, why?"

"And we're going live-on-tape?"

Becca shrugged. "Can't go live, and we have to shoot them. We've got no other choice."

Gunther nodded and turned to walk out.

"Hey Gunth," Becca called to him. The Norwegian turned and looked back at her. "I am expecting these will be aired at some point, so they have to look as good or better than anything we've done so far. Got it?"

He nodded. "Got it." He stepped out and then stepped back in. "Oh, do you know if anybody's heard from Lawton?"

Becca shook her head. "Lawton?"

"Yeah, Andy Lawton, the technical director. No one's heard from him in two days, and we've got two AWOL production assistants who've apparently found better things to do as well. If this is going up tomorrow night, we need to get Andy in here soon or find another TD by morning."

"Keep trying to get a hold of Lawton, and let me know by noon what the status is," Becca said.

"Will do." Gunther walked out.

Brooke looked at Becca, wide-eyed.

"Okay," Becca said, holding her hands out as if to stop everything. "I'll admit that's a bit of a coincidence."

"Becca," Brooke said, trying her best to stay calm. "I think our crew is under attack." She stood up. "What if some whacko is out there with a vendetta against our show and is taking them out, one-by-one?"

Another knock came at the door. It was Allen Morrall, the studio head. "Hey Becca, sorry to interrupt, but someone from the FBI is here to talk with you."

"The FBI?" Becca said. "Why does the FBI want to talk to me?"

Allen put his hands on his hips. "Well, the FBI doesn't run their plans by me for approval before they do anything, so I can't answer that question."

Becca shook her head and rolled her eyes. "No. Stupid question." She stood. "Okay, send him in."

A young thirty-something man stepped through the door wearing a perfectly pressed black suit, white shirt, and blue tie. His dark black hair was combed to one side, not a single strand out of place. He looked at Becca and then at Brooke. She noted his slightly off-center smile and the dimple in his chin.

"Hello, I'm Special Agent, Matthew Vecoli." His voice was soft, with a slight roughness to it. "I was hoping I could have just a few words with you."

Becca stood and motioned to a chair. "Sure, come in."

Vecoli walked over and shook her hand. "Thank you." Then he turned, smiled shyly, and shook Brooke's hand. "It's a pleasure to get to meet you. I'm a big fan."

"Aww, thank you," Brooke said. He held her hand for an extra moment as their eyes connected, which was okay with Brooke. Until now, she had no idea that the FBI had agents who looked like male models.

Becca, always the buzz kill, sat back in her chair. "So, Agent Vecoli, why is the FBI interested in this case?"

Agent Vecoli let go of Brooke's hand and took a seat. "Let's just say, I've been asked to look into it."

Brooke took a seat in the chair next to him. "Is it because the crime happened in another country, so federal authorities have to be involved?"

Matthew looked back at her with his crooked smile. "Something like that."

"Well, what questions do you have for us?" Becca asked,

trying to keep the meeting moving along.

"First of all, looking online, I noticed your show has a rather extensive questionnaire for contestants to..."

"Cast members," Becca said.

"Excuse me?"

Becca shook her head. "Their called cast members. Everybody's been getting that wrong this week. They call them contestants, applicants, hopefuls. This is not a game show or a job interview. It's a reality-based television show, and those who come on the show are selected by our casting department. The correct term is cast member."

Agent Vecoli stared back at her, mouth slightly open, waiting to see if she was finished.

"I'm sorry," Becca said. "I'm sure you can imagine this week's been very emotional for all of us. I hear these things said about our show and I'm given no opportunity to correct them."

"I'm sure it must be very frustrating for you," Agent Vecoli said.

Becca shrugged and nodded.

"Well, I was wondering if I might be able to get my hands on copies of Chris Haddock's and Kristine Bullock's applications."

"Do you have a warrant?" Becca asked.

Again, Agent Vecoli looked a little surprised. "I can get one if I need to. Is there a reason you don't want to cooperate with the FBI?"

"None that I can think of," Brooke said, glaring at Becca.

Becca sighed, shook her head, reached over, and hit a button on her phone.

"Alanna...shit. She stood up. "My assistant isn't here. I'll go see if I can find someone from our casting department." She walked out the door. "I may stop by legal as well."

Agent Vecoli swiveled his chair in Brooke's direction. "It appears the stress is getting to her."

Brooke scoffed. "The stress is getting to all of us. And now we have crew members missing."

"Missing?" Agent Vecoli leaned forward. "What are you talking about? Who's missing?"

"Becca's assistant, for one," Brooke said. "Who just so happens to be the sister of my make-up and hair girl. Neither one is answering our calls."

She started holding up her fingers. "And now two PAs, the technical director, and a cameraman who's been missing for two days now..."

"Have you contacted the police about this?"

"Not yet. But this is the first day the sisters didn't come in, and we just learned about the TD. So, I'm thinking we probably should."

"The TD?"

"Technical director." Brooke said. "He's the guy in studio control who pushes all the buttons on the panel with the colored lights and controls all of the camera shots and graphics that go live on the air."

"Ahhh," Matthew nodded his understanding, but Brooke was sure he didn't, nor did he probably care. "But the show isn't on the air right now, correct?"

"Well, no, but there is still production going on because of contractual obligations."

"But are you on tight deadlines—the same schedule as if it were to be broadcast each week?"

"Actually, no. Without an impending air date every week, the production schedule has slowed to a crawl."

"Then perhaps these missing individuals just aren't taking things as seriously without all the pressure on them."

Brooke shook her head. "Perhaps, with the production assistants and Lawton, but not Ben, our cameraman, or Fiona and Alanna. They've always been dependable. And I know they'd call in."

Agent Vecoli shrugged. "I still don't think I would rush to the police just yet. They don't take missing persons too seriously until at least a week, or something like that. But I'll tell you what...if it will make you feel better, I'll look into it."

"You would have time to do that?"

Matthew shot her a killer smile. "For you, I will make the time."

Brooke smiled back.

"And perhaps," Matthew said sheepishly, "you could somehow find the time to allow me to take you to dinner?"

Brooke giggled—something she did when she was nervous. And being the host of a national live television show, she didn't get nervous that often. But this man in front of her—his looks, his swagger and this question that she didn't see coming—definitely made her nervous, in a giddy, high school kind of way. "Don't you FBI guys have rules about fraternizing with suspects or witnesses or something?"

Matthew shrugged. "As far as I know, you're not suspected of any crime, and you haven't witnessed one either. So, neither of those rules would apply. You're just a very beautiful woman, who's caught up in a really shitty situation, and you're trying to do the best job you can. I just want to support that."

Brooke smiled. "You're sweet."

Matthew blushed, making him look even cuter. "And I'll be honest...I'm a fan. I can't believe I'm actually here talking to you, so to get a chance to take you to dinner would be a real honor for me."

"Okay, good news," Becca rushed back into the office, killing the mood. "There were several copies of Chris Haddock's and Kristine Bullock's applications right on Alanna's desk. I swear that girl is my very own Radar O'Reilly."

Matthew jumped from his chair and Becca handed him the copies. "Here you go. Is there anything else I can do for you?"

"Nothing at the moment," Matthew said. "But if I think of anything I'll let you know." He held out his hand.

Becca shook it. "All right then. Have a good day!"

Matthew turned to Brooke and held out his hand. "It was a pleasure to meet you, Miss Winthrop."

"Yes, it was," Brooke said, shaking his hand. "And the answer to your question is, yes."

Matthew's killer smile grew even larger. "That's terrific. I'll be in touch."

"I'll look forward to hearing from you then," Brooke said.

"Becca. Bad news." Gunther rounded the door frame and rushed into her office. He stopped when he saw Matthew. "Oh, I'm sorry. I didn't mean to interrupt."

"It's okay, Gunth," Becca said. "What's up?"

Gunther sighed, shifted his weight, and put his hands on his hips. "George just called. He went over to Andy Lawton's house to check on him. The front door was ajar, the place had been all turned over, like with broken lamps and glasses and shit. And there was blood on the floor and the wall."

Chapter Seven

Special Agent Matthew Vecoli stepped out of the studio office building into the hot California sunshine. The events of the last few minutes had him rethinking his decisions. He walked out to his rental car, a Volkswagen Jetta. He smirked, thinking there was no way he could pick up Brooke Winthrop and take her to dinner in a piece of crap like that. Maybe he could swap rental cars for the night or something.

Climbing in, he closed the car door and recoiled at the stifling heat that had built up in just the few minutes he was in the studio. He turned the key and cranked up the AC. Then he pulled out his phone from his breast pocket, hit a contact, and held it to his ear.

After a single ring, the call was answered. "Tell me you got them."

"Yes sir. I got them."

"Good. So let me know what your people find out."

"Sir...we need to talk," Matthew said.

"We can talk when you bring me the report."

"Sir..." Matthew was always intimidated by this man and still got nervous to cross him in any manner. "When I was in there, they just got word that their TD...er...technical director, seems to have been beaten and physically removed from his home."

"Yeah?" came the gruff reply.

"Well, when this started, we didn't talk about anybody getting hurt or harmed in any way."

"He's not harmed. He just had a headache when he woke up. The man's fine."

"Sir," Matthew said, shaking his head and looking to the second-floor windows of the office he just came from. "I work for law enforcement now and..."

"Don't get your panties in a bunch, Vecoli. Get me the report and walk away. I will never mention that you had any involvement in this."

Matthew looked down at his steering wheel, traced around the VW logo with his finger. "But...sir,"

"Matthew," replied the gruff voice now sounding desperate. "I need you. I need your help with this. Please tell me you're still with me. I promise you, everything will be okay."

Matthew sighed. He owed this man so much. Practically his very life. He knew he couldn't turn his back on him now. "Yes, sir. I'm with you."

"Excellent. Let me know when you have the report. Deliver the hard copy. We don't want anybody tracing your email to mine." Then the call clicked dead.

Vecoli looked at his phone screen. Yes, the call had definitely ended that abruptly. He slid the phone back into his breast pocket and shook his head. "Matthew, you dumb shit. What have you gotten yourself into?" He threw the car in gear and drove out of the lot.

CHAPTER EIGHT

Detective Brett Ostrowski used his hips to close the door of his silver Dodge Charger. His hands were full. He had a bean burrito in one and an afternoon coffee in the other. When the door didn't close all the way, he turned and slammed his behind up against it. Coffee splashed out of the sip-hole in his cup. He checked his reflection in the window to make sure it didn't stain his new shirt or tie. All seemed clean, even the little paunch over his belt that usually caught drips and crumbs when he ate in the car. He never wore his jacket because, even in winter months, L.A. was too damn hot for that. And he liked to roll up his shirt sleeves. He thought it made him appear busy. His head was shaved because that's what you did these days when your hair was falling out. The best way to hide a bald patch was to make it bigger. He had tried hair paint once, but after the merciless ribbing he got from his colleagues, he never made that mistake again. He turned and trudged into the Los Angeles Police Department Headquarters, chewing on his burrito.

Captain Vargas had texted and told him to come in. Ostrowski felt the captain was worried about him these days. After thirty-four years on the police force, he had spent the last fifteen with Paul Sykes. Paul had retired a couple of weeks previous and the captain must've texted Ostrowski ten times each day since. "Where ya at?" "Did you get your lunch?" "Did you make it to the crime scene?" "Are you coming back to the station?" And just the simple "You okay?" Ostrowski wasn't sure if, in losing a partner, he'd gained a mother. But it didn't bother him too much. The captain had always had their backs; worrying about his people just showed he cared.

"Yo, look at Detective Ostrowski," said Sargent Hampton at the front desk. "I don't know what I'd do if I didn't see food in your hands."

Brett chuckled. "I'd tell you to screw yourself, Hampton, but I don't talk with my mouth full." He took a big bite from his burrito and cheered the sergeant with his coffee cup as he walked by. Sargent Hampton smiled and saluted.

Ostrowski reached the elevator just in time. "Thud foor, pweesh," he said, with his mouth disgustingly full. The young female cadet hit the three-button and glanced up at him warily. Ostrowski smiled and shook his head. "Sowy." He took a drink from his coffee to wash the burrito down as fast as he could.

When the doors dinged and slid open, he stepped off the elevator and into the hallway lined by offices with floor-to-ceiling windows. Ostrowski walked to the end of the row and entered the captain's office. "Hey, Cap...oh." The captain was sitting at his desk, and a young well-dressed, female detective sat in the chair across from him. "Sorry to interrupt. I'll wait until you're free." He started to back out, but the captain waved him in.

"Detective Ostrowski. No come in, we've been waiting for you." He gestured to the woman. "I'd like to introduce you to Detective Shaneel Johnson."

Ostrowski sized her up when she stood and turned to him. She had on a clean, crisp new navy-blue suit with a white blouse. She wore just enough make-up to look faux-natural. With her hair cut short and tight, she definitely projected a serious image. She held out her hand and flashed him an all-business smile. But Ostrowski couldn't get the obvious joke out of his head and he started to laugh.

Shaneel Johnson looked confused and pulled her hand back.

"Something funny, detective?" the captain said.

Ostrowski settled down to a chuckle. "Wait until I tell the guys at the pub that today I walked in on the captain and Shaneel." He laughed again.

Shaneel and the captain looked at each other and then back at Ostrowski. He realized they didn't think it was the least bit funny so he settled down.

"I'm very sorry." He nodded at Shaneel. "I just 'Muskrat Love' moments like this." He laughed again, surprised that they didn't even smile. When he calmed himself, he asked, "I'm sorry, did someone die? Because that was pretty funny."

"Nobody died, Ostrowski," the captain said. "Let me try this again. Allow me to introduce, Detective Shaneel Johnson, your new partner."

Now nothing was funny. "My new...what?"

Shaneel held her hand out once more. "I've been looking forward to meeting you, Detective Ostrowski. When I found out we would be working together, I did a little research. Three-time recipient of the Police Commission Distinguished Service Medal. I feel privileged to be working with an officer of such distinction."

He looked over at Shaneel, and then down at her hand. "Oh." He went to shake it, but he was holding the burrito. He tossed it on the captain's desk, splattering refried beans and salsa across it. Ignoring the mess, he shook her hand. "Pleasure," he said. But his tone indicated something else entirely.

"Captain," Ostrowski said, trying his best to smile. "Can I have a word with you alone for a minute?"

The captain looked up to Shaneel. "Can you give us a moment, Detective?"

"Certainly, Captain." She glanced at Ostrowski, and then walked out the door, closing it behind her.

Ostrowski slouched into a chair as soon as the latch clicked. "Ken, what are you doing to me?"

The captain held up his hands. "I don't want to hear it, Brett. She's excited to work with you, and I don't like you out there on your own."

"No. It's been great," Ostrowski leaned across the desk. "This is the best time I've had on the job in thirty years. It's been liberating. Sykes used to fart in the car all the time. I don't have that problem anymore."

"Brett, I want you to have a partner. That's all there is to it."

"Okay." Ostrowski fell back into his chair. "But does it have to be someone so young?"

"She's the one who happened to be available. What do you expect me to do?"

"Well," he said, snapping his fingers, "my mama told me, 'you gotta shop around.'"

The captain rolled his eyes and gestured to the door. "Get the hell up and get her back in here."

Ostrowski stood, shuffled over to the door, and opened it. "Detective Shaneel."

She walked in. "It's Johnson."

"What's that?" Ostrowski said.

"It's Detective Johnson. Shaneel is my first name. If we're going to be working together, shouldn't you know how to properly say my name?"

"Yes, I should," Ostrowski said, staring at the captain, wishing he had laser beam eyes at that moment. "Sorry, Detective Johnson."

The captain tossed a sheet of paper to them. "I've got one for you two." Shaneel picked it up. "Head out to that address. It looks like someone's starting to go after crew members of that crazy marriage show."

"Will do, Captain," Shaneel said. She turned to Ostrowski. "You have a car?"

Ostrowski nodded his head toward the door. "In the lot."

"I'll wait for you down there. It will give you another minute to talk to the captain alone. If you need to." She walked out.

Ostrowski grabbed his burrito off the desk, however, he was strangely not hungry anymore. He headed for the door but before he left the office the captain called for him. "Hey, Ostrowski."

Ostrowski turned.

"Keep your chin up. Maybe love will keep you together." The captain winked and then smiled for what seemed like the first time since the early nineties.

Ostrowski couldn't bring himself to smile back. He just slogged out.

Detective Johnson was waiting for him outside the parking lot door. "Get all your complaints out the way?"

Ostrowski dumped his burrito and coffee in the trash can. "Complaints?"

"I'm assuming that's why you needed to talk to the captain alone. You're either upset that I'm black or that I'm a woman...or both."

"Black?" Ostrowski shook his head. "No, my last partner was black, and I loved him like a brother."

"So, you don't like being paired up with a woman then."

Ostrowski stopped and faced Johnson. "No. Listen, I don't have anything against you. Congratulations on making detective. I'm happy for you. It's not that I didn't want you as my partner. I didn't want another partner at all, woman or otherwise. I'm an old fart who spent the last fifteen years with another old fart. And now I very much like my alone time. I can think whatever I want, say whatever I want, eat whatever I want, and not even have to contain bodily functions without offending someone." He turned and headed to his car.

"I guess I can understand that. You get in a groove, and then someone else comes along and that groove has to change in a major way."

They reached the car. "You understand?"

"Yeah. I understand." Johnson walked around to her side of the car.

Ostrowski spoke to her over the roof. "So, if I were to slip up here and there and perhaps say the not-so-politically-correct thing or something, you'll give me a pass?"

Johnson opened the door. "Oh, hell no. I'll see your ass in HR." She slid into the passenger seat and closed the door.

Ostrowski looked to the heavens and sighed. Then he climbed into his side of the car and started it up. "What's the freaking address again?"

"6132 Eleanor Ave. Apartment 2."

Ostrowski punched the address into his phone, set it in its holder, and drove out of the lot.

For a while, the only voice heard on the drive was the female voice of Ostrowski's Android phone telling him where to turn. After a few minutes, he glanced over at his new partner. She stared straight ahead with her jaw clenched tight. He suddenly felt bad for acting the way he did. "Look, I'm sor..."

"No." She held up a finger and shook her head. "You don't have to talk to me. Just talk with yourself or whatever it is you do. I'm not even here. I just ask that you give me a warning before you release a bodily function so I can roll down the window."

"I'm trying to apologize here."

Shaneel looked over at him. "For what exactly?"

"How about, for acting like an ass and for pouting because I didn't get my way?"

"Mmmmm hmmm?"

"Uhhh. I suppose I could add, for making you uncomfortable on your first day as detective when you should have been excited and proud."

"Anything else?"

Ostrowski glanced over at her. "Look, you're my new partner, not my new wife."

Shaneel's mouth dropped open. "Oh, you are really bad at this. And there's your first slip-up."

"I slipped up already? How?"

"If I were a man having an issue with you, you wouldn't have made a wife comment."

Ostrowski laughed. "That's where you're wrong. I'm equal opportunity inappropriate."

Shaneel sat back and crossed her arms. "Well, you're right about one thing—you're definitely better off alone."

"Thank you for your understanding."

She looked out her window. "That explains the three divorces."

Now Ostrowski's mouth fell open. "Holy crap. You really did do your research."

"I'm a detective."

The car was silent for a while until Ostrowski spoke. "How about you? How many divorces have you had?"

Shaneel shook her head. "I'm still married with one son, four-years old."

"Nice."

They arrived at the apartment of Andy Lawton, a square, two-story tan building. Andy's apartment was on the first floor toward the back. The police had already taped the place off and a crew was inside taking pictures and dusting for prints. The detectives got out of the car and one of the officers standing out front nodded a hello. "Hey, Ostrowski. You breaking in a newb?"

"Nah." Ostrowski gestured a thumb toward Shaneel. "Her folks are on vacation this week. I told them I'd watch her till they got back." Many of the officers laughed. Ostrowski smiled and patted the man's shoulder as he passed.

Shaneel walked up to the officer and held out her hand. "Hi, I'm Detective Johnson."

"Welcome Detective. I'm Officer Malouf." He shook her hand and nodded toward Ostrowski. "You're working with the best."

Shaneel pulled out a pen and small notebook. "That's what I hear."

"Yeah. He knows how to think like the bad guys. Knows what they're going to do next. It's amazing."

With a polite smile, Shaneel nodded and prepared to write. "Do you know if anybody heard or saw anything?"

"No, ma'am. I checked with all the neighbors, and they didn't hear a thing."

Ostrowski headed into the small apartment to find three CSIs already at work. One was taking pictures, the other was dusting a side table for prints, and the third appeared to be collecting hair samples from a large bloodstain on the floor with tweezers.

The apartment was studio style—the kind where the love seat opens up to a small bed, and the kitchen, living room, and dining room are the same room. The place looked like a battle site. The walls were speckled and smeared with blood, and all the furniture in the room had been shoved around. A lamp from the side table had fallen and broken, and the small white shade had been trampled into a twisted mess. A torchiere lamp, in the opposite corner, had tumbled and shattered onto the floor, but the glass had been stumbled through and kicked around the room. Ostrowski thought this was where much of the blood had come from. Obviously, the combatants had rolled around in the shards, cut themselves, then slammed each other up against the walls. All but one of the wooden chairs around the small table were overturned. The one kicked against the far wall had one of the legs broken off it.

"Oh, my God," Shaneel said when she entered.

"Tell me someone heard something," Ostrowski said.

"Not according to Officer Malouf. He said he already asked all of the neighbors and they didn't see or hear anything."

"Bullshit. World War Three on the other side of the wall and they didn't hear a thing?" Ostrowski shook his head. "They're just too chicken-shit to talk is all."

"Well, look at this place. Can you blame them?"

Ostrowski wandered around a corner to find a large smear of blood across the wall at eye level. He pointed to it. "Looks like it got really bad here." A door to a small linen closet was open and hand towels had fallen out onto the floor. He walked into the tiny bathroom to find the mirror smashed. There was blood on the glass and several shards had fallen into the sink. Looking over, he saw the broken chair leg lying on the floor of the shower. "Hmmm."

"What?"

"I think I got it." He pointed to the chair leg. "Our victim had been making his assailant pay for the intrusion with that chair leg. But this is where he was disarmed. The assailant had had enough and smashed Lawton's head into this mirror. Lawton somehow managed to get into the hall, but his assailant slammed him up against the wall. Then he threw him across the room onto the floor over there." He pointed to a bloodstain on the floor where the CSI was working. "He obviously hadn't intended to hurt Lawton at all when he came here. But he wasn't going to leave without him."

"Why do you say that?"

Ostrowski pointed to the hand towels on the floor. "Because I'm assuming Lawton finally lost consciousness where he fell over there. His assailant opened this linen closet, quickly grabbed a towel or two, letting others spill out onto the floor, and tried to stop the bleeding."

He walked back out into the main room. "My guess is that

he tied the towel around Lawton's head, lifted the body over his shoulders, and walked out the door, not concerning himself with closing it afterward."

He pulled out his phone and hit speed dial.

"Hey Ostrowski," answered Captain Vargas, his voice on speaker phone.

"Hey Cap, did you say that someone was going after the crew from that marriage TV show?"

"Yes, someone from the show called and there are like four or five crew members who haven't reported for work in a few days. But this is the first report of anything that resembles violence."

"Well, it's violent all right. We need to check the homes of every crew member that's gone missing, and we should put squad cars out in front of the homes of the other employees."

"There's too many crew for that, Ostrowski. We don't have enough cars."

"Then I'd get the crew into one safe location until we get this figured out. I'm not sure why, but this guy seriously wants people, and he's not taking no for an answer."

CHAPTER NINE

The ESPN Sportscenter theme played on her phone—a ringtone she hadn't heard in a long time and to be honest, it was still a little too soon to hear it now. "Ba da da, ba da da." Brooke picked her phone off the counter. There was the smiling face of Jake May, looking tough in his Cleveland Browns uniform, ready to pass the football, scanning downfield for a receiver. He was the all-American hometown hero, who fell from grace hard. "Ba da da, ba da da." And she took the brunt of that fall, right in her left eye. She clenched her teeth, tapped the screen, and lifted the phone to her ear. "Hello?"

"Hey, Brooke." He was quiet, calm. But she could hear his nervousness, recognized the tinge of sheepishness in his voice.

She could also feel the tightness in her gut. Just the sound of his voice made her feel uneasy. "Hey," she managed to get out.

"I don't mean to bother you; I've just been watching the news and everything and..." He was struggling. He couldn't finish a sentence. "I just wanted to make sure you're good is all."

"Uh, yeah, uh…." *Crap. Now he knew she was struggling too.* "I'm good. We're working it out. It'll be okay."

"Oh, that's good. I just knew how upset you'd be at something like this."

"Yeah. It's been difficult." *Should she have admitted that to him?* "I never want to see anyone get hurt...obviously."

"Yeah." Nervous laughter. "Obviously."

"But we'll get through it and get back on the air here, eventually."

"Okay. I've just seen people say some pretty mean things about you so..."

"I know. I'm good." She needed to end this conversation. She didn't want him to get any idea there would ever be any kind of reconciliation. "So, thanks for checking up on me." *Probably shouldn't have thanked him for that.*

"No problem. I don't know if you heard, but I'm now the football coach at Walkerville High School. The school board agreed to give me a shot."

"I did hear. And I wish you all the best."

The doorbell rang. *Thank God.* "Jake, I have to go. I have a date." For some reason, she loved telling him that.

"Oh. Okay. Ahhhh....have...fun."

"Bye." Brooke clicked off the phone, threw it in her purse, and ran to the front door of her Santa Monica condo. She was now second guessing her decision to go out with Matthew Vecoli. When she started with Jake, she had similar feelings, like champagne bubbles pinging through her belly, and things eventually became a nightmare. No. Worse. Could she possibly be gullible enough to fall for another good-looking guy and risk the chance that the same thing could happen again?

The doorbell rang a second time.

Brooke paused her hand on the doorknob, wondering what would happen if she just didn't answer. She would stay in, she would be alone, and she would be safe. But she would always be wondering...what if? What if she had opened the door? What if he was as good inside as he looked on the outside? She had spent too much time with Becca to risk the "what-if" questions in her life. They would plague her until the end of her days. Not that she was the risk taker that Becca was—not even close. But there was no way she could sit back and wait for the sure thing, because Jake had been the sure thing, and look where that ended up.

The doorbell rang a third time.

Brooke turned the knob and pulled open the door. Matthew Vecoli greeted her with his simmering smile. "Hey, Brooke."

How ironic. He used the exact same two words that Jake had just used. Yet the reaction in her gut was night and day different. Where Jake's voice made her feel like sheltering from the coming storm, Matthew felt like the shelter.

He stood on her porch, perfect hair, perfect smile, perfect teeth, wearing black jeans and a blue shirt, opened one button too many.

"How ya doin'?" he asked, with his silky voice that had the perfect touch of rasp.

Brooke worked her mouth to speak but no words came out. She had to breathe first. She tried again. "I'm doing well." She grabbed her white knit wrap, draped it over her open shoulders, and headed out the door.

Matthew walked her down and opened the passenger door of a simple silver Jetta. Very sensible.

"I'm sorry about the ride," Matthew said.

"Don't be. Jettas are fine cars." She nodded and climbed in. "Thank you."

"Yes, but someone as beautiful as you deserves a Caddy." He closed the door, got in on his own side and started the car. "Given my ethnicity, you could've probably guessed that I can't think of a better place to eat for a first date than an Italian restaurant. So, I've picked a good one."

Brooke smiled. "Sounds great." She let a moment pass before adding, "First date, huh?"

Matthew glanced over and blushed. "Oh, I may be presuming too much. It's not really a first date until there's actually a second date. It's just 'going out.'"

"We'll have to see," Brooke said. Becca would be proud of her. She let him know her expectations were high with that one simple statement. Becca always told her to make them work for it.

When they reached the restaurant in Beverly Hills, Matthew dropped the car off with the valet and escorted her into Vincenzo Osteria. Brooke had heard of it. It had a reputation of being very good *and* very pricey. She tugged at his arm. "Matthew, this is too expensive. We don't have to eat here."

"Hey not to worry," Matthew said. "This place belongs to a very good friend of my uncle. He's the one who set up our reservation. C'mon. You're gonna love it." He put his arm around her shoulder and guided her into the restaurant.

"Wait here." Matthew said, and he walked up to talk to the hostess. She gestured toward a counter farther back where a short, older gentleman with glasses was staring intently at white slips of paper that he held close to his face.

Brooke became aware of another couple standing to her left. "Yep, that's her." She avoided looking in their direction, but she knew they'd recognized her. She heard the woman say, "I can't believe she even has an appetite after everything she's done."

Matthew leaned over the counter and said something to the man who looked up, smiled, and cried out, "Heeeey..." followed by a long string of very fast Italian words. He threw off his reading glasses, ran around the counter, and hugged Matthew. Then the two walked over to Brooke.

"Belissima!" said the old man when he reached her. "Bonjourno, benvenuta!" Grabbing her shoulders, he reached up and kissed her on each cheek.

Matthew chuckled. "This is Vincenzo. He's my uncle's friend who owns this place."

"Oh," Brooke wiped her cheek with her wrap. "Nice to meet

you, Vincenzo."

Vincenzo just stared up at her smiling. "Belissima."

"He's going to hook us up with a table." Matthew tapped the old man on the shoulder. "Hey, Vincenzo. Che ne dici di un tavolo?"

"Ahhh." The old man chuckled and walked away. "Seguimi. Andiamo."

Matthew smiled at Brooke and waved her forward. She walked behind Vincenzo, overhearing the woman in the foyer say, "Well, who do I have to kill to get a table?"

The interior of the restaurant was filled with dark wood, red cloth, and violin music. The booths had soft cushions and high backs, allowing a secluded feel.

Matthew ordered a bottle of Brunello and the chicken marsala for them both. Once the wine was delivered and poured, they had time to relax.

Matthew raised his glass, "Here's to...?"

"Kristine Haddock," Brooke said and clinked his glass.

Matthew smiled. "To Kristine." They both sipped their wine, which tasted exquisite.

Brooke spun the wine around in her glass, then watched the legs slide down the sides. "So, tell me something about Matthew Vecoli that very few people know."

Matthew chuckled. "Going right into interview mode, huh?"

Brooke smiled and shrugged. "I guess it's who I am."

Matthew looked up at the ceiling, contemplating the question. "Well, let me think about it. Ahh." He snapped his fingers and pointed at her. "I played Sancho Panza in *Man of La Mancha*, in high school."

Brooke paused a moment, then laughed out loud, glad she didn't have wine in her mouth.

Matthew raised his shoulders and his hands. "What? Is that funny? I was a hell of a good second to Don Quixote."

"I'm just picturing you singing on stage in tights and puffy shirts."

Matthew laughed then, too. "It was something to see, I promise you." He picked up his wine again and cheered her. "That little stint on stage makes me respect the hell out of you and the work that you do."

"It does?" She took another sip of wine.

"Hell yeah, it does. It's not easy getting up in front of people and trying to perform. Not only are you nervous as hell to screw up, but you're putting yourself out there for any and all to have an opinion about you." He took a sip of his wine. "I heard the lady at the front door when we walked in here."

Brooke offered a half-hearted smile. "Yeah. That's the fame portion of the job. That's what makes the job so glamorous."

Just then their salads arrived. They both decided to go with the fresh ground pepper.

After the waiter left, Matthew spoke. "Do you mind if I ask you something?" He speared some lettuce with his fork. "You were the darling of GINfo with your very own show. Why did you leave a big-time news gig where you got to see the world to do a reality-type show where you're stuck here in godforsaken L.A.?"

Brooke finished chewing her lettuce and swallowed. "A few reasons combined. First of all, when everything had blown up so dramatically between Jake and me and I was more news than any story I could cover, it was just hard to do that job anymore. Becca had been working on this concept basically since we graduated from the University of Pennsylvania. And she finally got all of the stars to align, and when Derek McGregor green-lighted *I Do or I Don't*, it just didn't make any sense to stay at GINfo anymore. It was just time to leave."

"Makes sense I guess." Matthew nodded. "So out of all the stories you covered at GINfo, what was the most memorable?"

Brooke swallowed. "I get asked that a lot. You'd think it

would be some meeting with a head of state or a movie star or something, but it's an easy answer for me. It was in this podunk town in Michigan where this little autistic boy had one person in the world he loved the most, and that man just happened to be in prison."

Matthew pointed his fork at her. "I remember that. You're talking about Delton Hayes and Noah Higgins, right?"

"Yes. In fact, I was done doing any actual live location reporting by that time because I was doing *Deep Dive*, but when I heard the governor was involved I demanded to be onsite at the prison the day Hayes was released." She slipped a forkful of salad in her mouth.

Matthew nodded. "Yeah, I can see that. It was quite a story."

"My turn," Brooke said, washing her salad down with a sip of the Brunello. "How does a singing manservant end up in the FBI?" She giggled.

Matthew blushed. "Bad or good fortune? I don't know." He plucked a tomato from his salad and popped it in his mouth. Washed it down with wine. "That was my sophomore year in high school. And I only went out for the play because the girl I had the hots for was playing Dulcinea."

"Really?" Brooke said. "You must have been really good to get Sancho Panza on your first audition."

"Oh yeah." Matthew reached for a piece of bread. "I was very good. If I'd had the courage to stick with it, we would probably be doing some big Hollywood show together right now." He pulled the bread apart and proceeded to butter half of it. "But I was chicken shit. And as soon as some guys started teasing me about it, I folded like a cheap tent. I didn't do another play."

"That's a shame."

"It is. I let peer pressure guide my every move. Let's just say, after that, I made some real bad friend choices. Just after high school, with no direction in my life, I ended up with the wrong crowd and found myself on the receiving end of an ambush, where the lot of us were beaten nearly to death. Actually, one kid lasted three days in the hospital, and then he did die."

"That's horrible."

"So, my dad and my uncle yanked me from bed one morning and dragged me, kicking and screaming with a good number of four-letter words, I might add...," he said chuckling. "Threw me in the car and drove me straight to the Marine Corps recruiting office and signed me up."

Brooke grabbed a piece of bread. "You poor thing."

"Nah. As much as I hated them that day, it was the only choice I gave them. I was too wild for my dad to deal with."

The bread was warm and the butter melted right into it. "I didn't know the Marines would even sign someone up under duress like that."

"Well, my uncle has always been well connected." He chuckled and gestured to the room. "As you can see. So, he knew the guys they were taking me to, and they hooked me up, no problem. Before I knew it, I was property of the U.S. Government and on a bus to Parris Island, South Carolina."

"That's insane."

"It was what it was. Like I said, I gave my dad no other choice. I had the whole world figured out by eighteen, and my dad was an idiot. My choices were going to get me killed. It was the only thing he could do and it ended up being the best thing for me. I came up against a sergeant down there who did nothing less than save my worthless life."

"How'd he do that?"

"By smacking me upside the head until I started thinking straight. If it weren't for him, I'm sure I would either be dead or locked away."

"It's good to have people like that in our lives."

Matthew stared off into the distance and nodded. "Yeah, it is. I'd do anything for him." He grabbed his glass of wine. "Anyway, after I got of the Corps, I somehow got into Quantico, and here I am now."

"Still the property of the U.S. Government," Brooke said.

Matthew laughed. "Whatever works, I guess."

"So, are you still letting others make your decisions for you?"

"What's that?"

Brooke dabbed at the dressing on her plate with the bread. "You said you let others guide your every move."

"Oh no." Matthew put his hand over his heart. "All my decisions are made right here. Which is why I'm sitting in this lovely establishment right now with the prettiest girl in the city."

Brooke smiled, grabbed her glass, and held it up. "Here's to your heart."

Matthew grabbed his glass and clinked hers. "Here, here."

They both sipped their wine and an older couple approached the table. "Excuse me," the man said. He was tall, walked with a slight hunch, and had a comically bushy mustache. "Aren't you the girl from that show where the two people who just meet, get married?"

Brooke put down her glass and looked up. "Yes, I am, sir. But we're eating so..."

"I thought so," He said. "Don't you at all feel ashamed of yourself? And now that a girl has lost her life because of the stunts you folks pulled..."

"Hey, pal. That's *enough*." Said Matthew, not at all concerned about keeping his voice down. "Move along."

"And you!" He turned to Matthew. "You obviously have no self-respect. Just out chasing skirts. Not caring about what type of person she is?"

"You know what Pops?" Matthew stood to his full height of six-two, reached into his back pocket, pulled out his credentials, and flashed them to the man, whose eyes grew wide. "I've actually been appointed to protect her from harassing assholes like you. So, if you don't want to end up in a cell for the night, you'll move your judgmental, piece-of-shit ass from my sight this very minute."

Matthew's words had their intended effect. The man said nothing else. He scowled and nudged his wife forward. They scurried out of the room quickly.

"Assholes." Matthew sat back down. "They don't know anything about you."

Just then two waiters sat steaming plates of chicken marsala on the table in front of them. Brooke looked at the food and then up at Matthew. "Do you mind if we box this up and go? I'm suddenly not very hungry."

When Matthew pulled into Brooke's driveway, there was a police car waiting for them. Both doors were open and a uniformed leg was sticking out of each side. The two officers stood and greeted them when they got out of the car.

"Evening, ma'am," the taller one said.

"What's going on, officers?" Brooke said.

"We have orders from downtown to take you to a safe location, Miss Winthrop."

"Is that really necessary?" Matthew asked. Both officers looked over at him and didn't answer. Matthew held his hand out. "I'm Special Agent Matthew Vecoli. I'm with the FBI."

One of the officers shook his hand. "When downtown tells us to do something, we don't ask if it's necessary. You understand how it is."

Matthew nodded. "Yes, I do."

"Is it Andy? Did they find him?" Brooke asked. "Is he.... hurt?" She couldn't bring herself to say dead.

"All we know is that there is reasonable cause for concern," the other officer said.

"Then I won't hold things up." Matthew turned to Brooke and handed her the two boxes of chicken marsala. "Well, here's food for you when you get there."

"You keep one of them," Brooke said.

Matthew shook his head and pulled his hands back. "No. I want you to have it. Trust me, this is going to be better than anything you'll find wherever you're going."

Brooke smiled. "Thank you. This has been nice."

Matthew leaned in and hugged her tenderly. "Yes, it has been. Call me later when you're settled."

"I will." Brooke felt that there may have been more than a hug between them at this point had the circumstances been different. But the appearance of the officers and the prospect of police protection had completely killed the mood.

"Good evening officers," Matthew said, shaking both their hands. "Keep her safe."

"We will, Agent Vecoli."

Matthew got back into his Jetta and, with a final wave, drove off.

"Would you like us to escort you into the house, Miss Winthrop?"

Brooke shook her head. "No, give me ten minutes or so to pack a bag and I'll be right out." She unlocked the door, clicked on the lights in the entryway, and headed straight for the kitchen. Throwing her purse on the counter, Brooke opened the refrigerator, placed the food boxes on the bottom shelf, and grabbed a bottle of water.

She noticed her hands shaking when she opened the bottle. She sighed, realizing she was about ready to cry. She leaned against the counter to collect herself. She wondered if Andy Lawton was still among the living and contemplated her own part in his current situation.

She thought of the many years she and Becca had worked

to get this show produced. The weeks spent on video calls, hammering out details, arguing about particulars. Finally molding it into something that not only sold to the network but also to the nation in huge numbers. Brooke always referred to it as a "labor of, and about love." And now, in a matter of days, all their hard work had fallen completely apart. Like they had built their castle out of tissue paper, and it disintegrated with the first rain.

Sniffling, she grabbed a napkin, wiped her nose, and headed into the bedroom. She pulled an overnight bag out of the closet, set it on the bed, and opened the lid. Grabbing her robe and nightgown off the chair, she tossed them in and went back to the closet to pick out clothes for the next few days. She just needed something simple to get her to the studio. As long as they were in production, there was an entire wardrobe department responsible for clothing her in the right outfits.

As long as they were in production. Brooke scoffed at the thought. It was true they were still shooting shows, but once the contractual obligations were met, Brooke was fairly certain the network would deep-six the entire thing. She doubted another network would pick it up. She couldn't even see another show like this being made, with all of the horrible backlash in the media. The Queen Bs might just be responsible for eliminating an entire genre of programming.

She grabbed a couple pairs of pink and lime green sweats, underwear and socks, walked out, and tossed them into the bag. Then headed into the bathroom. She kept a small toiletries bag in the closet in there. All of her make-up was taken care of too. A chill ran up Brooke's spine.

"Oh, my God." She looked into the mirror and spoke aloud to herself. "What if whatever happened to Andy, had also happened to Fiona and Alanna? What if that's why they're putting us in protective custody." Brooke fought back the tears filling her eyes. She continued her task with a purpose this time. Surely there was someone, wherever they were going, who would give her some answers. She just needed to get there.

She grabbed a hairbrush, toothbrush, and toothpaste put them in the bag and headed back out into the bedroom.

A rough, strong hand fully grabbed the back of her neck and pushed her down onto the soft bedspread. Brooke screamed but her voice was completely muffled. She tried to turn her head and felt a poke in the side of her neck. Pure terror tensed every muscle and her body coiled to fight. But then the tension released instantly. Her limbs did not respond and fell limp.

Her world went dark and consciousness slipped away.

Edwards

Chapter Ten

Becca opened her eyes, and stared into the sleeping face of a man, lit by the flickering colors of the flat screen mounted on the wall of the hotel room. She looked toward the TV and saw a rerun of CSI SVU. Mariska Hargatay still looked hot after something like 53 seasons, she thought.

Head pounding, bladder screaming, Becca dragged herself from the bed wearing only panties. She trudged toward the bathroom, passing an empty bottle of vermouth and an open jar of green olives on the way.

That's right. Dirty martinis. That explains the headache.

She kept the bathroom dark while she did her business, knowing the light would just aggravate her head.

Grabbing one of the hotel fluffy robes from the closet, she threw it on, walked back to the bed, and looked at the guy. Mark, or Marty or something like that. Martin. It was Martin. That's right. She met him in the lobby checking in. Martin who drank martinis. It was funnier last night. Now it wasn't funny at all because he was drooling his martinis all over her pillow.

Becca reached down and tapped him on the side of the head.

91

Nothing.

She tapped him again, harder. "Hey, Ace."

"What?" He grunted.

"Playtime's over. Time to go."

"What time is it?"

"I just told you. Time to go."

Martin opened dreary eyes and looked around. "It's still dark out."

"I don't care," Becca said. "I want my whole bed to sleep in, so it's time for you to get out of it."

Martin dropped his head back to the soggy pillow. "Don't be a bitch."

"What did you say to me?" Becca grabbed his hair and pulled.

"Ow ow ow ow." Martin was awake now.

Becca dragged him out of bed by his hair, letting go when he sprawled onto the floor.

"Dammit. That hurt." He picked himself up and glared at her.

"Oh, you wanna get tough?" She pointed to the door. "All I gotta do is scream and there are two cops standing right outside that door who will bust in here and drag your ass straight to jail. So go ahead and try it."

Martin curled his lip and turned away.

"No? Then grab your shit and get out of here."

"Can I at least go to the bathroom first?"

"You take one step toward that bathroom, and I'll start screaming."

Martin turned back to her. "Really. You're going to be that way?"

"You can piss in your own room."

Martin grabbed his shirt and pants. "I wasn't going to piss."

The thought of what he just said made Becca's stomach churn. "You sick bastard." She pushed him toward the door.

"Uhh, can I get my clothes on first?"

"No." She opened the door and shoved him into the hallway. Martin stood there in his boxers looking at the police officers who flanked her doorway.

"Sir, we have decency laws" said the red-headed officer. "You need to put your clothes on now or you will be arrested."

Martin struggled to put a leg into his pants. "I need my shoes."

Becca grabbed his shoes and threw them at him.

"Ow! Are you seeing this, officers? Isn't this assault or something?"

"Dude," scolded the other officer, tall and fit. "When you hook up with a stranger in a hotel without knowing anything about her, this is what you should expect." He shook his head. "Decisions in life and all."

Still struggling with his pants, Martin shuffled down the hall. "You should be protecting the rest of us from her, not the other way around."

The officers looked back into the room at Becca. "Don't stand out there and judge me," she snapped.

"No ma'am. We're only here to guard you, not judge you," said the fit-looking cop. He nodded to her. "Are you all right?"

"Yes. Thank you."

"Have a good rest of your night, ma'am."

"Thank you. You, too."

The officers glanced at each other and then looked back out to the hallway.

Becca closed the door and sat down on her bed. Seeing the officers standing there made everything seem more real. She was here because people were getting hurt. People were getting hurt because of her relentless ambition. Because of the decisions she'd made. "Decisions in life and all," the cop had just said. They cautioned Martin about hooking up with a stranger, but she had been just as reckless. She was reckless with everything, not giving a shit about her own life, but now she was hurting the people around her. What if her recklessness were to get Brooke hurt somehow? She would never forgive herself. She needed to be more responsible—more caring. She couldn't just explain everything off by saying "they knew what they were getting into." Because the truth was, they probably didn't.

Becca looked up at the door and a feeling of deep gratitude gripped her. Two men were standing out there with one purpose, to protect her from her own decisions. She walked over to the door and opened it.

Both officers turned back to her. "Everything all right, Miss Dodge?" said the redhead.

"Yes. I just wondered if you could use anything. I could call room service and put it on my card. Anything you want? Coffee or something?"

Both officers glanced at each other and smiled. Then the redhead looked at Becca, "No, thank you, Miss Dodge. We're just fine."

Becca looked at the other officer. "You?"

"I'm all good but thank you."

"Well, thank you for being here. Good night."

"Good night, ma'am."

Becca closed the door and took off the robe, pulled an oversized t-shirt from her bag, and threw it on. She went into the bathroom, downed three Tylenol, and climbed back into bed, drawing the covers up close.

CSI SVU was still on, but Becca had no desire to watch any more drama right now. She grabbed the remote and clicked through the channels, stopping at some home renovation program. She found it amazing, the different types of reality shows being produced right now. People loved this shit. Nobody liked working on their own house, but everybody seemed to like watching other people rip walls out of other houses only to find mold growing or hidden hornets nests the size of Kenmore refrigerators. The worst problem they could come across was a cracked foundation. But that was it. Nobody died from a cracked foundation. It just cost them a shitload of money to repair it. Then the budget was shot and the house became an Ikea dream-house after that because there were no more funds for the good stuff.

Becca thought about what it would be like to produce a show like that. Perhaps nobody even dressed up to come into work. Perhaps the required dress was jeans and flannel shirts. Brooke would look good in a flannel shirt. But Brooke looked good in anything.

The truth was that *I Do or I Don't* would probably never again see the light of day. Becca felt it was really dead. The only show to truly go out on top. There is a day when everyone expects the plug will be pulled on a show, but never when it's television's highest-rated show two-thirds of the way through the first season. Becca knew it was time to start thinking about the next project and right now a home-reno show seemed fun somehow. She would just need to figure out how to sexy it up.

Something hit hard on her door. Becca jerked upright in her bed. She pulled her covers up close.

Sounds of a struggle, and then a bang on her wall. Feet shuffled followed by another slam. There were three small swift bumps on the door, and she heard something slide down it.

For a brief moment there was silence, then Becca heard the distinct sound of a card inserted into the key slot on her door, the plink-click of the lock, and the handle was turned. The door swung open slowly and Becca lie back in her bed, her ears pounding as loud as the door banging a few seconds ago.

In stepped a stocky man, with short, cropped, mostly gray hair. He wore a dark suit and tie, but Becca knew the last time she saw him he was wearing a military uniform. It was on the set of *I Do or I Don't*, and he was giving away the bride, Kristine Bullock.

"Miss Dodge?" Sgt. Duncan Bullock said, in a low scratchy

voice. "Please come with me." He raised a handgun and pointed it at her. "We have a show to produce."

CHAPTER ELEVEN

Sgt. Bullock directed Becca into the bathroom, instructed her to get dressed, and closed the door. She threw on her jeans and a pair of flip-flops and heard noises of hard work and heavy breathing in her hotel room. She grasped the edge of the counter firmly and looked at herself in the mirror, trying to judge what the woman was feeling who stared back at her. Becca had garnered the nickname "Tearless and Fearless," during her self-destructive period at the University of Pennsylvania. But the woman in the mirror didn't fit that description. She looked scared. And for good reason. This wasn't some stupid dare or college prank. She wasn't staring down some dumb-ass thug on the street who truly had no backbone and showed it if you pressed him. This was a father who had lost both of his kids, and he considered her responsible. Not only that, but he was also battle-tested on the fields of war. He had a reputation of being tough and apparently proved it by going through two armed police officers without firing a shot. This wasn't somebody Becca could just stare down. She had met her match with Sgt. Bullock. Beyond that, this was personal. His second child was dead, and he was ready to make her and everyone else pay. Crimes of the heart were hard to curtail.

"All right, Miss Dodge," she heard him say. His voice was quiet and muffled through the door, but it still made her heart stop.

"Come out and bring your bag."

Becca tried to swallow but discovered her mouth was completely dry. She tried to catch a breath and found that difficult as well. She looked once again at the woman in the mirror convinced that this was the last time she would be seeing her... alive.

"Come on out," the voice said. More agitated now.

Becca felt that if she were to have any chance of surviving this, making him more agitated was not the way to go about it. She nodded to her reflection, and with a shaky hand, clutched the doorknob and turned. Exiting the bathroom she saw two unconscious police officers lying on the floor of her room, their hands zip-tied behind them, their faces bloody. The eye on the fit, taller one was already swollen so large she wasn't sure he could even open it if he were awake.

"Get your bag and let's move," Duncan Bullock fiercely whispered. He stood by the door, his pistol aimed in Becca's direction. She saw her bag on the bed, all zipped up and ready to go. She looked back at Bullock, looked into his eyes, at his resolute stare, and she suddenly felt as if she had to fight to catch a breath. She considered running back into the bathroom and locking the door, but her mind raced through the consequences of that action. That would launch him into a rage and he'd do one of two things: kick in the door and either physically drag her from the room or kill her right there.

"Come on, let's go," he said, clearly not willing to put up with any shit.

Becca recalled him saying that he wanted to produce a show. Obviously, he had no intention of killing her—right now anyway. He had something to prove. By going with him she had a chance to think of some other way to escape. She would take the time. Becca grabbed the overnight bag and hurried out the door.

"Stairway to the right."

She turned and walked at a brisk pace down the hall. She'd hoped someone would open their door so she could run into their room and lock this lunatic out. Then she would have time to call 911. But it was late. No one was awake right now. Otherwise they would have come out when they heard all the ruckus when Bullock took down the police officers.

They had almost reached the end of the hall, Bullock's gun in Becca's back, when they heard the ding of the elevators behind them. They both looked back to see two more police officers get off the elevator. They looked confused, not seeing their colleagues standing in the hall, and then seeing Becca at the other end with another man. Both officers crouched and pulled their guns. "Freeze!" one shouted.

Bullock hooked Becca's arm into his and dragged her the rest of the way toward the stairwell, using her as a shield. Becca could hear the two police officers running behind her. One screamed into his radio microphone, "Officers down! Assistance required! Back stairwell. Suspect getting away with Becca Dodge!"

Bullock crashed into the stairway door, slamming it hard against the cement block wall, and headed down the steps. Becca couldn't run as fast in flip-flops and lost her balance a few times. She'd drop to her knees and bounce painfully down the steps, but the steel grip and cast-iron arm of Bullock never let her fall. He lifted her back up, practically wrenching her shoulder out of its socket, and kept running at an amazing pace down the five flights of stairs. They were already down two flights when the police came through the door on the fifth floor.

"Stop!" they yelled. Becca thought that was about as useful as standing next to a train track and screaming, "Slow down!"

Bullock kept up his relentless pace. Becca thought he'd probably been in worse situations in whatever wars he'd fought and wasn't too concerned about the level of competency on his heels. As they neared the bottom, the two officers had only managed to gain a little over a floor and were well behind them.

Bullock headed out the hotel's back door to a waiting black SUV. It beeped when they arrived, unlocking it. Bullock swung open the back door and pushed her toward the seat. "I'm sorry about what I'm about to do. I was only going to cover your eyes."

"What do you mmm..." A heavy crack on the back of her head cut Becca's words short, and she slumped forward. She felt Bullock shove her all the way in and heard the clunk of her door close. Becca could only lie there, hovering just above unconsciousness, while she listened to the sound of struggles outside. A body slammed up against the car. A gunshot rang out and several thumps. A silent pause and then a blaring siren in the distance.

The driver's side door opened and someone jumped in, revved the engine, and threw the car in gear. The car took off like a shot and swung around corners like a carnival ride, throwing Becca's limp body off the seat. Gunshots and skidding tires faded into the distance as consciousness and the pain in her head slid away.

It seemed only minutes later that the car door opened again. Becca felt herself being pulled out and hoisted over a shoulder. With a steady gait, someone carried her through the cool night air, her arms hanging down, swaying gently. She could hear doors being opened, felt herself being gently let down by firm strong hands onto a soft surface that protested with the squeak of springs and wires. She realized instinctively that she was lying on a cot. She was covered by a warm fleece blanket. The light went out, a door was closed and locked, and Becca fell back into an agitated sleep.

Chapter Twelve

Brooke's eyes fluttered open. She looked around, experiencing that initial disoriented moment when you wake up and don't recall exactly where you are. Her bare surroundings were bathed in a soft light that was diffused through parchment paper taped to the window of a door. The room was beige. A large gray metal desk and chair were pushed to the opposite wall of the tiny room. And the air had a harsh metallic tinge to it. Brooke bolted upright, horrified when she realized she *was* truly disoriented with no idea where she was. She was on a cot, covered with sheets and a blanket. She had on the same dress she wore on her date with Matthew. Her bag sat on the floor next to her.

The cot creaked when she stood. Testing her wobbly legs, she shuffled her way to the door and tried the handle. It was locked. She knocked gently. "Hello?" There was no answer. She carefully picked at the tape, loosening an edge and ripping it free. She ripped a small section of the paper back, about the size of an eyehole in a door, to expose the window. Brooke put her eye up to the paper and looked through. She saw the craggy face of a man, staring back at her.

Brooke screamed and jumped back, tripping over the chair and landing on her butt on the hard cement floor. She heard keys unlocking the door, so she scooted over to the cot, grabbed the blanket, and pulled it down in front of her.

The door opened, and a man walked in. "Good morning, princess," he said with a great deal of disgust in his voice. "You have to give me a minute to get here before you start ripping the place apart." He set a package of Pop-Tarts, and a bottle of orange juice on the desk. "There's your breakfast." He gestured to the door. "The paper's on there for your privacy. If you don't want privacy, then go ahead and rip it off."

It took Brooke a moment to place the face and the voice. "You're Kristine Haddock's father."

He turned to her, emotionless. "Yes. And *you* are the reason she's dead." He walked back to the door. "Eat your breakfast, you're going to need your strength. Opening arguments of your trial start today."

"My trial?" Brooke felt her face become hot, afraid to be locked in the room again. "Mr. Bullock, please. Can we talk?"

Bullock chuckled. "No need to be nervous, darling. The whole thing is going to be run by the very same rules you and your friend set up. If you're truly blameless, you have nothing to worry about." He gave her a wink, closed the door, and locked it.

Brooke looked up at the Pop-Tarts and OJ. She realized all she'd eaten since yesterday afternoon was a side salad. She reached up, grabbed the Pop-Tarts, saw they were blueberry. Frosted. Pop-Tarts were a guilty favorite of hers. But she couldn't eat now. Couldn't even think about eating. She placed them back on the desk, climbed up onto the cot, and pulled the covers up to her shoulder. And cried.

Chapter Thirteen

The pounding of Becca's head hammered her back to consciousness. The pain kept her from lying flat any longer. She sat up, threw her legs over the cot, and cradled her aching head in her hands.

Looking around, she scanned the room—a beige shithole that looked like a factory office from the eighties. It even had the gray metal desk and an old chair on wheels pushed against the wall. The place was dimly lit from the outside. The door had parchment paper taped to the window. She wasn't sure if it was meant to stop her from looking out or someone else looking in. It took a moment to figure out it was the latter because she could easily rip it down if she wanted.

The door unlocked, and in walked Duncan Bullock, with a small shopping bag. "Good morning, glory. I brought breakfast."

"Fuck you," Becca said. The pain in her head was replacing her fear with a smoldering anger.

"Got a headache, huh?" Bullock pulled a bottle of Tylenol, and a bottle of orange juice out of the shopping bag and tossed it on the cot next to her. He placed a pack of Pop-Tarts on the desk. Then he pulled out another object, ripped the package open, and jammed the wrapper and bag into his pants pocket. He cracked the package and shook it up. "I'm sorry about the crack in the head last night. The situation warranted a quick neutralization to take care of more pressing matters." Bullock reached over and placed the emergency cold pack on the back of her head.

Becca flinched when he touched her and smacked the ice pack out of his hands, sending it sailing under the desk. "Don't touch me, asshole."

Bullock backed away. "So that's the way you want to be? I show you a kindness that you don't even deserve, and you act like that?"

"Like what?" Becca said, raising her voice. "Like someone who's been kidnapped and....neutralized?" She squinted from the pain in her head caused by the yelling.

"No. Like the rich, little entitled princess that you are," Bullock yelled. "You have a little lump on your head, but my daughter is dead. *Dead!*"

Becca's fear rushed back.

Bullock turned to the door. "You need to get your shit together, Queen B. The trial starts today."

"Trial?" Becca said. "What trial?"

"*Your* trial. The one to determine if you're responsible for the death of my little girl."

"You're setting up a kangaroo court?"

Bullock scoffed. "Something like that. But we're using your rules."

"My rules?"

"Yeah. We're going to broadcast this extravaganza. Perhaps we'll call it, 'I Did or I Didn't.'" Bullock walked out and slammed the door. Keys rattled and the lock clicked.

Becca dropped her pounding head back into her hands. She wondered if Brooke was safe or if he had beaten her senseless as well.

She reached down and popped the top on the Tylenol, jammed her fingernail through the foil covering, and ripped the cotton out. She dropped four into her hand, threw them into the back of her mouth, and swallowed. Then she cracked open the orange juice and drank half of it in one gulp to wash them down.

She crawled under the desk to retrieve the cold pack, then clambered back onto the bed, and held it on the back of her head. She knew she needed to get over her headache to be as sharp as possible to get through this.

She was a good producer and knew she would need all of her negotiation skills on this one.

Edwards

CHAPTER FOURTEEN

After several hours, the door unlocked.

Brooke hadn't moved in all that time. She looked up from under the covers of her cot.

Duncan Bullock stuck his head in. "Time to get dressed. Show's gonna start pretty soon."

"Get dressed? In what?" Brooke asked.

"In whatever you brought for clothes." Duncan closed the door, then opened it again. "You've got five minutes." He closed the door and locked it.

Brooke sat up and grabbed the bag next to her bed. She unzipped it and recalled she had only brought sweats—lime green and pink. She had no idea what Bullock was talking about, this show that was about to happen, but she didn't want to be seen in sweats. She stood, looked at her dress to see if it was at all camera-ready. It was a wrinkled, crumpled mess. Sweats were definitely the better option. Pink it was.

Stripping out of the dress, she threw the sweats on and was brushing her hair when a knock came at the door. "Are you decent?"

She flinched at the sound of his voice and the hairs stuck out on her arm. "Yes," she said, but it came out barely audible even to her. She realized she was so frightened she was going through the motions, doing what she was told, with no thought to the consequences. "Yes," she said again, louder this time.

The door unlocked and swung open. Bullock was a step outside of the door, holding a large knife. "Come out, and I'll take you to the restroom before we go to the studio."

Brooke looked at the knife, it gleamed in the yellow, halogen light outside the room. It had a long blade with a portion of it serrated. Brooke's feet couldn't move as if they were fixed to the floor. She pointed at the knife. "Why do you have that?" she asked with a quivering voice.

Bullock held it up in front of his angry face. "To make sure you know I'm serious. I'm extremely adept at using this thing," he said, twirling it around in his hand. "If you try to get cute or brave, I'll just take care of business right now, and we won't worry about the show." He gestured to the left of the door. "Now let's go use the bathroom, so we can get this thing going."

Brooke tried to move, but she couldn't take her eyes off the knife. As long as he held that, she was sure her feet wouldn't be able to take a step.

Bullock seemed to understand this. He spun the knife in his hand and slid it into a holster on his belt with the same flare as an Old West gunfighter holstering his gun. He waved her out of the room. "Come on girl, break a leg, before I break it for you."

Brooke shuffled forward on heavy legs, exited the room, and turned left. They were in one end of an old factory. The space was large and dark with stained concrete floors, and the stench of machine lubricant hung in the stale air.

Bullock guided her down a hallway, walls made of cement block painted with a high-gloss paint that was once white but now dingy. Dark streaks marked it up here and there. On the left were two metal doors, rusted on the bottoms and embossed with black signs, "Men" and "Women."

"I'll be waiting right here," Bullock said. "Don't take forever."

Brooke pushed open the squeaky door and walked in. It slammed shut behind her with a thunk that echoed in the expanse of the old cement bathroom. The counter had four sinks facing a dirty mirror. In front of each sink was a red plastic cup with a toothbrush and a small tube of toothpaste. Names were written in black marker on each cup. Brooke's was first, then came Becca's. But she was surprised to see cups marked for Fiona, Allana and Lyssa, one of the production assistants who had gone missing. Brooke looked closer, all of the cups were wet, and had been used recently except Becca's. Perhaps that meant Becca hadn't been kidnapped—or it just meant that Brooke was brought into the bathroom first. If the show was about to go on, Becca was probably in the building.

Brooke used the restroom, then washed her hands and brushed her teeth. The mirror was covered with a hundred years of filth, and she could barely see her reflection—but what she could see wasn't good. She did the best she could to clean up her smeared make-up and arrange her hair into something at least agreeable to the eye.

When she was finished, she walked out. True to his word, Bullock was waiting for her. He jerked his head down the hall. "This way."

Brooke walked along, flanked by Bullock, through a door into what was obviously the front office area of the factory, or whatever this building was. She caught a glimpse of the lobby through the thin window in the door as they passed by. Floor-to-ceiling windows revealed that it was night out. Bright light poles lit up a big empty parking lot, and another factory building was across the street.

A small plastic oil drum sat next to the door to the lobby with wires attached to the handle. On top was a black box with a green light.

Bullock guided Brooke down a row of identical offices to a locked door. He pulled out his keys, opened the door, then stood back to let her enter a large conference room. A long table was tipped on its side and shoved up against the far wall. Three brown vinyl chairs, probably from the lobby, were positioned, TV show style at one end of the room. Fiona sat in a standard chair along the wall, Ben Hufnagel stood next to two tripods at the near end of the room, and Andy Lawton—his head wrapped round with a wide, white bandage and sporting a baseball-size black eye and a bruised, scabby face—sat at a computer next to Ben.

"Oh my, God," Brooke said. Her eyes filled with tears when she saw them all safe, and in Andy's case, still breathing.

"Start on her make-up," Bullock said to Fiona. "I'm going to go get the last member of the cast." He closed the door and locked them in.

Brooke rushed to Fiona, who stood to greet her. They hugged and cried for a minute before Brooke pulled back and asked, "Are you all right? Have you been hurt?"

Fiona shook her head. "No, just frightened."

She turned to Andy. "What happened to you?"

Andy looked up from his computer screen. "I was stupid enough to fight back. Turned out to be a bad idea. He's pretty tough for an old guy."

She looked up at Ben. "You?"

Ben shook his head. "He was on me too fast. Put a gun right to my forehead." Ben placed his finger just above his left eye. "The worst thing that happened to me was soiling myself."

Andy chuckled. Ben looked down at him and smiled.

"I'm glad you can all laugh about this," Brooke said. "I'm not finding a whole lot funny."

"It's not funny," Ben said. "But I have to do something. And I think laughing and standing tall beats rolling up into the fetal position and crying."

"You should probably sit down here so I can get to your make-up," Fiona said. "He doesn't do angry well, apparently."

Brooke went over to the set of three chairs and took the middle one. Fiona reached into a plastic shopping bag and pulled out a tube of foundation.

"Obviously he knows very little about make-up." She squeezed a little out on her middle finger. "This shit is discount brand from some dollar store, and there are no sponges for me to even apply it." She dabbed and smeared Brooke's face.

Brooke looked up at Fiona. "What about Allana?"

"She's all right. She's back in the room."

"Why is she not here with us?"

"I don't think she's supposed to be here at all. She was scheduled to be out of the house on a date at the time Mr. Bullocks burst in, but she popped back to grab something, and he had no other choice but to nick her too." She threw the tube of foundation back into the bag and pulled out a powder compact.

A jangle of keys was heard outside the door, and the lock clicked. The door opened and Becca walked slowly in, concerned eyes darting back and forth to scan the room. Her expression melted into one of relief as she recognized those around her. When her eyes locked on Brooke, they reddened instantly. "You're okay!" She rushed over, dropped into the chair next to hers, pulled her close, and squeezed tightly.

Brooke squeezed back. "I'm good."

"Make her up too," Bullock said. "I'll be right back, and we can get going."

He slammed the door shut and locked it again.

Becca pulled back and addressed the others. "Everyone is good?"

Fiona and Ben nodded. "As good as we can be under the circumstances," Ben said.

Becca looked at Andy. "Lawton?"

Andy stuck a thumb in the air. "Terrif."

"You don't look terrif."

Andy patted the bandage on his head. "Apparently the guy is as good a medic as he is a raging lunatic. He got me fixed up pretty well after nearly taking my head off."

Becca rubbed the back of her head. "I'm afraid I know what you mean."

"What are you talking about?" Brooke reached up and felt a large lump on the back of Becca's head. "He hit you?"

"That's not the word he used. He *neutralized* me. And he beat the shit out of about five or six cops whose only job was to protect me from crazy-ass people like him."

"Are you serious?" Ben said. He rolled his eyes and shifted his weight. "Who the hell *is* this guy?"

"He's Kristine Haddock's father," Brooke said.

"I know that. I'm talking about his other life. Are we stuck here in the warehouse from hell with Rambo or something?"

The door unlocked and opened again. Bullock gestured to others outside the door. In walked the two production assistants, Mike Riser with his surfer-tanned skin and sun-bleached hair and a terrified Lyssa Brandt who looked cold wearing flip flops, shorts, and a sleeveless Black Lives Matter t-shirt.

Brooke thought they had to have been taken at the same time. They'd become a couple during the run of the show, and were inseparable, referring to themselves as "salt and pepper."

"Stand over there," Bullock said, gesturing to the wall. "We need to have a talk."

Mike and Lyssa scurried across the room, jammed their backs against the wall, and huddled together close as if they wanted to conserve body heat. Bullock closed the door, inserted a padlock, and clicked it shut, tugging on it to make sure it was locked. Then he turned and addressed his captive audience. "Okay, let's talk ground rules here." His voice was low and rough. His tone flat, serious, no-nonsense. "There isn't anybody who knows where you are, so don't plan on a rescue anytime soon. This is an old stamping plant with several exits. I have wired every door. Each wire is connected to its own drum with enough ammonium nitrate to level this whole building. So, if you're thinking about sneaking out of here in the middle of the night or something, you will end up killing yourself and everyone else."

"Shit, you are crazy," Becca muttered.

Bullock looked over at her, expressionless. Stared at her for a moment, then continued. "If you're thinking about jumping me, ambushing me, trying in any way to cause me harm, I think Mr. Lawton here can tell you that would be a bad idea."

Andy lifted his middle finger to Bullock.

Bullock was unphased by the gesture. "I retired as a gunnery sergeant from the marines, and I had a special talent for hand-to-hand, so if you oppose me...," he slowly looked around the room, letting each person fill in the pause with their own idea of the horror he could inflict. "I will not lose. I've brought you here because I require your special talents. You have all had the misfortune to work on the television program *I Do or I Don't*...the show responsible for the death of my daughter." Bullock put his hands on his hips and looked at the floor, collecting himself.

Brooke felt herself wanting to cry, but she couldn't determine what the source of the tears truly would be—empathy for this man's pain or fear for the predicament he was putting her and her friends in.

"So now I want to put together a little show of my own." Bullock said, pointing at Fiona. "She has enough make-up. Get started on the other one."

"I've still got to do her eyes and lipstick," Fiona said.

"Hurry the hell up," Bullock snapped.

Fiona jumped. Brooke rubbed her shoulder, to calm her. "Just do my eyes, Fee. I can put on my own lipstick."

Fiona started to sniffle and rummaged through the plastic bag for the eyeliner.

"It's okay, girl," Brooke said. "You got this."

Fiona looked up, eyes red, and mustered a sad, crooked smile. She nodded and began applying the liner.

"We're going to produce our own version of the show," Bullock said. His voice was quiet, almost tired, and scratchy like it had been overused for years. Worn out. "Only this time the contestants will be our illustrious Queen Bs." He gestured to Becca and Brooke with a smile, which looked more like a sneer.

"What?" Becca scowled. "Are you saying that we're the couple here?"

"Oh, no," Bullock said, wagging his finger. "What I'm saying is that we're going to go through the show with you two as the contestants. And you can see everything that is wrong with it. How twisted it is. How it can invite every low-life and cretin in the world for their fifteen minutes of sick fame."

"And then what?" Becca said. "What are you going to do with it once you have it recorded?"

"Then we're going to broadcast it on the Internet for the whole world to see."

"So a low-life cretin like you can get your fifteen minutes of sick twisted fame?"

Bullock never broke his stare at Becca. The center of his brow sagged, and Brooke could see the veins pulse in the side of his head. Everyone froze and a deep, oppressive silence smothered the room. The only sounds Brooke heard were her own heartbeat and the rapid breaths from Mike and Lyssa.

Brooke looked at Becca. True to form she was still "Tearless and Fearless," doing her best to hold her own against this monster. But even the strong and sure Becca finally withered under the weight of his stare. Her defiant expression wilted, and her shoulders sagged.

"You said we were going to have a trial," Brooke said, trying to break the tension and save her friend.

Bullock's stare snapped to her. "You're in it." He gestured to the cameras. "This show is the trial."

"I don't understand."

"Your stupid show is broken up into segments. Every episode is exactly the same. There's nothing new or extraordinary about one from the other. So, we will go through each segment and see where things can drop through the cracks. How you can put individuals like my daughter in harm's way. If you can prove to me that's not the case, then my bad, and you walk out of here." He walked his two fingers in front of him.

"And if we can't?" Becca said, a bit meeker now. "Which I'm assuming is the case."

Bullock's eyes narrowed. "Then you'll get the opportunity to say 'hi' to my daughter."

"Wait, what?" Lyssa's s voice squeaked out. "But what about us? We didn't do anything wrong. We shouldn't even be here."

Bullock pointed at her and spoke quietly. "Shut up."

"No, man. She's right," Mike said. "We didn't kill your daughter, *they* did." He jerked his head in Brooke's and Becca's direction. "They're the ones responsible, not us. This is a stupid internship."

In two quick strides, Bullock was on Mike, hand around his throat, pinning him hard to the wall.

Lyssa, screamed and dropped to the floor, buried her face into her knees, and wailed.

Mike couldn't talk, couldn't breathe. His wide terrified eyes looked into Bullock's.

"You're through with your little tantrum, understood?" Bullock said in his quiet scratchy voice. "You're going to calm your little girlfriend down, and you're going to do your work." He shook his head slowly from side to side. "I'm not asking. Don't make me have to talk to you again." Bullock released his grip and the intern dropped to the floor, clutching at his throat, and gasping loudly. Lyssa cried out, then reached over, curled into him, and whimpered.

Ben glared at them both in disgust. "Nice," he whispered.

Bullock strode back into the center of the room as though nothing had happened. "The rest of you are just here to crew the show. Once we've completed all four episodes, you will be free to leave. I have no issue with anyone here other than these two." He pointed two fingers at Brooke and Becca. Then he clapped his hands, rubbed them together, and turned to Fiona. "So, let's get Miss Dodge made up, and we can get this show going."

CHAPTER FIFTEEN

"I get losing your daughter and all is going to cause some people to go a little crazy but pulling something like this is unbelievable."

So said the voice of Gino, the very rude DJ who woke Ostrowski. The clock/radio alarm went off at precisely 6:30 am every morning. Ostrowski wanted badly to hit the snooze button and shut Gino up. If he'd still been working with Sykes, he probably would have. But now he had Shaneel Johnson to keep him on his toes.

"Oh, no. It wasn't just the daughter he lost," said Gino's morning partner, Jade. "He had a son die of leukemia a few years back."

Ostrowski rubbed the sleep from his eyes. *Mornings with Gino and Jade* was his show of choice to wake up to—not because they were incredibly good or talented, but because they seemed to be less stupid than all the others. And on the rare occasion they actually played a song, it was an oldies tune, which reminded him that he used to be young once.

"Yeah, but still," Gino said. "How does that justify doing

something like creating your own show on the Internet and calling it a trial?"

He rolled over and jumped from the bed, his spine cracking at every vertebra when he straightened. Ostrowski sighed, stretched, and shuffled off to the bathroom, listening to the rhythm of his knees and ankles as they creaked out the percussive beat that he referred to as the "first walk of the day—an old guy's march."

"I don't know," Jade said. "It seems a little over the top for a guy, especially a military guy. He's supposed to be this hard-nosed sergeant. You'd think he'd have it a little more together than that."

Ostrowski yawned and looked at himself in the mirror. What a mess he was first thing. He had sunken eyes and a twelve o'clock shadow—he was supposed to look refreshed in the mornings, not like an extra from *The Walking Dead*.

"And the women look completely terrified. They're sitting with a psycho and trying to look non-plussed, but you don't buy it. You can see they're about to lose it."

Ostrowski thought he looked like kids these days. They wanted to have hair on their face and shave everywhere else — everywhere else. They wanted the stubbly face of a thirty-five-year-old and balls that looked like a five-year-old's. It didn't make sense to him.

"Good morning," Gino said. "If you're just joining us, and you've been completely unconscious the last few hours then I'll let you know what we're talking about. Many of you know that Becca Dodge and Brooke Winthrop had been abducted, along with several members of the crew of the TV show *I Do or I Don't*."

"What the hell?" Ostrowski had been ignoring the radio. He kept it on in the mornings basically so it wasn't always so quiet and hoping for a song. But when he heard the names of the women in the case he was working on, he snapped to attention. He walked out, sat on the bed, and listened.

"Overnight a YouTube link was sent to many of the major

media outlets showing Becca and Brooke, the Queen Bs as they have been dubbed, sitting in what looks like a set from an old cable company talk show," said Jade, laughing.

"It does," Gino said. "Anyway, they are sitting there with the father of Kristine Haddock, the bride from the show who was recently killed by her newlywed groom in Costa Rica."

"Holy shit," Ostrowski said. He grabbed his phone off the charger and flicked it on. There were twelve missed calls from "Rook," his name for Shaneel, and another seventeen missed calls from Cap. "Son-of-a..." He jumped up and ran back into the bathroom to get ready.

Ostrowski managed to get his teeth brushed and not much else. He threw his clothes on and drove to the station, listening to Gino and Jade discuss the video of "Bullock and the Bs," as it was now dubbed. Fans were calling in saying all manner of crazy things. "Good for him. People need to be held accountable and the justice system never does it." "I feel for him and all, but nobody has the right to do that to those poor women." "What if we just burned the network building down right now — stop the garbage they broadcast every day."

Ostrowski shook his head. "What crazy assholes." He clicked off the radio and parked, ignoring that his car wasn't remotely between the white lines. He rushed into the headquarters building and sprinted up to the third floor. He met Captain Vargas on the way to the briefing room.

"What the hell happened to you?" Vargas asked.

"I got in a fight," Ostrowski said, breezing past him.

"Who with?"

"You don't know her." Ostrowski rushed into the briefing room, now jammed with people. "What the hell is going on with this video I've been hearing about?"

"You haven't seen it yet?" Shaneel Johnson said, who was leaning over a table looking at printouts of pictures.

"No, I haven't seen it yet. Why would I watch it without you?

119

We're partners, aren't we?"

Shaneel stood straight and looked at the captain, who followed several steps behind Ostrowski.

"You watched it without me, didn't you?" Ostrowski put his hands on his hips and did his best to look hurt.

Shaneel backed up a few steps and crossed her arms.

"Well, what the hell have you been doing?" she said. "I've been trying to get you on the phone all night and all morning."

"Cut the crap, Ostrowski," Vargas said. "You snooze you lose, and I know you've been snoozing." He turned to the guy in front of the laptop. "Go ahead and run it for 'Rumpled-Old-Skin' here.

"Nice," Ostrowski said. "The love is underwhelming." He pulled out a chair at the table across from the monitor on the wall and took a seat. Shaneel sat across from him and spun her chair to face the monitor.

"This was sent to every major network and media outlet at about four this morning," the captain said. "It exploded immediately. Traffic so heavy it shut down the Internet site." He nodded to the tech guy in front of the laptop who hit the space bar.

After a fifteen-second commercial for stress medication, a picture of Kristine Haddock appeared on the screen, accompanied by an echoey and distant voice-over.

"This is Kristine Bullock, my daughter. She was kind, cheerful, loving, beautiful to the core. Until the day she decided to go on the TV show known as *I Do or I Don't*."

Bullock had chosen a photo of Kristine on the beach, laughing as she ran through the waves.

"This show turned out to be the worst decision of her short life. For she put her hands in the fate of these two women."

The video cut to the front page of the *Hollywood Ledger* featuring pictures of Becca Dodge and Brooke Winthrop. "These two are responsible for letting a man onto their show, who would eventually marry and then kill my daughter."

The shot then went to a close-up of Duncan Bullock. He continued to talk.

"That man, Chris Haddock, is now in jail in Costa Rica; he will be dealt with by the authorities there. But he is the end result of a crime that was perpetrated long before he came along—the crime of putting my daughter into harm's way." The camera zoomed out to reveal a somewhat disheveled Brooke and Becca. Duncan sat to their right.

"I have those two women, sitting here with me today." He glanced over. "Miss Becca Dodge, and Miss Brooke Winthrop."

The women took each other's hands when he mentioned their names. They were clearly not happy to be there, fear certainly resonating on Brooke's face. Becca stared mainly at Bullock in disgust.

Bullock turned back to the camera. "Over the next few days, we will be running a little experiment. I have the belief that their show attracts the bottom feeders of society, and that they don't bother to weed out the worthless pieces of shit who want their fifteen minutes of fame. They tell me I'm wrong about that. So, we're going to devote a single program to a separate segment of their show. For example, the first segment that always came up on *I Do or I Don't* was the application portion of the show. The part where the contestants weeded through the applicants to find their own perfect match. And *that* will be the topic of tomorrow's broadcast. Thank you." Bullock nodded to the camera, and the picture faded to black.

"Well, that has tune-in written all over it, doesn't it?" Ostrowski said.

"You're kind of a sick bastard, you know that Ostrowski?" Vargas said.

"Well, what do we know about it?" Ostrowski asked. "Did we check the IP address and trace the location?"

"Couldn't," Shaneel said. "He used a virtual private network.

According to the address our guys got, he would have to be on the third floor of Digital Lock Security Systems in Concord, California."

"Where's that?"

"Just outside of San Francisco."

Ostrowski put his arms up on the table and rubbed at the stubble on his face. "Then we'll just have to see what we can figure out from the video."

Shaneel tapped at the folder of images with her pen. "Already on it."

Ostrowski didn't know whether to admire his new partner or be irritated with her. He was pleased that she was on the ball, but she didn't have to be so damned smug about it. Then he remembered being a rookie too—about 127 years ago and recalled trying to impress everyone around him—and decided to give her a pass. He smiled and patted the chair next to him. "Well, come on over, partner. Let's see what we're working with."

Shaneel glanced over at the captain, then dragged herself up from the chair, around the table, and plopped down next to him. She slid the folder between them.

There were three screen shots printed out. The first was a close-up of Duncan Bullock, the second was a wide shot showing Bullock with Dodge and Winthrop, and the third was a blow-up of a seam in the wall behind them.

"Doesn't give us much to go on, does it?" Ostrowski said.

The captain leaned against the table next to them and crossed his arms. "Not a whole lot, no."

Shaneel tapped at the blow-up with her pen. "Typical industrial office wall. Could be a warehouse somewhere."

Ostrowski sat back in his chair and cradled his fingers behind his head. "Or could be an office in practically every single strip mall in the southland.

The captain harumphed. "Yeah, that's probably true. I didn't think of that."

Ostrowski smiled on the inside. He got that one without any coffee. "So, with nothing to go on, we wait for crazy dad's next upload. In the meantime, let's see what we can dig up on this hot shot. Find out who he really is."

The captain turned to the guy in front of the laptop. He nodded, jumped up, and rushed out of the room.

Ostrowski sighed, slapped his knees, and stood. "Come on, Johnson. I'll buy you a coffee and a donut."

"I don't like donuts," Shaneel said.

"I don't either," Ostrowski said. "But being on the police force, we're required to keep up appearances."

CHAPTER SIXTEEN

"You've reached Duncan Bullock. Please leave a message."

Matthew Vecoli clicked off the call. "Son of a bitch." He paced back and forth in his hotel room, GINfo playing on the TV, discussing the big news of the day—the video that had been uploaded by Duncan Bullock earlier in the morning. They talked at length about what he said in his three-minute video and discussed multiple views on his intentions once this thing was over—which included ending the life of the two women.

Matthew paced, not knowing what else to do. He didn't know how to get hold of Sgt. Bullock, had no clue as to his location. He couldn't use the services of the FBI. He had already called in all of his favors there. He was now at a standstill, and that was a position he was not used to being in, nor was he any good at it.

His phone buzzed in his hand. The screen read, "Dunk." He tapped it and held it to his ear. "What the hell is going on, sir."

A tired, raspy voice spoke back. "What do you need, Vecoli?"

"We didn't discuss this, sir. You never told me this was part of the plan."

"Not sure you would have been so willing to help me if I had."

"You got that right."

"You've got nothing to worry about, Vecoli. Your part is done now, and nobody will ever know how you helped me, I promise you that."

"Sir, can I ask what you plan to do with Miss Winthrop, Miss Dodge, and the rest of the crew when you're done with your stunt?"

"Don't ask questions you don't want the answers to."

Vecoli pulled the phone away from his ear and squeezed it, wishing it was Sgt. Bullock's neck right then. He snarled and put the phone back to his ear. "Sir, there is something you need to know. I have feelings for Miss Winthrop. So I'm asking you to release her as soon as possible."

There was silence.

"Sir?"

"I'm sorry, Vecoli. You should have never gotten involved. And just so you know, this is the last time I'm answering this line. Now I know you're no longer on my side, I'm not taking a chance you'll get your FBI friends to coordinate my location."

"Sir, I..."

But Bullock cut him off. "I'm sorry, Matthew." The call beeped dead.

"Sir?" Matthew said. "Sir?" He looked at the phone and saw the call was over. He quickly hit the button and listened for the ring. "You've reached Duncan Bullock..." Matthew growled and threw his burner phone against the wall of the hotel room. It left a dent and shattered, scattering across the bed and the floor.

CHAPTER SEVENTEEN

Ostrowski winced when the quarterback got sacked on the two-yard line. He was sitting in the war room watching the replay of his beloved USC Trojans take it on the chin in a crushing defeat by the Oregon Ducks from the previous Saturday.

Shaneel Johnson walked in. "Okay, I just got off the phone with someone at Langley. They said they'd be sending..." She stopped in her tracks when she saw what was on the screen. "*What* are you doing?"

Ostrowski slapped his forehead. "Ugh. With everything going on this weekend, I never got to catch this game."

"We have a huge crime of national interest going right now, and all you can think to do is watch football highlights?"

Ostrowski turned and hit the space bar on the computer. "Trust me, they're not highlights. Oy vey!"

"Weren't you going to call his wife?"

"Yes, but I didn't want to call her at the crack of ass. I wanted to give her a chance to get up first." He looked at his watch. "Okay, 11:30. There's a good chance she's up." He gestured to a chair. "Have a seat you can listen in on this."

Shaneel crossed her arms and sat down.

Ostrowski pulled his phone out of his pocket, located the text Shaneel had sent him with Mrs. Bullock's phone number, and hit the dial button, keeping it on speaker. The phone rang twice before a woman's voice answered with a tired, "Hello?"

"Good morning, Mrs. Bullock. I'm Detective Brett Ostrowski with the Los Angeles Police Department. First of all, let me please express my deepest sympathies for everything you're going through. I can't even imagine how difficult this must be for you."

There was a pause on the other end before a weary, "Thank you, Detective."

"I do have to ask you a few questions, though. Do you have a moment to talk?"

"I'm not sure I have any more information for you than I've already given to the FBI."

"The FBI has already contacted you?"

"Yes. I spoke with them yesterday."

"Is that so?" Ostrowski raised an eyebrow to Shaneel. She shrugged and shook her head. "Well, if you don't mind, I have just a couple of things to ask and I'll let you be. Is that all right?"

"I guess, Detective."

"First of all, could you tell me when your husband first went missing?"

"Let me think," Corrine Bullock said. "We were down there on the show on a Tuesday. They left the following Wednesday, and on Thursday she...fell. It wasn't until the following Wednesday they discovered that Chris Haddock had pushed her. And Dunk took off the very next day. So, it was a week ago, last Thursday."

Ostrowski realized that this poor woman would frame time around the day her daughter was killed from now on. People always thought about dates based on major events in their life. It has been three years since his last divorce, six since his father died, seven since his second marriage, and fourteen since his mother died. Whenever somebody asked him about when something happened, he always tried to wedge his answer into one of those time frames.

"So, about ten days ago then." He nodded at Shaneel and mimicked writing with his hand. She opened her folder, grabbed a pen, and started taking notes.

"Yes. I guess about then..." The woman's voice trailed off.

"Did he say anything to you before he left?"

"He said he loved me. Then we went to bed. The next morning I woke, and he was gone. There was a note on the kitchen table that said he loved me and his life with me, and thanked me for twenty-eight of the best years of his life." Her voice quivered.

"I'm sorry," Ostrowski said. "This all must be very difficult. Just a few more questions."

"Thank you, Detective. It is."

"Did he say anything in the day leading up to his departure? Anything that would give some indication of his intentions?"

"This is what the FBI wanted to know. All I can say is that when Kristine...died, Dunk cried. In all the years I've been married to him he's only cried twice, once when Daniel passed away and then that day when Kristine died. He was down for days. But when they discovered it was Chris Haddock who killed her, he became enraged. We have a punching bag in the basement where he always worked through things. He always called that his 'thinking time,' and he spent hours beating it that day."

"I see." Ostrowski looked up at Shaneel. She nodded and continued to write.

"And then when Costa Rica said they wouldn't extradite Chris Haddock, Dunk grew very angry. He said we deserved justice. I guess that was when he went down and started punching the bag. Because I remember him being very calm when he came back upstairs. He said that Haddock was actually just a symptom of the problem, and that the real issue here was the show that had put her in danger, to begin with. He said the 'Queen Bitches,'—pardon my language. I'm just saying it like he did, and of course, he was very angry."

"Not a problem, Mrs. Bullock."

"He said the 'Queen Bitches' were the ones to blame. Said they needed to be put up on charges, but that nobody was even going to look at their part in this. He just said the show was the real crime here."

There was a pause, as Ostrowski waited for more, but nothing more came. "And that is all he said?"

"Yep. That's pretty much it."

"He didn't say anything about how they should pay, or that he was going to take matters into his own hands or anything like that?"

"Nope. Nothing like that," Mrs. Bullock said. "In fact, he didn't say much at all after that. He went back downstairs for another hour or so, but he wasn't punching the bag. I didn't know exactly what he was doing, but I heard him puttering around down there for quite a while. Then he came upstairs. We ate a real quiet dinner. Watched a little TV. Then I took an Ambien and went to bed. The next morning I woke up and found the note."

"And did you ever discover what he was doing in the basement?"

"Yeah. I went down there and found that he'd been going through his military gear. Had stuff spread out all over the place. I saw that he'd taken a couple of his guns and things."

"And you didn't call the police when you saw this?"

"Of course not." Mrs. Bullock sounded upset. "I wasn't going to call the police on a man who just felt like he lost everything. I went on the news, told him I loved him, and I wanted him to come home."

"Good. You did everything right, Mrs. Bullock." Ostrowski said. "You tried to take care of things, with as much understanding and love as possible."

"Yes. That's what I was trying to do." Her voice sounded extremely tired now.

"I'm going to let you get on with your day, Mrs. Bullock."

There was a sarcastic chuckle. "Such as it is."

"But if your husband contacts you, or you think of anything else, please give us a call at this number. Do you have it?"

"Yep. It's showing up right here on my phone. I will, Detective."

"Okay. Take care, Mrs. Bullock."

"Thank you."

Ostrowski tapped the call off and looked at Shaneel.

"FBI's already on this. Did you hear anything about that?"

Shaneel shook her head.

"Hmmph." Ostrowski spun his phone around in his hand. "They usually contact us first when they're investigating something in our jurisdiction."

"But the Bullocks live clear up in Concord, California. Would the FBI need to contact us for that?"

"True, but the crime and the investigation are down here. They would definitely contact us. At least they always have in the past." He shrugged. "Unless they called the captain, and he didn't let us know about it." He hit the space bar and the football highlights came back to life. He spun around and leaned back in his chair.

"What are you doing!" Shaneel said. "We have a case to solve."

"This is my thinking time. Let me know when you're ready for some lunch."

Chapter Eighteen

Heavy footsteps grew closer, and then she saw a shadow on the paper covering the window. A manila folder was slid under the door. The shadow stood back up and walked away.

Becca sat up from her cot, put her feet on the floor, and looked at the folder. She already knew its contents. These were the applications of the men that Bullock had filled out.

When they had finished shooting their opening segment the previous night, Bullock had the foresight to shoot the opening to his next show, which was to introduce the selection segment. Becca had to admit that was a good move. As sick and twisted as this whole thing was, Bullock did know how to produce.

The cot creaked when she stood. She picked up the folder and read the note on the cover, written in Sharpie, "5 apps, pick 2." That was a change from her show. They gave each cast member ten applications, and they were supposed to pick three. If any of the choices of the men and women lined up, they were selected to be matched on the show. Becca didn't know where this was going. Did this mean that these five guys were out there somewhere getting ready to go on a date with her and Brooke? Perhaps they were staying in their own rooms in this very facility. Did Bullock have a conference room set up somewhere with candlelit tables and Pop Tarts on fine china?

She tossed the folder on the desk, sat down, and thumbed through the applicants. The first one actually looked promising. Henry Munson, a dentist from Chicago. Apparently, he had a business mind too, because he also owned a building in the city where he rented out space.

The next one was a lawyer from Colorado. A regular outdoorsman—he loved to ski in the winter and hike and camp in the summer.

The door unlocked and Bullock shoved in Ben Hufnagel, who was holding the small video camera. "Don't do all the work before we get a chance to take the shots," Bullock said. "You know how this works." He tapped Ben on the shoulder. "Go ahead, you got five minutes. Make it look real, just like you do on your show." He closed the door, locked it, and they heard him walk away.

"What the hell are we doing here, Ben?" Becca asked.

Ben shrugged. "I guess I'm getting some b-roll."

"No. I mean why are we doing what this guy says?"

"Ummmm, because he'll kill us if we don't."

"I think he's going to kill us anyway"

"Not me." He twirled his hand for her to turn. "Spin back around and sit up at the desk. Let me get some shots of you right there."

"Are you serious right now?" Becca stared at him. "You're going to go along with this until he kills Brooke and me, and then you're going to be okay just walking away?"

"Becca, we've got five minutes to get these shots," Ben said. "Four now. So please let's just get this done."

She spun around and looked back at the papers. "Okay, but don't think you have a spot on my crew after this is all over.

"I can get another job," Ben said. "I can't get another life."

Becca gritted her teeth and rested her head on her hand. She looked down at the papers while Ben stood behind her and got an over-the-shoulder shot. Then he moved to the other side of the desk and knelt down, capturing a low-angle medium close-up, probably doing a slow push-in to a closeup, to make it look like she was concentrating.

But she wasn't concentrating. She couldn't even read the applications. Her head was whirling, and her stomach felt sick. Becca had been through a great many things in her short life. But Ben's lack of any concern for her stung as badly as any betrayal she'd had to deal with.

Becca had considered herself a good producer. She felt she showed concern for her crew. She gave them a long leash, empowered them to make their own creative choices, and many, as in the case of Ben, she gave complete control of their schedule. As long as the show got out each week with as minimal amount of stress as possible, she didn't watch their clocks.

"Put your finger on one of the lines," Ben said. "Like you just spotted something interesting."

Becca followed his suggestion while he stood several steps back and shot a medium-long shot.

Becca felt like crying. So much for the "Tearless and Fearless" moniker she'd been given so long ago. She had now felt both emotions in sequential days.

"What if you took the folder over, sat on the cot, and leaned against the wall while you flipped through a couple pages?" said Ben, the consummate cameraman, always looking for the next good option.

"Why don't you kiss my ass," Becca said.

"What?"

The fact that he actually looked surprised, infuriated Becca. "What do you mean, what? You piece of shit, traitor." She jumped from her chair. It rolled across and slammed against the door.

"Becca we're all trying to get through this the best we can,"

Ben said.

"No, you're trying to sell me out to save your own feeble little ass." She pulled back her left foot and let it fly, hitting him perfectly in the balls.

It happened so fast, Ben never had time to even flinch. He let out a wail and collapsed into the fetal position on the floor. The camera clattered and bounced along the cement, and Becca saw the viewfinder go dark. She felt satisfied. She'd accomplished the proverbial "two birds with one stone."

Keys rattled, the lock clicked, and Bullock opened the door, brandishing the knife. He looked at Ben whimpering on the floor. "What the hell is going on in here."

Becca shrugged. "I think he's done."

Ben cried out. "She just kicked me in the nuts."

Bullock looked at her and sighed. "Did you get any shots?"

"A few," Ben said between his huffs and his puffs.

"Then get the hell off the floor and get out of here."

"We could use more shots," Ben said.

"Just go." Bullock continued to stare Becca down while Ben struggled to his knees, picked up the camera, and pushed himself to his feet. He shambled past them out the door. "I think she broke the camera too."

Becca smiled at Bullock.

He shook his head and stepped backward toward the door. "Get busy and make your picks."

"You know what?" Becca said. She reached over, closed the folder, and threw it at him. "You can take your picks and shove them up your ass! I'm not doing the trained monkey thing any longer." The papers flew out of the folder and floated every which way to the floor.

Bullock watched all the papers skitter to a stop, then glared at Becca.

"What're you going to do, beat me up? Are you going to put

a battered woman on camera? That will really help your cause, won't it?"

Bullock shook his head. "Nope. There's a young lady here that wasn't supposed to be. When she asks me why I'm breaking her fingers, I'll tell her about your defiance." He stepped out.

Becca felt her face grow warm and dread rush over her. "No. You leave Alanna alone, you coward!"

"This is going to cost her one finger. Your actions moving forward will decide the other nine." He closed the door and locked it.

"NO!" Becca screamed. She grabbed at the handle, tried to turn it, yanked on it, hoped to tear it from the door. But it held firm and fast. Becca pounded the metal door with clenched fists, screaming for Bullock to leave her friend alone, but there was no response. She ripped at the paper covering the window, saw only the cement floor under the yellow halogen light way above that faded into the darkness of the vastness of the building. She looked both ways, still pounding. She heard only footsteps.

Becca turned her back to the door and slid down to the floor, considering—no hoping—that Bullock used Alanna as a threat to keep her in line. He couldn't truly be that kind of a monster.

A distant scream, piercing through the thickness of the fabricated walls, proved her wrong. It was definitely Alanna's. It was followed by an agonized cry, and wails of "Why? Why? Why?"

Becca pulled her knees to her chest, clamped her hands over her ears, and wept, muttering, "You miserable bastard."

She looked at the papers scattered about the floor of her room and realized she had the power, and the responsibility to stop it. She crawled on all fours, gathered up the applications and the folder, and climbed up onto the bed.

Out of the corner of her eye, she saw Bullock peering in the window. She dared not look at him, for fear she would do or say something that would cause more harm to Alanna. She stared down at the open folder hoping that would be enough for him.

Apparently, it was. He silently moved away from the window.

Becca slumped over, buried her head in the pillow, and cried. Miss "Tearless and Fearless," was now both crying and afraid.

But none of it was for her.

Chapter Nineteen

Brett Ostrowski and Shaneel Johnson sat in the war room, eating their In-n-Out burgers, while they waited for the rest of the team to arrive for a follow-up meeting. They sat in silence. The only sound in the room was that of their soft munching and the occasional rustle of the French fry bags.

Ostrowski looked mainly at his hamburger, glancing up occasionally to see if she was looking at him. If she was, he gave her a polite smile and looked back down at his hamburger.

Shaneel finally spoke but he was in the midst of chewing and thinking about the Kings game, and he didn't hear her. He looked up and covered his mouth with his napkin. "What's that?"

"I asked when you're thinking about retiring."

Ostrowski sniffled and shrugged. "Haven't given it much thought." He continued to chew and then wondered what motivated her to ask such a question. Perhaps she didn't like working with him and wanted to start some sort of countdown clock until the day she didn't have to deal with him anymore. Or maybe she was just attempting small talk. "Why?" he decided to ask.

Shaneel held up a finger, took a drink, and washed the fries out of her mouth. "Because working with you is brutal. And I was hoping you were retiring soon just like your previous partner so I could have someone from this century show me the ropes."

Her honesty felt like a ball-peen hammer up the side of his head.

"Oh, okay. I was just wondering if you were trying to make small talk or not." He took another bite of his hamburger and stared intently at the remains of a squashed fly on the ugly sky-blue wall that somebody had killed and didn't find the need to wipe away. The conversation ebbed once again, but he was left to contemplate that the only thing his new partner wished of him is to be gone. "I don't get it," he said, with his mouth full. "I have been trying very hard to be pleasant and work with you, and you say something shitty like that to me."

"Pleasant?" Shaneel said. "Apparently you think pleasant is just making jokes about everything. Constantly."

Ostrowski raised his hands and his shoulders. "It's not? You don't like to laugh?"

"Yes, I like to laugh." Shaneel put her finger down on the table in front of her. "But you know what else I like? I like to *learn*. I like to discuss things, books we've read, movies we've watched. I like to be asked about my day. I like to be treated as an equal. You care more about a damned three-day-old football game than you do about me."

Ostrowski opened his mouth to speak but she held up a finger to stop him. "You make another wife comment and I'll kick your ass."

"If I'm being honest," Ostrowski said. "You're no joy to be around either. You're so damned serious every minute of every day. The job is too grim to be like that. But you walk around here constantly like you've got a corn cob up your..." Ostrowski stopped himself.

"What? Up my what?" Shaneel said. "You can be so damned

glib when it's all just a joke. But when you have a real point to make, you're completely tongue-tied because you're so old you don't even know what's appropriate to say anymore."

He hated the fact that she was right.

She sat back and crossed her arms. "Let me help you. Corn cob up my ass is acceptable. Corn cob up my fat ass is *not* acceptable. Maybe this is what we need from now on. You to stop talking and me to fill you in on the proper vernacular for the twenty-first century. The correct phrase you're looking for Detective, is..." The door opened as Shaneel finished, "...corn-cob up my ass."

Captain Vargas walked in followed by a man and a woman, both in suits. "Are we interrupting something?" he asked.

"Nah," said Ostrowski, shaking his head. "We're just talking about the types of things we put up our ass."

Shaneel spun her chair and looked out the window at the clear sky and pursed her lips.

"Who we got here?" he asked the captain.

"This is Special Agent Ramirez and Special Agent Cameron from the FBI."

Shaneel scoffed.

Ostrowski stood and held out his hand to shake, then realized it had mustard on it. "Oh, hold on." He wiped it on a napkin and held it out again.

"Pleased to meet you." Special Agent Cameron shook his hand first. She was a young blond woman, late twenties, early thirties, and, Ostrowski had to admit, "pleasant."

Special Agent Ramirez, on the other hand, was just the opposite. He had dark steel eyes, graying hair on the sides, and a heavily pockmarked face. Ramirez shook Ostrowski's hand firmly and nodded.

Shaneel walked over and shook each agent's hand politely then sat back down.

"They have a profile on Duncan Bullock, and I wanted them

to share it with you two." The Captain said.

Ostrowski gestured to the chairs. "Let's hear it."

They all took seats, Ramirez at the head of the table, opening a folder in front of him.

"Duncan Bullock was a gunnery sergeant in the Marine Corps. He saw real combat in Kuwait as part of Operation Desert Storm. Earned a silver star when one of his men was shot up pretty bad. Bullock carried the private over his shoulders, three miles to an aid station. Got him there just in time to save his life. But eight months later, that same private was ripped apart by an IED." Ramirez let that statement hang there.

"So....are you saying he went off the rails then?" Ostrowski asked, wanting to get on with it.

"On the contrary," Ramirez said. "Though Bullock took that hard, he took the loss of all of his men hard. He is a very caring and protective individual. When the whereabouts were learned of a small nest of Iraqi soldiers hiding out in a building in Kuwait City, Bullock led a recon team to get eyes on the scene. He was to radio back any intel, so a proper plan of attack could be made, maybe a Tomahawk missile sent through their front door. But when someone radioed in that it looked like they were manufacturing IEDs at that location, Bullock made it his personal mission to take out the building. His men were very loyal. They attacked and neutralized the enemy site without losing a single soldier."

"Pretty impressive," Vargas said.

"That's not all. Witnesses said they saw Bullock kill five men in that building with his bare hands." Ramirez let that one hang out there, too.

Ostrowski was growing tired of his dramatic pauses. "So, are you trying to tell us these women are in the hands of a crazed killer or what?"

"Not crazed," Ramirez said. "Capable. Focused."

"Well, we already knew he was capable. He took out five of

L.A.'s finest, and hardly broke a sweat."

"His name had always been, 'Dunk,' or 'Sergeant Dunk,'" Cameron said. "But after that, his men started calling him 'Slam Dunk.'"

"This all very interesting," Shaneel said. "But how does it help us?"

"We're giving you the context of the man you're dealing with here," Cameron replied. "He is a fix-it type of guy. A do-it-yourselfer. He lost a son to leukemia five years ago. He struggled with that. Realized there was no one to point to. No one to blame."

"You can't go take out an entire building of cancer," Ramirez said.

"So, he needs someone to blame here," Ostrowski said.

Ramirez nodded. "Exactly. He's not going to sit idly by and watch justice be done. As Agent Cameron said. He's a do-it-yourselfer. And with Haddock being prosecuted in another country, he's going to look for the next person in line who is responsible for the death of his daughter."

"Brooke Winthrop and Becca Dodge," Vargas said.

Both agents nodded at him.

"And I suppose, being a gunnery sergeant, the man has mad skills with just about everything," Shaneel said.

"Sgt. Bullock was a quick study. He was top rated in firearms, munitions, and explosives."

"Add technical skills to that now, too," Cameron added. "He's been working for Digital Lock Security Systems as a training and development specialist since leaving the military."

Ostrowski sat back and crossed his arms. "Which means he has the know-how to pull off all this putting a show online without the possibility of tracing the IPN."

Again, both agents nodded.

"Fantastic," Ostrowski said, looking over at the captain and Shaneel. "We're dealing with Super Sarge."

Edwards

Chapter Twenty

Brooke scanned each of the applications thoroughly. A man who ran a nonprofit company that organized fundraising events for other nonprofits in British Columbia; a lawyer in Colorado; a doctor in Iowa; a dentist in Chicago; and a social worker in San Francisco. Since they were essentially the same applications taken from the website of *I Do or I Don't*, they were very detailed with all of the vital information filled in.

Brooke tapped her fingernails on the hard surface of the old metal desk. She had it narrowed down to three, but she was supposed to come back with her top two choices. She was trying hard to decide which one to drop. But, thinking logically, she wasn't sure why she was being so painstaking. She was sure she wouldn't be dating the man or men. It felt like a trap. She and Becca would make their choices, and he would crap all over them and tell them why they were stupid.

Even so, just like everything in life, if she was given a task to do, Brooke was going to see it was done to the best of her ability. She didn't put much stock in luck, considering success to be a result of determination and hours on task.

She had already set aside the social worker and the dentist. She looked over the doctor in Iowa once again.

Her door unlocked, and Bullock opened it. "It's show-time."

Brooke tossed out the Iowa doctor, not being a big fan of Iowa anyway. She picked up the last two papers and stood.

"Those are your choices?"

She nodded. Handed him the papers.

He waved them off. "No. Bring them with you." He nodded toward the door. "Let's go."

Brooke walked out and headed down the hall, heard him, felt him, shadowing her. Could feel his heavy breath on the back of her neck. It made a chill run up her spine, and she picked her pace up to increase the distance.

Bullock unlocked the makeshift studio, and Brooke entered. He slammed the door closed right behind her, and she took her seat. Fiona was there waiting for her, ready to apply the foundation as soon as she sat down.

"Have you talked to that traitorous friend of yours?" Fiona said.

"Traitorous? Who are we talking about?"

Fiona pulled back and looked at her amazed. "Then you don't know?"

Brooke looked at the others, then back at her. "Know what?"

Fiona leaned in, seething, and practically hissed the words out. "Becca has been causing all manner of trouble. She pushed Bullock so far, he went in and broke one of Alanna's fingers to teach her a lesson."

"What?" Brooke gasped. She brought her hands to her mouth. "That's horrible."

"So please tell that bitch to keep herself in line," Fiona said.

"Wait. Are you blaming Becca for Alanna's finger?"

"She's the reason he broke it. Said she was out of control and this was the only way to get her to stop."

"Fee. Becca didn't break Alanna's finger. She loves Alanna."

"She really showed love today. She let Alanna be her sacrificial lamb."

Brooke put her hand on Fiona's shoulder. "Come on, Fee. Please don't blame Becca for Bullock's actions."

Fiona pulled away from her. "So, you're sticking up for her, are you? Top dogs sticking together and all, while the little people pay the price for all your shit?"

"Fiona, no..."

"That's why we're here in the first place. Because you and she screwed up. And now we all have to suffer for it." She pointed at Ben. "Becca's already shown her true colors. She attacked Ben when he was following orders."

Brooke looked over at Ben. He was scowling. "What happened?" She asked.

"Kicked him in the bullocks!" Fiona said. "Dropped him like a wet rag. All he was trying to do was get the shots he was ordered to get."

Ben shook his head, and he looked away.

"We're all just trying to do our best and stay alive, and she lines us up for the slaughter."

The door opened, and in came Mike and Lyssa. Bullock looked at Brooke, who was trying her best to hide her shock.

"Why doesn't she have any make-up on yet?" he asked.

"Chatting too much," Fiona said, and she started applying the foundation once again.

"Hurry it up. I want to get this shot before it gets too late." He slammed the door shut and locked it.

Brooke said no more. She stared at the scuffed ends of her black flats, hoping that she would one day have the chance to go to a shoe store again.

Fiona was silent. There was nothing more to say. Somehow a very distinct line had been drawn between them—a line neither of them drew but was drawn for them. It was a bold and brazen line, and Brooke wasn't sure it could be erased once this ordeal was over.

Fiona finished with the foundation and started in on her eyes.

Brooke wondered how all this would play out from this point on. Bullock had done a very good job of setting the blame for everyone being here on herself and Becca. Would they now get the blame every time he decided to do something cruel to someone else? Was he now immune to their wrath even though he was the perpetrator?

Becca entered through the door and walked over to the chair. She plopped down hard as if she could barely make it that far before giving out. Her face was white and her eyes red. She was clearly not holding up well.

Brooke would have worried that something was seriously wrong with her had she not found out about Alanna. She realized that Becca must be sick about what happened. She couldn't say anything to the others. Aside from the fact that Bullock was now in the room, the crew's harsh attitude had already determined her guilt and were ready to sentence her.

"Enough on her," Bullock said. "She's the pretty one anyway. Dodge needs the help. Go do her make-up."

Fiona froze, hand in the air. She looked like she was playing the children's game freeze tag and she'd just been touched.

"What?" Bullock said. "What the hell's wrong with you, make-up?"

"Not a thing," Fiona said. "She put the eyeliner back into her plastic bag and rolled her chair over to Becca. Then she pulled out the foundation and began applying it a little more firmly than she had to Brooke. Becca's head would sway back from the pressure, but she was too far gone to even notice.

"I see you both have your papers," Bullock said. "We'll wait until we're rolling to reveal who you've chosen." He walked over to the table with the computer and picked up a folder. "Are you all

148

set with the video file?" he asked Lawton. Andy raised his thumb and continued to stare at the screen.

Fiona started on Becca's eyes a bit more gingerly now. Brooke was relieved to see that. She was afraid Fee wanted to stick the pencil through Becca's eye.

Fiona quickly finished the eyes and the lips and backed away.

"Okay, let's get this going!" Bullock yelled. He sat down in his chair and rolled it over next to Brooke. Mike took his spot at the camera over Becca's shoulder, and Lyssa stood next to Ben.

"Count us in," Bullock said.

Ben held up his hand and counted, "Five, four, three," He brought his last two fingers down silently and pointed to Bullock.

"Welcome everyone, to our second episode. As I said in the introduction, we are going to examine each of the segments of the show *I Do or I Don't* in depth. We are going to look at the faults in the production and see how things were destined to fall through the cracks—all of which led to the death of my daughter." He glanced over at Becca and Brooke and then back to the camera. "The first segment of the show was always a pre-produced selection segment. This was where each of the contestants was given a set of applications to go through. They would pour over these documents to try to determine who, on paper, looked like they were the perfect soulmate and life partner. Amazing isn't it, how all of that can be determined by a simple little questionnaire?" He smirked at the two women, shook his head, and looked back at the camera.

"In the spirit of the show, I had five men fill out the very same applications that they," he said, gesturing to Becca and Brooke, "use on their show. I then gave them both the five applications to peruse on their own. Here is our pre-produced segment."

Music started through the computer speakers, and Andy spun his monitor around to face Brooke, Becca, and Bullock. In the small box on the screen marked "Program," Brooke could see the shots that Ben had acquired earlier of her in her room, pretending to go over the sheets. There were a few shots of Becca as well, but it was mostly of Brooke. She wondered if that's because Ben had been incapacitated before he could get his work done. When the video was finished, Andy swung his monitor back around, hit the space bar, and pointed a finger at Bullock.

"It does appear that the two ladies gave a great deal of thought to this task. Let's see if that was truly the case." He swiveled his chair to face them. "Miss Winthrop, how did you come up with your choices?"

Brooke glanced down at the pages in her hand and thought about it. She looked up at the little consumer camera that Ben had on the tripod and froze. She felt silly. She had commanded entire studio audiences and networks and looked white supremacist thugs and religious radicals straight in the eye when she interviewed them for the news, never backing down. But here, having to divulge the slightest little bit about herself, racked her nerves.

"Miss Winthrop?" Bullock urged.

"I...just...picked the ones that looked the best."

Bullock looked at the camera and nodded condescendingly. "Seems logical, I guess." He turned to Becca. "And Miss Dodge, how did you choose your two candidates."

"I picked the top two sheets of paper." Becca rested her head on her hand.

Brooke could feel the tension in the room. There was a very palpable dislike and distrust of Becca from all of her crew. If the recording hadn't been rolling, Brooke was sure they would have all turned on her that very moment.

Bullock chuckled. "Very scientific of you." He looked at Brooke. "Would you please share with the audience your top two choices?"

Brooke held the papers up and read off them. It was easier than trying to talk right now. "I chose, Thomas Brandt, a lawyer from Colorado." She flipped the pages. "And Richard Pridgett, who runs a nonprofit in British Columbia."

"Interesting," Bullock said. "You went with money, with the lawyer, and then a good-hearted nonprofit worker. There's a little bit of a dichotomy there. But something tells me, with the shoes you like to wear, the lawyer would probably win out." Bullock chuckled.

Brooke added in her own nervous laughter.

Bullock looked over to Becca. "And who were your top two sheets of paper?"

"The dentist from Chicago and the lawyer from Colorado," Becca said, head still resting on her hand.

"Very good." Bullock opened the folder on his lap. "Now all of these were excellent choices...," he looked at the camera and held up a finger to make his point. "...on paper. But as you will see, anybody can look good on paper." He looked at Brooke. "For example, let's take your wonderful man who ran the nonprofit in Canada. Richard Pridgett was not actually his true name." Bullock held up a picture. "His real name was Robert Pickton, and he was a serial killer convicted of at least forty-nine murders. He ran a nonprofit to lure in female victims to his farm, where he killed them and fed them to his pigs."

Brooke gasped. Brought her hand to her mouth. Said nothing.

Bullock nodded at Becca. "Your dentist? Turns out he was the very first serial killer in the United States." He held up a picture of a man in a bowler hat with a large puffy mustache. "His name was Dr. H.H. Holmes and he owned a building in Chicago, which became known as the 'Murder Castle' because it had special rooms where he locked women inside, gassed them, and then dissected their bodies while they were still alive."

Becca looked nonplussed. Brooke sighed heavily and wiped at an eye.

"And the lawyer from Colorado who you both picked, was none other than the most charming and good-looking serial killer of them all." He held up a familiar picture to everybody. "Ted

Bundy." Bullock put the pictures back in the folder, tidied the edges, and closed it. "So, you see, choices on paper are perhaps the worst choices of all."

"Bullshit," Becca said.

Brooke looked at her, hoped her concerned stare would get Becca to stop. She could feel everyone else in the room tense at Becca's tone.

"Excuse me, Miss Dodge. Just what is it exactly, that you consider bullshit?"

"All you did was change a few names on the applications. You didn't have anybody vet them. We use a team of individuals who go through an entire, thorough vetting process. Nobody gets on the show without multiple layers of scrutiny, the first of which is a background check. If any of them had changed their name because they were serial killers, that would have been caught, like, in the first five minutes."

"Good point," Bullock said, smiling at Becca. He had obviously been expecting that objection. "But not a single one of these individuals had any criminal record until, of course, it was discovered that they had committed multiple murders. All of their background checks would have come back squeaky clean."

"Is your argument right now that Chris Haddock is a serial killer? That he has killed multiple times before this?"

"Oh, I know he's killed before," Bullock said. "I have proof of that."

"What?" Becca said, the air rushing from her lungs like she'd been punched. Brooke felt her face flush and began to feel faint.

"Yes, he has killed under another name." Bullock was delighting in closing his trap. "Chris Haddock is a very sick individual. I can't confirm any human deaths, but I was able to get my hands on a video from the Internet from years ago. It was, of course, taken down right away. But as you know, nothing is ever lost or deleted, right?" Bullock turned to Andy. "Mr. Lawton, can we play the clip that was uploaded by 'Little Darwin'?"

Andy hit the space bar and spun the monitor back around. The picture showed a sink, and in walked a very young Chris Haddock. He was easily eight or ten years old, but definitely the same individual. In his hand he had a small gray mouse, hanging by its tail. He held it over the sink, letting its little legs kick for a second, before dropping it in with a thunk. The mouse quickly regained its bearings and scurried around. Chris reached up and turned on the hot water. Steam rose from the stream, as the mouse squealed in agony.

Horrified at what she was seeing, Brooke glanced over at Becca to get her take on it. No longer tearless and fearless, she was pale with sweat rimming her hairline. Her mouth hung open and she stared disbelievingly at the monitor.

The hot water torture of the mouse went on for several minutes Each time the mouse tried to scurry up the side of the sink to get away from the scorching heat, Little Darwin flicked him back into the scalding bath once more.

Eventually, young Chris turned off the water, then grabbed a spatula and used it to corral the now-lethargic mouse to the center of the sink and push it down into the dark hole of the drain. The video then showed him reaching up past the camera for something.

Brooke put her face in her hands and heard the garbage disposal turn on.

CHAPTER TWENTY-ONE

Brett Ostrowski stood by the door of the War Room, coffee in hand, waiting to hand it to Detective Johnson when she walked in. Today would play out differently because he was going to kill her with kindness from the start. He would hand her the coffee and then ask her how her night went.

He knew that Bullock's next video would be released today, so he was up and out of the house by five. He listened to the radio and found out it *had* been released, but that it was taken down right away due to disturbing scenes. Gino and Jade had been speculating all morning long about what could be so disturbing to have the video be intercepted and quarantined.

Ostrowski knew he would be able to see it here today, no matter what it contained, so he arrived before everyone else.

Sure enough, Detective Johnson was surprised to see him when she walked in. But when he handed her the coffee, she couldn't grab it because she had a large green smoothie already in her hand.

"No problem." Ostrowski shrugged and gave it to the captain.

"Thanks, Ostrowski," Vargas said. "Make sure your stomach

is settled, because I've seen the video, and it's a shocker."

"What's so shocking?" Shaneel asked.

Benchley, the tech guy, stuck a USB drive in the side of the war room computer and fired it up. There was a steady stream of police officers and office workers and the room was soon filled to bursting. Everybody wanted to be one of the few who managed to see the train wreck.

The monitor on the wall flashed to life, and the smiling, yet crazy-eyed face of Duncan Bullock appeared. "Welcome everyone, to our second episode. As I said in the introduction, we are going to examine each of the segments of the show *I Do or I Don't* in depth...."

The war room remained silent while the two women disclosed their picks and Bullock shot them down. There were little murmurs here and there, but nobody wanted to be the one to make too much noise and miss out on what was being said.

Multiple gasps were heard when Bullock looked at Becca Dodge and said, "Oh, I know he's killed before. I have proof of that."

Then came the video of Little Darwin, a.k.a. Chris Haddock, torturing the mouse. The viewers in the room had all manner of reactions. Some cursed the kid, others gagged, and still others wept.

When the garbage disposal went off, the camera cut back to the two women. Brooke Winthrop had her face in her hands and appeared to be crying. Becca Dodge stared disbelievingly into the distance, most certainly at the monitor in the little makeshift studio.

"I also have a file here containing a psychiatric review of Chris Haddock from right around the time this video was taken. It says, and I quote, 'The subject exhibits signs of narcissistic and socio-pathetic tendencies.'"

"Where was this review? And why didn't we get a copy of it?" Becca asked.

"It was filed away. Disclosure acts and HIPPA laws kept it silent," Bullock said, holding up the sheet of paper. "And if you are an extreme narcissist, and you want to go on national television, why would you let something like this get out?"

"But…. how did you get hold of it?"

"Because I did my due diligence. Something that your staff failed to do. And now my daughter is dead."

Bullock turned to the camera as it cut to a close-up of him. "And that will conclude today's segment. See you tomorrow." The screen faded to black.

The room remained completely silent for a moment. It was Ostrowski who made the first sound. "That was sick."

With the silence broken, the room erupted with comments, curses, and criticisms. The captain stood, whistled, and waved his hands down to silence the room once more.

"Right now, I don't know who I'm madder at," Ostrowski said. "I'm starting to wonder what my next steps should be. Do I still try to get to this Bullock? Do I want to arrest these two women? Or do I want to buy a plane ticket to Costa Rica and put a bullet in the head of that little bastard myself."

"You only have one choice, by the letter of the law," Captain Vargas said. "But I'm not saying I disagree with you."

"I'm almost embarrassed for those ladies," Shaneel said. "But I want to know how he got hold of those files when they weren't available for the crew of the show."

A quiet voice came from the far corner of the room, next to the window. "Because I helped him get them."

All heads craned around, and the crowd parted, to see the well-dressed man with the perfectly combed dark hair, arms crossed, leaning on the windowsill.

"And just who might you be?" Vargas asked.

"I'm Special Agent, Matthew Vecoli."

Chapter Twenty-Two

Matthew Vecoli sat in the war room of the Los Angeles Police Department and slowly sipped the bitter, old coffee that was just given to him by an office worker at Captain Vargas's orders. He glanced across the table at what could have been a law-enforcement diversity poster—a Hispanic captain, a black female detective, and an aged white detective who was unshaven and bald as a cue ball.

Breaking the awkward silence, Ostrowski stood up. "Hey GQ," he said. "You're easy on the eyes and all, but we need you to actually speak now. It sounds like you have a lot to answer for."

Vecoli looked back down at his cup of coffee and nodded. "Yes. I do." He reached up and loosened his tie. "I don't know who I'm more disappointed in right now—Sgt. Bullock, or myself for listening to him."

Ostrowski sighed. "With the lives of two innocent women hanging in the balance, forgive me if I don't feel sorry for you."

"Look," Vargas said, with an annoyed glance over at Ostrowski. "Why don't you tell us how you got involved with Duncan Bullock."

"We met fifteen years ago, when I served under Sgt. 'Slam Dunk' Bullock in Iraq. He literally saved my life in the corps."

"Were you one of the men who gave him that nickname?" Detective Johnson asked.

"No." Vecoli shook his head. "That was before my time. But I was on a one-way road to self-destruct-ville. If Sgt. Bullock hadn't come into my life, I'm sure I'd be dead now."

"And Bullock twisted and manipulated your gratitude to get what he needed out of you," Ostrowski said.

Vecoli let that statement sink in a moment, then took a deep breath and nodded.

"And just what was it he needed from you?" Captain Vargas asked.

"He called me the day the news broke about his daughter's death being a murder instead of an accident. Said he wanted to post some stuff about the show. He wanted the world to see how they were negligent and didn't protect his daughter, or any woman that went on the show for that matter. He asked me to look into Chris Haddock—see if there were any warning signs that they ignored. Things like that."

"So, you unleashed the full power of the FBI on the case?" Detective Johnson asked.

"I had a few people who owed me favors. And a few others who I didn't mind owing favors to."

"And it never occurred to you that this was the wrong thing to do?" Vargas said.

"You don't get it," Vecoli knew he sounded agitated. He got that way when he felt he was being judged. He took a moment, realizing he'd better get used to the feeling. It was going to be happening a lot from now on. He took another breath, sipped the bitter coffee and began again. "When the sergeant called me, he was crying. I'd never heard anything like that before. The strongest man I ever knew was now hurting so bad he was in tears," said Vecoli, putting his hand on his heart. "I would have done anything for him at that point. I just wanted to help take the pain away from the man who had done so much for me."

"So why come to us now?" Ostrowski said.

"Because what's happening now is not why I helped him. Sure, I knew he was going to use whatever information I gave him against them, but I didn't know he was going to set up his own court. I had no idea he was planning on kidnapping a bunch of people and creating a circus. And I certainly didn't know he intended to kill Winthrop and Dodge."

"Can you contact him?" Vargas asked.

Vecoli shook his head. "Not anymore. I had a burner he'd sent to me, but I tried calling him a couple times to persuade him to stand down and he kept hanging up on me. After he told me he would no longer answer my calls—thinking I'd use the phone to locate him—I threw it against a wall and smashed it."

"Please tell me you know where he's holding everyone," Ostrowski said.

Vecoli looked back at his coffee and shook his head.

"For the love of Pete," Ostrowski crossed his arms and sat back in his chair.

Johnson turned and looked at Ostrowski. "Aren't you supposed to know where he's at?" You're the super-detective who instinctively knows the next move a bad guy's going to make."

Ostrowski held up his index finger. "One, I don't consider Bullock a bad guy. He's a grieving father who's in a lot of pain. And two..." He pulled down his index finger and raised his middle finger.

"All right stop this," Vargas berated them, a raspy growl in his normally calm voice. "Do I have to pull you two off this case? It's too high profile to risk you screwing it up by nit-picking each other."

Ostrowski and Johnson sat back and looked at the table like three-year-olds being scolded by their mother.

"Sorry Captain," Johnson said.

"Yeah, sorry Cap," Ostrowski said. "We're still in the negotiation phase of our young relationship."

"Well, I'm declaring the negotiation phase over. Effective immediately." He turned back to Vecoli with the same intensity. "You do know there are going to be repercussions for your involvement in this, don't you?"

"I do, but I'm here to ask a favor from you." Vecoli sat back. "I'm asking you defer reporting my involvement until this is over. Once you find Bullock, I may be able to help diffuse the situation."

Chapter Twenty-Three

"Have a seat and wait," Bullock said. Then he closed the door.

Brooke was in another room in a separate section of the plant. This room was well lit, though smaller than the studio they had been shooting in. Yet it had the same beige, metal walls. Two chairs were set at a small table in the center of the room. The chairs were slightly larger and looked more comfortable than the old office chairs they had been using. Brooke thought they were probably from the main desk in the lobby. They were both faded lime green, and the vinyl was cracked from years of sitting in the sun.

There was a camera on a tripod facing the chairs, against the far wall. Two more cameras sat on tripods behind each chair. Brooke knew how this worked. The far camera captured the two-shot, or wide shot, and the two behind each chair would capture the medium close-ups of Brooke and Becca as they talked. Wires ran from each camera through a hole that had been cut in the wall. She was sure that was where Andy was. He would be switching between the cameras and recording the program on the other side of that wall.

Brooke selected the chair on the right, because she felt that was her good side, and she would look best in the wide shot. She felt a little better about herself this time as Fee was brought to her room and had time to do a proper make-up job, as opposed to the five minutes she got before the previous two segments. She took her seat and waited.

She could tell, just from the way the room was set up, that this was the question segment. On the show, this segment was designed to break the ice between the man and the woman. They would learn things about each other, such as life goals, aspirations, values—things that help or hinder the compatibility issue. In Brooke's estimation, it was the most important segment for the couples because they could find out answers to important questions to determine if the person was worth pursuing long before any emotional connection had been made.

The door unlocked and Becca was led into the room. She looked lethargic. Not weary exactly. She just looked like she was tired of fighting. Becca had always been a fighter. It's why she made it to the top in Hollywood. She fought for everything she got, and she fought harder than everyone else.

But this was taking a toll on her. When they made eye contact, Brooke could tell the fire in her eyes was dimming. To think that their life's work was somehow wrong, tainted everything they had worked so hard for, every future dream they had. It looked to Brooke like Bullock was winning this battle of wills.

He guided Becca over to the other chair and she dropped into it. Then he laid a folder on the table with the word "Questions" written on it in black marker.

"I'm sure you two can figure out what we're doing here now. This is the 'questions' segment of your show, where your guests get to ask five questions of the person they picked from a piece of paper. These are five questions that you chose for them— questions that they didn't even get to choose themselves. And they determine the rest of their lives. That's pretty bold on your part, don't you think?"

Brooke and Becca looked at each other, not saying anything.

"Don't you think it's pretty presumptuous of you to think you can come up with the perfect five questions to cover the entirety of someone's life?"

Again, Brooke and Becca did not answer.

"Well, anyway," Bullock continued. "Since we didn't have any more serial killers for you to sit down and chat with, we are stuck doing the question segment with you two together." He leaned down and tapped the folder with his forefinger. "Here's your questions. I will leave the room so you two can talk, without me leaning over your shoulder. I'm hoping you'll actually speak or you'll be letting America down." He backed toward the door and put his hand on the knob. "Alanna Gates is hoping you talk as well."

Becca snapped her head toward him and glared. Brooke saw the fire in her eyes reignite. If she could have, Becca would've shot fireballs from her eyes to kill him.

Bullock opened the door slowly, stepped out, and closed it quietly.

Brooke leaned forward and picked up the folder. "Becca, we need to do this."

"Oh, of course we need to do this, Brooke," Becca snapped. "Because what America doesn't know, is that Mr. Holier-Than-Thou will actually torture an innocent girl if we don't play his sick little game." Becca's fire was back with a vengeance now. Bullock was stupid. He had her on the ropes, but then he said something to energize her again. Bringing up Alanna was like blowing on dying ashes. They heated up and burst into flame once more.

Brooke opened the folder to find two sets of index cards wrapped with rubber bands with each of their names on the first card. She pulled out the set with Becca's name on it and handed it to her. "Becca, let's just do this." She wanted to get Becca to stop before she said something that could really get Alanna hurt and have the team turn on her even more.

Becca snatched the set from her hand, pulled off the rubber band, and threw it on the floor. She slipped the first card to the bottom of the pile and looked at it the first question. "Who goes first?"

"Go ahead and ask me the first question."

"Okay then, pretty girl, how do you define success?"

"Well...." Brooke wasn't expecting that one. But she had worked in news long enough to know that these videos were probably viral monsters out beyond these walls. And after the previous day's video, she was fairly certain they were losing the battle of public opinion. She needed to use this segment to make a stand and regain some of that dwindling support.

"I think that's an easy one. For me, it's a two-part answer. First, you need to find happiness. It doesn't matter what that path looks like because it's different for everybody. But you have to find your own happiness. Once you have achieved that, your next responsibility is to help others find happiness. That was the reason you and I started our show to begin with—to help those who weren't having any success finding their special person. I thought if we could help locate that individual, it could get them on their own path to happiness. What could be more successful than that?"

Becca's hard face eased slightly, and a small smile formed. "You have an amazing view of life and one of the best hearts I know."

Brooke smiled back but didn't know what to make of it. Did Becca really believe that, or was she just posturing for the audience? Becca knew this business and knew how to work a room like nobody Brooke had ever seen. She looked at her first question card for Becca. "Okay, your first question is the same thing. "How do you define success?"

Becca looked at her for a moment, appearing to let the answer gel a little bit before she began to talk.

"I always think there has to be a measurable. Something

to compare your own creation with. No, I don't mean that you necessarily need to compare yourself to others, or other's achievements. What I'm saying is that you set predetermined goals for yourself, strive for those goals, and whether you reach them or not is how you determine success."

"And if you don't reach them?"

"It's never a question of reaching them or not," Becca said. "Because there's no giving up. Success is always a given. Reaching that goal will never be in doubt. Reaching that goal within a specific time frame is the thing. And if you don't make it, that just means you weren't successful at that time. And that's your opportunity to figure out the stumbling blocks, figure a new strategy to deal with them, and go again. You will be successful if you don't stop. If you don't quit. The only time someone is not successful is when they stop reaching."

"That is a remarkable way to look at it," Brooke said. Becca's smile grew a little brighter. She was probably thinking the same thing Brooke was—that Bullock was most likely seething because his questions, would-be digs, had actually worked out to be great momentum builders for the two.

Becca looked down at her sheet for the second question. "Is it okay to harm others for personal gain?" Becca rolled her eyes.

"Absolutely not," Brooke said, not wanting to let that linger out there and have people question any sort of pause. "It is never okay to harm anyone in any way, especially for personal gain." She stopped then because Brooke knew the balance. Saying too much on something like that is almost as bad as saying too little. It can quickly be perceived as defensive, as if you've got something to be defensive about. She looked down at her next card. "How many people are you willing to take down to get to the top?"

Becca chuckled. "I don't take anyone down. I've never needed to. My abilities can stand on their own. I go past people, but I don't have to take anyone down. If they can't stand with me or keep up, they get left behind. Am I competitive? Hell, yeah."

She chuckled again and ran her fingers through her hair. "That question sounds like it came from someone who wasn't able to keep up and rather than deal with his own failings, he makes it sound like it's someone else's fault. The world generally doesn't work that way. It's not the fault of the rhinoceros that the dodo bird is extinct." She shook her head and looked at her next card. "If you believe marriage to be so important that you need to have a show about it..." Becca shook her head. "Never mind."

"Becca, we need to do this," Brooke said. "Ask me the question."

"No," Becca said. "The only purpose of the question is to be mean and hateful. Let's keep going. Let's see what mean, hateful thing he has for me next."

"Becca. Ask me the question before Alanna gets another finger broken."

Becca scowled, looked at the camera behind Brooke, and then the one against the far wall...glared at them both, then looked back at the card. "If you believe marriage to be so important that you need to have a show about it..." She looked up at Brooke, then back down to the card. "then why are you not married yourself?"

The question took the wind out of her for a moment. Was it possible Mr. Bullock didn't know what she had just gone through with Jake May? It seemed unlikely. And if he did know, then this question was crafted to be hurtful. "Well," she began. "Obviously I did think marriage was important. As many people already know, even though my marriage with Jake didn't go very well, I felt strongly enough about it to try to make it work—to my own detriment. No, it doesn't work out every time, but I do think it's worth the effort. And when Jake and I were happy, those were the best days of my life. I am hoping to find someone else someday. Until then, I have truly enjoyed helping others discover the happiest days of their lives."

"I know, honey," Becca waved the card in front of her. "This is mean-spirited, dirty shit." She flung the card over her shoulder and it slid to a stop in the corner.

Brooke took a breath and looked at the next card. She read it to herself first, then looked up at Becca. "Okay, keep cool."

Becca nodded. "Oh, I will." She scooped her hand toward her. "Bring it."

Brooke looked back at the card. "Many Americans think you should face charges of negligent homicide. How do you respond to those accusations?"

Becca tilted her head down and stared directly at Brooke, eyes narrowing slightly while she prepared her answer. Then she shifted her gaze directly into the camera and spoke calmly.

"What happened to Kristine Haddock was a tragedy of remarkable proportions. And if we would have had the chance to go over every piece of data, it is a certainty that Chris Haddock would never have been a cast member on our show. But we did not have all of the facts. And the real shame here is that we did not even have access to all of the facts. And since we did not have access to all of the facts, it cannot be considered negligent homicide, can it? Negligent homicide would be when a corporation lets tainted food get shipped even though they know it's bad or companies that dump toxic chemicals into groundwater reserves—things where people actually die because someone has knowingly caused harm. It's not negligence if someone doesn't know the facts, it's ignorance. And to my knowledge, there is no such thing as ignorant homicide." Becca lifted her head, crossed her legs, and sat back. "But if we want to discuss breaking laws here, we can talk about how someone managed to get protected files, somehow circumventing doctor/patient confidentiality rules and HIPPA laws. Oh, and what about kidnapping and torture? Is there a card here that asks my opinion on those topics?"

"Easy, Becca." Brooke did not want this to get out of hand. "You've done a good job of answering the question. Now give me mine."

Becca snarled and took a deep breath. She flipped the card

169

and read the next question, then threw her head back in disgust. "Oh, come on!"

"Ask the question, Becca," Brooke said.

Becca sat forward and held the card out in front of her. "Okay, Brooke. Would you be willing to be a contestant on your show, now knowing you could possibly be matched up with the worst kind of person imaginable?" She tore the card up and let it drop to the floor.

"Yes," Brooke said.

"You don't have to answer bullshit like that."

"Yes, I do," Brooke said. "Now just let me do this, please."

Becca crossed her arms and sat back in the chair.

Brooke gave her a moment to settle, then continued. "I know what happened was not only a tragedy but also a fluke of disastrous luck. I understand that the chances of something like that happening again on our show are probably one in a billion. So, if I were to go on my own show to find someone, I would and could do it without hesitation, knowing that others are working diligently behind the scenes to keep me safe." She confirmed her comments with a curt nod to the camera. Then she looked at the next card for Becca—read it and froze.

Becca tilted her head. "What? Say it."

Brooke jabbed her tongue in her cheek, knowing that this was going to be bad. But she decided to go with it anyway. There was no way she was going to be responsible for Alanna's knuckles. She looked at Becca and read: "If someone dies as a result of being a contestant on your show and then your show jumps ten rating points, do you feel joy or remorse?"

Becca's eyes grew thin and she sat forward slowly. "Are you fucking kidding me? That's the question? Do I feel joy or remorse when someone dies on my show?" Becca shook her head vigorously. "That's it." She stood up. "I'm done."

Brooke reached over and grabbed her arm. "Becca, no. We have to finish this."

"Oh, you're damn right we have to finish this." She threw her cards in the air, and they scattered around the room. "I'm going to finish this right now." She kicked her chair and it tumbled backward, knocking over the tripod that held Brooke's camera sending it crashing to the floor.

Brooke jumped from her seat. "Becca, no!"

"Oh, yes." She picked up the tripod, collapsed the legs, and held it like a club, with the camera at the end. "The only thing I'm remorseful about is letting this piece of shit waste our time like this." She reeled back and, ignoring Brooke's screams, swung the tripod, smashing camera into camera, destroying them both.

"This damn show has just been canceled!" Becca cried. She stomped to the back of the room, unclipped the camera from the last tripod. Held it high above her head, and slammed it down with all her might, to the concrete floor.

Brooke stared at her dear friend, the woman she had known for nearly two decades. But now she didn't recognize her. Becca's face was beet red, and she was panting like an angry tiger. She was lost in a rage that had gotten the best of her, had sapped away any sense of rational thought. Becca, who always struggled to stay in control of any situation, not only lost the situation but lost control of her own self.

All Brooke could do was drop to her knees on the floor and cry.

Chapter Twenty-Four

Andy Lawton had been told to set up the computer in the cleaning closet. It was next to the room that was going to be used for the questions segment. Ben had already done the camera placement and ran the cables through a small hole in the wall that Bullock had made. All Andy had to do was roll the old tool cart in there, plug in the cables to the switcher interface, and he was ready to record.

He hated being in the cleaning closet—not just because it was a tiny room. Though he was not completely claustrophobic, he still liked his spaces a little bigger, but this was also the room where Bullock had been living. It had a creaky cot on one corner and a mop sink in the floor on the opposite corner. The room smelled of old cleaners, sweat, whiskey and piss—but mostly sweat. The floor in and around the mop sink was wet, leading Andy to believe that Bullock uses it to try and wash down, but it wasn't working. Bullock was starting to smell very ripe, as were they all by this point. But the air in the room also carried the distinct odor of urine, which made Andy wonder if Bullock stood next to the sink and pissed right there, then ran the water a little bit to wash it

173

down. Either way, the stench made his stomach turn.

Both Andy and Bullock watched the question segment as it was recorded. Bullock leaned in to watch the monitor. The man's whiskey-filled breath—on top of the room odor—made Andy almost heave. He covered his nose with his hand and his shirt while Bullock stayed glued to the monitor. With each card, he nudged him, "Okay, watch this."

When Becca became angry, Bullock chuckled. But when she went nuts and started smashing the cameras, Bullock jumped up. "That damn bitch!" He tripped over his cot and kicked his bag—sending it careening across the floor—as he rushed out of the room.

Bullock slammed the door closed and locked it, and Andy heard him bang on the very next door and unlock that. He listened to the muffled screaming through the prefab metal walls, happened to look down at the bag, and froze. There, tucked inside a partially open pocket, was the Wi-Fi adapter. It looked like a USB drive with a small antenna. That was what Bullock had been using to connect to the Internet and upload the shows they were creating.

Without hesitation, Andy dove for the bag, grabbed the stick, and plugged it into the back of the computer. It recognized the adapter immediately. Andy clicked on the Wi-Fi locator tab and saw that it had automatically connected to a router known as Plastek Dynamics R1.

Andy heard Bullock drag a screaming Becca out of the room and down the hall. She was fighting and cursing all the way. He would soon be back, so Andy had to work fast. He opened up a browser, then a new tab, and clicked on the email accounts. Typing in his email address and password, he waited for his account to open.

Bullock stormed down the hall, slamming his fist into every door as he passed. Andy jumped when the loud boom came on his own door. "Let's go!" he heard the old man say to Brooke.

He hit the compose button and a new email window opened up. He typed in his mother's name, and her email address populated the "To:" box. In the Subject box he typed, "LET THE COPS KNOW." In the body of the email he wrote, we are being held near Plastek Dynamics. Then he hit send. It took a moment for the little "Message sent" announcement to fade in, but as soon as it did, Andy yanked the Wi-Fi adapter from the back of the computer and shoved it back into Bullock's bag.

He heard a door slam shut down the hall. He knew Bullock was on his way back and would be there within seconds. He closed the email tab, clicked on the settings menu, and selected "Show all history." It took a moment for the history to populate.

Keys rattled outside the door, and then one found its way into the lock.

Andy selected his two addresses for the day, the default address when you open a tab, and his email account.

The lock turned and the door opened. Bullock stormed into the room, fury, and rage twisting his face.

Andy hit delete, and the proof of his indiscretion disappeared. "The cameras are dead then?" said Andy nonchalantly closing the browser just as Bullock fell onto his cot in eyeshot of the screen.

Andy squirmed, leaned forward, and sighed, believing he came from within a split second of death.

"What the hell's wrong with you now?" Bullock growled.

"I...," Andy shrugged, tongue-tied. "I have to...take a leak."

Bullock pointed over to the corner. "Just piss in the mop sink. I do it all the time. Then we have some editing to do."

Chapter Twenty-Five

Radio hosts, Gino and Jade were carrying on about Becca Dodge and her anger issues.

Ostrowski knew he'd see the next uploaded video in the war room as soon as he got in, so he didn't bother watching it when he woke up. Instead, he turned up the radio in the car. "I want to feel sorry for her," Gino said. "But I just can't."

"I'm the same way," Jade replied. "She's been kidnapped and all but seeing the video from the day before and the kind of creep they let on their show, now she's seems way too defensive."

The application-picking segment did hit several other sources on the web and was seen by pretty much everybody who wanted to see it. Ostrowski knew that would be the case. The Internet usually finds a way to get what the Internet wants, and there's no way to stop it anymore.

"I know, right. I should be all, 'You go girl!' and 'Yeah, woman power!' but I'm like, 'Come on. You screwed up. Just own it.'"

"And for her to go off the rails like that. I mean, it kind of shows she knows she's in the wrong here. Don't you think?"

"Oh, for sure," Gino said.

Ostrowski pulled into the parking lot and turned off the car. Listening to the riveting commentary of his two favorite deejays, he was almost sorry he didn't fire up the video earlier.

He grabbed his coffee and headed into the headquarters building. Ostrowski didn't bother buying the captain or Shaneel any morning coffee this time. His grand gesture the previous day didn't work out so well.

The halls were suspiciously empty, and he wondered where everybody was. He didn't think he was that early. His question was answered when he saw seemingly the entire department stuffed into the war room. He chuckled when he entered. "Welcome everybody, to today's episode of 'I Did, But I Shouldn't Have."

Ostrowski squeezed through the door and walked to the one empty chair saved for him at the table, in between Shaneel and Vecoli.

Shaneel snapped her fingers. "Shoot, I was hoping you would have gotten me a coffee today, too."

Ostrowski scoffed and smiled at her. Whatever he did with her was somehow going to be wrong. He was coming to terms with that. "Sorry 'bout that." He took his chair, looked over at Cooper, and nodded. Cooper hit the space bar and the room became instantly silent.

The monitor faded from black to a close-up of Bullock's face.

"Hello. I'm Duncan Bullock. Today's program mimics the questions segment of the show *I Do or I Don't*. Normally this segment is between a prospective man and woman. Since that is not the purpose of our program, we are just going to look in as producer Becca Dodge and host Brooke Winthrop ask each other questions regarding the show and their relationship to it. I hope you will find it enlightening."

The scene dissolved from Bullock to a wide shot of a room with the two women facing each other across a small round table and a metal door with a small window was positioned in the center of the far wall. Brooke Winthrop held up a pack of cards. "Becca, let's just do this."

Becca Dodge leaned forward and snatched the cards from her hand and looked at the top one. "Who goes first?"

"Go ahead and ask me the first question."

The camera cut to a close-up of Becca. "Okay then, pretty girl, how do you define success?"

The camera cut to a close-up of Brooke. "Well, I think that's an easy one. For me, it's a two-part answer. First, you need to find happiness..." Brooke's answer held no shocking revelations. She answered it sweetly. The exact words you would expect to come out of her mouth.

Brooke then asked Becca a question. "How many people are you willing to take down to get to the top?" Becca chuckled.

The camera cut to a close-up of Becca. "Am I competitive? Hell, yeah!" She chuckled again and ran her fingers through her hair. "That question sounds like it came from someone who wasn't able to keep up, and rather than deal with his own failings, he makes it sound like it's someone else's fault. The world generally doesn't work that way. It's not the fault of the rhinoceros that the dodo bird is extinct."

The camera cut to a close-up of Brooke. "You've done a good job of answering the question. Now give me mine."

The camera cut to the wide shot showing both women. Becca threw her head back. "Oh, come on!"

"Ask the question, Becca," Brooke said.

Becca sat forward and held the card out in front of her. "Okay, Brooke. Would you be willing to be a contestant on your show, now knowing you could possibly be matched up with the worst kind of person imaginable?" She tore the card up and let it drop to the floor.

"Yes," Brooke said.

"You don't have to answer bullshit like that."

"Yes, I do," Brooke said. "Now just sit back and let me do this, please."

Becca crossed her arms and sat back in the chair.

Ostrowski was surprised at how belligerent Becca Dodge was acting. It didn't seem like someone who was suffering a great deal. She was acting like the bully.

The camera was on a close-up of Brooke. "...could do it without hesitation, knowing that others are working diligently behind the scenes to keep me safe." She confirmed her comments with a curt nod to the camera. Then she looked at the next card for Becca.

The camera cut to a close-up of Becca, while Brooke asked the question. "Many Americans think you should face charges of negligent homicide."

The camera cut to a close-up of Brooke. "How do you respond to those accusations."

The camera cut back to Becca. Ostrowski noticed something. There was something wrong. Something different. He would need to see this played back again.

Becca Dodge shook her head vigorously. "That's it." She stood up. "I'm done."

The camera cut back to the wide shot. Brooke reached over and grabbed Becca's arm. "Becca, no. We have to finish this."

"Oh, you're damn right we have to finish this." She threw her cards in the air. "I'm going to finish this right now." Becca kicked her chair and it tumbled backward. A camera on a tripod fell into the frame, crashing to the floor.

Brooke jumped from her seat. "Becca, no!"

"Oh, yes." She picked up the tripod. "The only thing I'm remorseful about is letting this piece of shit waste our time like this." Brooke screamed and jumped out of the way. Becca swung the tripod out of frame to the left, and another camera came crashing down.

"This damn show has just been canceled!" Becca yelled. She stormed up to the camera taking the wide shot. For a brief moment, the view consisted of Becca's enraged face, then everything went shaky. There was a slight hesitation, and Ostrowski thought he could make out a wall seam sideways, but then there was a scream, the screen blurred, and then went black.

The room erupted in chatter immediately. Ostrowski tried twice to get Cooper to rewind the recording but the crowd drowned out his words. He finally jumped to his feet and raised his hands. "I'm actually going to do some work for the next few minutes, so if you're going to remain in here, I need you to close your damn mouths. Otherwise, get the hell out!"

The crowd went silent, and then immediately the bulk of them wandered out, cursing at Ostrowski, someone muttering, "Who does Ostrowski think he is."

"Who are you, and what have you done with the guy who called himself Detective Ostrowski?" Shaneel said with a smile.

Ostrowski glanced over at her, and then did a double take. Shockingly, she was smiling.

"What?" she asked, looking down at her shirt.

Ostrowski shook his head. "Nothing." He was sure if he were to say anything regarding her smile, he would screw it up, and she would just scowl at him again. He pointed to the screen.

"Cooper, run that back to the wide shot, where we first see the women."

Cooper did as he was told.

"There," Ostrowski pointed to the screen and addressed the captain. "We can now rule out strip malls and office parks."

"Why? What do you see?" Asked the captain.

"Look at that door." Ostrowski jumped up, rushed around the table, and pointed at it. "That is one big, heavy-ass door. It's metal. The only reason you need a big, thick door like that is because you're in an office and you want to keep out the noise of the huge pieces of machinery chunking away right on the other side." He traced the opening of the window. "You have a small window, probably very thick to keep the noise down too." He tapped the monitor with his knuckles. "Our girls are being held in some sort of abandoned factory."

"Our girls?" Shaneel said.

"Did I say that? I meant to say, the women are being held..."

The captain sighed. "Well, that shortens the list a lot, but it's still a huge task to investigate every abandoned factory in the southland. I don't know if it's even possible in three days."

"Perhaps I can use some of the resources of the FBI," Matthew said. They all looked at him as if he'd been enough trouble already.

"I think I'd start with City of Industry," Ostrowski said. "It just seems the most logical place to find an old factory." He pointed to the screen. "But that's not all. These girls, especially Becca Dodge, are getting a raw deal here." He rolled his finger in front of him. "Cooper roll it forward to Becca's first answer."

Cooper rolled the footage to the point where Becca started answering, then rolled it back to Brooke asking the question. "... willing to take down to get to the top?" Becca chuckled. Then the camera cut to her, sitting forward. "Am I competitive? Hell, yeah."

"Stop it there," Ostrowski said. He pointed to the monitor. "Edited for content. Bullock edited this video to make her sound like a thug."

"How do you know that?" Shaneel asked.

"Roll it back a second," Ostrowski said to Cooper.

Cooper did, then played it one more time. Brooke asked the question, then Becca chuckled, and the camera cut to her.

"Stop it!" Ostrowski said, practically jumping on him. When it was paused, Ostrowski spun to the others. "First she laughed and then the camera cut to her. But when it cut to her, she was not laughing."

"So, she stopped before the cut," The captain said.

Ostrowski shook his head and waved his hands back and

forth. "No. No. No. It doesn't work that way. When you laugh, you smile. You can't laugh without smiling." He did it and could tell how creepy he looked by the expression on Shaneel's face. "See. It doesn't work. Even if you stop laughing, the smile still takes a second or two to fade. It cuts to her right after the chuckle. There's no time for the smile to fade. And then she talks about being competitive. But that's not what the question asked. It asked her about taking people down. This was edited to make her sound offensive. I'm sure yesterday's show was too."

He twirled his finger to Cooper again. "Go to her second answer now."

Cooper rolled up to the shot of Brooke nodding to the camera, then the picture cut to a shot of Becca.

Ostrowski pointed. "There, she's sitting back relaxed—or something like it, and her hair, although messy, is messy in one direction because she just combed her fingers through it in that direction. Now roll it."

It cut to Brooke finishing the question and then back to Becca, sitting forward, before she started shaking her head and jumping up.

"And stop. There!" He pointed to Becca's hair. "The hair goes in the other direction. Also, she's leaning forward, with a totally different expression on her face."

"But she didn't like the question," The captain said.

"So, this woman is capable of going from zero to full-on rage quicker than Hitler?" Ostrowski shook his head. "No. The camera started on Becca, cut to Brooke briefly, then cut to Becca at a different point, maybe even a different question entirely." He shook his head and pointed angrily at the screen. "I'm telling you, the only purpose of these videos is to make sure these girls..." He looked over at Shaneel. "Women...get raked over the coals in the court of public opinion."

"To what end?" Shaneel asked.

"If I had to guess," Ostrowski said shrugging, "and I suppose that's what I'm being paid to do, I would have to say, so the world isn't so disappointed and horrified when he kills them in three days."

"Why three days?" Matthew said.

"Because that's how many more segments there are in the show. Five segments. This was the second. On the show, there are two more and then a wedding. These girrr...women aren't getting married, so..."

"Maybe it's a funeral," Shaneel said.

"He might be planning to kill them on the fourth show with the actual funeral ceremony, or even his own suicide, on the fifth," added the captain.

A uniformed officer appeared in the doorway. "Captain, we need you to come to the phone."

"Can it wait?"

"It probably shouldn't. There's a woman from Minnesota calling. She says she's Andrew Lawton's mother, and she just got an email from him telling her where they're all being held."

CHAPTER TWENTY-SIX

Jason Seevers needed a new pair of headphones. That's the only reason he was at Target that day. He and friends Javier and Omar from the San Dulcinte High School football team had been wandering around the store for nearly an hour, looking at sporting goods, hair products, even a very brief stop in the book section, before finally making it to electronics.

Javier and Omar went off to look at laptops while Jason scoped out a new pair of headphones. He stood at the counter, trying on each pair, and turning them up when a strange man caught his eye. The man wore a thin, gray, sports jacket with a hood pulled up over his head. This seemed odd, since it was 98 degrees outside and too hot for any kind of jacket, let alone a hoodie.

The man, who kept his head down, walked over to the video cameras and stopped. Jason took off the headphones and decided to get a better look. He took three steps and the man noticed him, looked up, and stared directly into his eyes.

Jason recognized him at once. He'd stared into that very same face in a close-up earlier that day. He turned and joined his friends over at the video games. "Hey, guys. Want to be heroes?"

"What are you talking about?" Omar said. "We *are* heroes."

"Shhh, keep it down." Jason cocked his head to one side. "You know how that bitch on the video this morning busted up all those cameras?"

"Yeah," Javier said. "Bitch went all crazy and shit."

"Do not look at anybody but me when I tell you this, got it?"

"What?" Javier said.

"Just keep your eyes on me until we decide what to do, got it?"

They both nodded.

"The dude that kidnapped them ladies and is doing all those videos, is here right now buying new cameras."

They both looked at him and smiled. "No shit?"

Jason nodded. "What say we take him down and gift wrap him for the cops?"

"Are you serious?" Omar said. "That dude took out five cops with his bare hands. He's like some super-soldier shit."

"That's because he knew they were coming, and they were probably some fat-ass, out-of-shape, donut-eating cops, just this side of retirement anyway. They weren't training for football every day of every week, and battle tested. Know what I'm saying?"

"Yeah," Javier said. "We take him by surprise, he'll never know what hit him."

Omar glanced over at the man, who was now stacking video camera boxes in his arm.

"Come on, man," Jason urged his friends. "We'll be on the news. All the girls will be all over us and shit."

Omar looked back at his friends and nodded.

"All right," Jason said. He stuck out his fist. "We on the news tonight, all over the world."

Javier and Omar both bumped his fist. "On the news," they

said together.

Jason nodded for them to follow him and the three headed for the sporting goods section. They all grabbed baseball bats and ran around the side of the store back to electronics. When they got there, their quarry was gone.

"Shit. He left," Javier said.

"Then we'll do this outside," Jason said. "Come on." He started to run and made it out onto the main aisle between sections when they spotted Bullock ducking in between shelves. They skidded to a stop. "He's not staying in the main aisles. He's hiding so nobody recognizes him."

Javier chuckled. "Too late for that, dumb shit."

Jason pointed and barked out directions. "He's headed for the self-checkout for sure. I'll go around home goods and get him where he has to come through. You two follow him and jump him after I knock him upside the head."

They nodded and, plan in place, all took off in hot pursuit. Jason ran around the outside, following the main aisle as fast as he could run. One woman yelped as he rushed by, and an old Target employee yelled at him. "Hey, slow down!" But he didn't. They would understand in about one minute.

He rounded the last shelving unit and was headed into position just as Bullock came through. Instead of slowing, Jason picked up speed and swung the bat at Bullock's head as hard as he could. Bullock, whose instincts were faster, ducked the blow. A display of canning jars on the shelf exploded into thousands of pieces.

Without hesitation, Bullock dropped the camera boxes, hit Jason with a solid fist in the center of the chest, stopping any chance the boy had of getting a breath. Then grabbed him by the back of the head and slammed it into the edge of a shelf. The boy's nose shattered, and a shower of blood and teeth rained down onto the floor.

Out of the corner of his eye, Bullock caught two more hostiles coming up behind him ready to swing. He launched himself at the first, rendering the now anemic swing completely harmless. With one hand he caught the bat and wrenched it out of the boy's hands. With the other he grabbed the boy's shirt, swung him around, and sent him hurtling down a shelf of glassware, breaking the majority of it and leaving the boy, writhing on the ground, bleeding, shards of glass sticking out of him everywhere. His high-pitched screams were unnerving.

The last boy hesitated for just a second. That was unfortunate for him. He actually had a clean shot on Bullock with a chance to do some damage, but he paused, giving Bullock time to grasp his bat firmly and block the kid's swing. The bats collided with a loud crack, that shocked the boy, but not Bullock. He pressed his advantage and backhanded the bat across the boy's jaw. Bullock felt it snap and the boy fell unconscious to the floor.

The store erupted into a cacophony of screams and shouts, and people ran panicked for the exits.

Bullock knew he had no chance to check out now. He grabbed one of the camera boxes and ran full speed, down the main aisles. He pushed past folks in the self-checkout, shoving still another teenager over the machine.

Bullock hit the manual doors, sending them crashing open, and fled into the parking lot. He made it to his SUV and pulled out slowly and inconspicuously as the siren-blaring cop cars pulled in and screeched to a stop. He waited for the cops to get out of their cars and run into the store before driving out of the lot, leaving the chaotic scene behind him.

Chapter Twenty-Seven

"Plastek Dynamics," Captain Vargas rushed back into the war room. "Cooper, find it on the map."

Officer Cooper quickly typed in Plastek Dynamics and clicked on "Maps." A satellite image appeared of an area with large blocks of buildings.

It looked to Ostrowski like an odd game of Tetris. But one of the blocks had the location marker on it—he always called "the upside-down teardrop." "There it is," Ostrowski said.

"Zoom in, Cooper," said Vargas. "Let's look at the buildings around it."

Cooper clicked the mouse wheel, and it appeared the camera was falling from the sky. Then it stopped and hovered closer to the Plastek Dynamics building. More upside-down teardrops appeared in light blue, with names next to them, such as Gilman's Foods, Hopper Hydraulics, LDR Logistics, and Kirasao Solutions. Moving in closer, more names appeared, but not all buildings had names.

"There are two buildings without names," Ostrowski said,

touching the screen with both hands. "One across the railroad tracks, and one right next to Plastek Dynamics. We need the skinny on those."

"I'm on it," Shaneel said, and she pulled out her phone. In minutes, she was talking to the Register of Deeds in City of Industry, and quickly got the information she needed. "The building right next door was just bought by a Chinese company and is in the process of being converted into a distribution center for medical supplies. The building across the railroad tracks was built as a stamping plant, which eventually went out of business. Ten years ago, it was purchased to be used as a warehouse but still hasn't been occupied. Want to know who bought it?"

"Who?" the captain asked.

Ostrowski smiled at Shaneel. This was a fine moment, the first time they were simpatico. "Something tells me...the U.S. military."

Shaneel smiled. "Nice work, Detective."

The captain clapped his hands. "Hot damn." He stepped in front of the monitor and ran his fingers along the road. "It looks like South Brea Canyon is the only road that accesses that particular industrial park." He snapped his fingers and pointed at Cooper. "I want all units to converge at this address. Someone notify the L.A. County Sheriff's Department. Get me Lt. Hostetler up here to discuss SWAT logistics, I want a mobile command center and a hostage negotiator on-site." He turned around and clapped once more. "Let's roll people!"

Just then a uniformed officer stuck his head in the room. "Captain, turn the TV over to GINfo. It looks like Duncan Bullock went shopping for more cameras, and three teenage kids decided to be heroes."

* * * * *

Less than an hour later, the parking lot in front of the old stamping plant was filled with dozens of squad cars, SWAT vans, an ambulance, a fire truck, and a Los Angeles County Mobile

Command Center.

Ostrowski, Johnson, and Vecoli walked through the maze of law enforcement to the MCC. A plump lieutenant was standing there, chewing on a cigar, and talking to his SWAT team. "...make no moves until you hear an order from me."

Vecoli walked up to him. "Make no moves at all, or we'll all regret it."

The lieutenant turned and looked at him. "Excuse me? I'm talking to my men here."

Vecoli pulled out his badge. "Special Agent, Matthew Vecoli, FBI. And it appears you have women on your team as well." He gestured to two women, suited up and ready for combat.

The lieutenant looked at the women on his team and back at Vecoli. Trying not to look annoyed, he put out his hand. "Lt. Eric Hostetler. Do you have something to add to this briefing, Agent Vecoli?"

Ostrowski waved to his captain. "Get everybody over here and listen to this."

The captain and the hostage negotiation team gathered to listen. Vecoli waited until they were all there before beginning.

"I served with Sgt. Bullock in Iraq. He is extremely capable of handling himself in both a firefight and hand-to-hand. But more than that, he has tunnel vision when he's on a mission. He set up this place to produce an online show. His mission is to denigrate these ladies before the whole world. Now I know we discovered the location before he expected us to, but that doesn't mean he didn't make contingencies for it. Like I said, he has tunnel vision, so he made sure that there was going to be no chance of interruptions. You can be absolutely certain he has made all necessary preparations to keep us out."

"What kind of preparations are we talking about?" Hostetler asked.

"I can't say for sure, but I wouldn't be surprised if every door in there is wired."

"Wired to blow?" the captain asked.

Vecoli nodded. "He is very good with all types of munitions, and he knows how things like that work. He currently works for a digital security company, so you can be sure he has eyes on us right now, and we have no way of seeing him. He will have a leg up on us on every move we make." He turned to Hostetler. "So, the reason I came to talk to you in the first place was to urge you and your team, to not bust the doors in and storm the place. He is ready for that, and it will lead to a lot of men down."

"Shit," Hostetler said. "This changes things." He turned to his team. "Okay, let's look at the map. We'll look for placements on surrounding buildings. I want 360 degrees of sharpshooters. We'll play the waiting game. It's just not as exciting."

Chapter Twenty-Eight

She had heard sirens from her metal-walled room before—distant and fading quickly. But to Becca, these seemed different somehow. They grew louder. Closer. And then they stopped. Several of them. They did not fade into the distance.

Becca stepped over to her door, peeled a corner of the paper back, careful not to rip it, and looked out. She could see into the murky darkness of the plant, brighter now in the light of day. But there was no sign of police, nothing to indicate that anything had changed with their circumstances.

Then Bullock ran by. She heard him unlock a door to her left, then heard it slam.

She realized she'd never seen Bullock run in the plant. He always moved slowly, methodically. Each movement measured and sure. But just now he sprinted across the plant floor and frantically opened the door. Something was up, and Becca was sure the sirens she'd heard had something to do with it. Perhaps their location had been discovered and this whole thing would soon be over. Becca would get her chance to see this thug dragged off in chains...or worse, which wouldn't break Becca's heart in the

193

least.

She had to sit and listen as he went into Alanna's room the previous night and slowly break three of her fingers—one for every camera she smashed. Alanna's screams were chilling and heartbreaking. Becca curled onto her cot with her pillow over her ears, but she still heard everything. She fell asleep in tears and woke up in a simmering rage.

She waited several more minutes at the window, but there were no more sirens, and Bullock never came back out. Perhaps he just had to take a shit in a critical way. She pressed the tape back in place and turned to walk back to her cot when she heard a door slam. She pulled the paper back once more and saw Bullock walking briskly and with purpose, arms to his side, almost marching. He pulled out his keys and walked past her door, stopping several doors down, unlocked the door, and pounded on it.

"Let's go. We need to talk."

He unlocked the next one, the next one, and the next one. Then hers, each time pounding and shouting something like, "Everybody out. Family meeting."

Becca pressed the paper back into place before she opened it and peered out. Looking to her right, she saw Mike and Lyssa, each coming out of their doors. When they saw each other, they hugged tightly. The next room farther down was Andy Lawton who stepped out, nonchalantly, leaned against the door jamb, and put his hands in his pockets.

Becca watched Bullock continue down the row, unlocking doors and shouting for everybody to come out. The sirens had certainly gotten him rattled.

Brooke, arms behind her back, emerged from the very next room to her right. When she saw her, she immediately strode over and hugged her for a full minute. The two held hands tightly, worried what was coming.

Alanna was next, she was hunched a bit with one hand

wrapped. When Becca saw her, she walked over and tried to hug her. "Alanna I'm so..." But Alanna winced, held up her arms as if to protect herself from an attacker and slowly backed away.

Fiona wrapped her arms around her sister and glared at Becca. "Stay the hell away from her. You've done enough." She pulled Alanna back and they stood over by Ben.

Becca watched the fear, anguish, and pain in Alanna's eyes. She crossed her arms, and with one hand pulled at her collar anxiously. She knew this was a relationship that would never be repaired, and she needed to let it go. She was trying to get a handle on all the emotions that were flowing through her at that moment. Sadness for the pain she caused Alanna, someone she deeply cared for, and grief for their lost friendship. She also felt tremendous guilt because she couldn't contain her emotions, and, finally, anger at the man who caused the pain.

With everyone out and lined up, Bullock paced back and forth in front of them, mouth closed, breathing heavily through his nose. His arms were behind his back as he walked. He looked at the row of captives and snarled. "I don't know if you're aware, but we now have some unexpected guests outside."

Becca crossed her arms at the sound of Bullock's voice. Her nails bit into her biceps and she glared at the man who was the sole source of everyone's suffering.

"I say unexpected, because I didn't think they would get here this quickly." He stopped and twirled his hand. "...if at all." He started pacing again. "This is such a random location, I was sure the authorities would struggle to find it. I told myself that they must be incredibly smart these days." Bullock chuckled. "Good for them. Their detective work is something really special. Top minds at the L.A.P.D." Bullock turned the other direction and shook his head. But then I got to thinking, 'What if they aren't that smart? What if they had a little help from...oh, I don't know... perhaps an elderly woman in Minnesota?'" He stopped and locked eyes with Andy Lawton.

Andy's mouth dropped open, and he ducked back into his room and slammed the door. Bullock was on it as it closed and beat against it with his shoulder. Every female in the room screamed, except Becca. Bullock managed to force the door open and charged inside. She heard Andy shouting, "No! No! No! Sorry! Sorry! I'm Sorry!" Then a crash.

A second later Bullock dragged a whimpering Andy out of his room by his hair. Andy groaned and kicked along with his feet to relieve the pull on his scalp, but it was clearly painful all the way.

Bullock lifted him up. "I work in computer security. You don't think I know what a key-logger is?" He jammed a fist into Andy's gut. The air rushed out so hard and fast, it sounded like a quick burst of a foghorn. Andy crumpled forward and dropped to his knees.

"What's more surprising, is that you didn't think through what could happen to you if I were to ever find out." He pulled back and hit Andy with a crunching fist into his face. Andy's head snapped back, he fell, and his head bounced on the cement floor.

"Stop it!" Becca screamed.

Bullock ignored her. He lifted Andy up by the front of his shirt like a doll. "Do you think I'm just playing around here? Did you think it was funny to put one over on me?" He held Andy, punching and backhanding him furiously. "Is this as funny as you thought it would be?" He lowered Andy to the floor and punched him several more times. Andy's face was red, with blood flowing onto the floor.

The anger within Becca ignited into a fiery rage. "Stop it!" she continued to scream. She took several steps toward Bullock. "Stop it! Stop It!" Continuing to walk until she was six feet from him, she yelled again. "Stop it!" Her fists were clenched, and now she stood in front of Bullock, ready to pounce. She was aware there was nothing she could do to hurt the man, but she would try. She was simply done with his brand of terrorism and she was ready to make her stand right here.

Bullock released Andy's unconscious body and let it drop to the floor in a heap. He stared at Becca, face bright red, breathing hard, like an angry bull ready to charge.

Becca stood in front of him, didn't flinch, fists clenched so hard they turned white. She breathed hard, her heart thundering in her chest.

After a moment Bullock relaxed and stepped back. Put his hands on his hips, looked at the others, gesturing at Becca. "Only one of you in this entire group has any balls. Only one of you has any fire in your belly to do something?" He looked at Becca, almost sporting a look of respect. "That is the very reason that you let her lead you down the wrong path. The path that led to my daughter's death." His eyes scanned the row of captives. "Because you're all like little lemmings. If someone tells you what to do, you just do it. But only one of you has the guts to shout the orders." He stared at Becca again, his look of respect turned into a scowl. "Now get back into your rooms and take a moment and think about what complete losers you all are to just sit back and watch this happen to one of your own, and the fact you didn't lift a finger to help him."

Nobody moved.

"Now!" Bullock shouted.

Slowly everybody disappeared back into their rooms.

Becca refused to move. She stood firm, fists still balled tightly, staring into the face of a man she knew could tear her apart. She wasn't sure what she should do next, but she'd sat in enough negotiations to understand she couldn't show a sign of weakness.

"Lyssa, get back out here," Bullock called.

A frightful Lyssa appeared in her doorway.

Not taking his eyes off Becca, Bullock pointed to the floor next to him. "I want you to come here."

Lyssa didn't make a move, other than to cover her mouth with her hands and burst into tears.

"Stop with the blubbering," Bullock said. He looked over at her frustrated. "I'm getting you out of here. But you're taking Lawton with you. He needs medical attention."

Mike ran out of his room and threw his arms around her. She hugged him tightly and cried, "I don't want to leave you."

"Andrews, back in your room. Lyssa, I'm not going to tell you again."

"I love you," Mike said. "Get out of here." He backed into his room.

"I don't want to leave you," Lyssa cried.

"You have to. Tell my folks I'm okay."

"Interesting," Becca said. "I usually only have to tell her something once. It would appear, Sargent, that I have more loyal followers in this room than you do."

Bullock's eyes narrowed. She saw he hated her just as much as she hated him. "Too bad you led them off a cliff," he spat out.

"Oh, considering your path is nothing more than terrorism and torture, I'd say my direction looks pretty good right now. Thank you," said Becca.

"Lyssa!" Bullock barked.

Lyssa jumped, and Mike closed his door. She slowly walked over.

Bullock placed a hand on his knife and spoke quietly to Becca. "Back in your room. Now."

Another thing Becca knew about negotiation was when to not press it. Alanna still had another hand, and an important rule of negations was not to push the deranged lunatic past his breaking point. She turned to walk back to her room. She saw Brooke standing in her doorway, teary eyes wide and terrified. She pointed for her to get back and stay safe. Brooke backed in and Becca stepped through her doorway and turned to watch what Bullock was going to do next.

Bullock instructed Lyssa on how to put her hands under

Andy's shoulders and drag him backward. She lifted him up and his unconscious head fell back and clunked on the floor. When she dragged him along, a thin layer of blood smeared across the cement. Lyssa cried all the way out of sight.

Bullock turned back to their row of rooms. He walked to the left, and Becca heard him lock the three doors of Ben, Fiona, and Alanna before getting to hers. He gripped the handle of her door and glared at her. "You try to be a hero again, and I'll stop playing with fingers and start going with throats." Then he slammed her door and locked it.

Becca dropped onto the cot. Her body shook uncontrollably, and she leaned forward and vomited.

CHAPTER TWENTY-NINE

One of the officers shouted, "Someone's coming out!"

Ostrowski, Shaneel, and Vecoli ran to the front of the barricade and found a police car to shelter behind. They watched a young black girl dragging out a body. Shaneel put a hand on Ostrowski's shoulder. "I'll be right back." She shot around the police car and ran up the sidewalk.

"Johnson!" Ostrowski yelled. He wanted to tell her not to go because the area had not been secured, but she was gone before he could even utter her name. Shaneel sprinted to the young girl's side and asked her to lower the body. She scanned it quickly and then stood again, giving the girl a big hug. She helped her hoist the body once more and both of them dragged it down the sidewalk, toward the line of law enforcement. Four paramedics were waiting for them. Two whisked the girl away, and the other two placed the man on a gurney and rolled it to an ambulance.

Shaneel walked back to stand next to Ostrowski and Vecoli. Ostrowski grabbed her arm and dragged her back a couple rows of cars before whirling on her. "Do I really have to explain to you how unbelievably stupid it was to run out into an unsecured area like that?"

"Nope," Shaneel said. "I know the rules. But I had a young girl hanging out there like a victim, trying to drag someone heavier than herself across the pavement. Just wasn't going to let it continue without doing something."

Ostrowski slapped his hand on top of the squad car they stood next to. "Cut the shit, Johnson! If you know the rules, then follow them. We are *not* to have this conversation *ever* again. Is that clear?"

Shaneel crossed her arms. "It's very clear. But what is this?"

"What is what?"

She smirked and gestured between them. "This is literally the first time since we met, you haven't been acting all class clown, and actually have shown some real emotion. What is that all about, hmmm?"

"Oh, don't do that." Ostrowski wagged a finger at her. "Don't go acting like I give a crap about you, Miss Thorn-in-my-ass. This has nothing to do with me. I know of a husband who doesn't need to be a single father, and a little boy who needs his mother."

That hit the mark. Shaneel's face went cold. She put her hands on her hips and looked at the ground.

Ostrowski spoke again with a much calmer tone. "Just be more careful, would you please?"

Shaneel nodded, still looking down like a scolded child.

Ostrowski was starting to feel like he was a little too harsh. He added, "And damn, are you fast."

Shaneel looked up and smiled.

"Hey, look at that," Ostrowski said, pointing at her face. "You actually *can* smile. Your face makes that shape. It looks good on you."

Shaneel chuckled and smacked his arm.

"I hope that wasn't too offensive."

"I can let it slide," She said.

"Detective Johnson," Captain Vargas came stomping over. "That was one of the most reckless..."

"Captain," Ostrowski put his hands up and stepped in the captain's way. "Don't talk to my partner like that. Besides, I've already discussed it with her. She understands, and she'll never do it again...when another angry father kidnaps two celebrities and holds them in a warehouse."

Shaneel giggled behind him.

The captain looked around Ostrowski at Shaneel and back. "Oh, *now* you two are thick as thieves? All it took was for her to act imbecilic, too? Now I have two assholes to worry about?" He pointed a finger at Shaneel. "Never again, are we clear?"

Shaneel smiled. "Clear. Thank you, Captain."

"Captain," Vecoli rushed over. "Right now, we're at a standstill, and Bullock is holding all the cards. Maybe I can fix the stalemate. I want to go in."

Chapter Thirty

Barely able to breathe, Brooke swallowed hard and knocked on the door to her office/cell. She had watched her dearest friend stand up to their tormentor. It was to no avail, but perhaps with two of them on Bullock, it might do some good.

When there was no answer. She knocked again.

Brooke could try a different tact. She would be nice. Not confrontational. She would be the good cop. She knew Bullock wasn't evil, he was hurting, and she would appeal to his humanity rather than try to bully him into ending this.

She reached up to knock again when she heard keys rattling outside her door. She stepped away as the door was unlocked and swung open.

Bullock stood back and jerked his head to the left. "Need to use the facilities?"

"Oh…ahhh." Brooke didn't know why it hadn't occurred to her that this would be his assumption. It's the only reason she'd knocked in the past. "No." Her voice quivered. She was hoping somehow, she could get it together enough to sound a little less terrified. "I was hoping I could have a word with you."

Bullock looked annoyed and shook his head. "No." He reached in and grabbed the door handle.

"Look," Brooke said, and she reached up and put her hand on the door. She wasn't sure who was more surprised at this, Bullock or her. But she knew this was probably the only time she'd get this chance. "I'm sorry. I know you're hurting. I can't even imagine how painful this all is for you. But you know none of this will bring your daughter back, and you're hurting those who love you as well."

Bullock frowned. "No. It won't bring my daughter back. Thank you for reminding me."

Brooke removed her hand from the door. "I'm sorry, I wasn't..."

"This isn't intended to bring her back," Bullock said. "This is intended to make sure that nothing like this happens to another poor innocent girl."

"I think you've already succeeded in that, don't you?" Brooke was falling back on her strength—interviewing. Just keep the conversation going, keep them talking until you get what you need from them.

"Honestly? No." Bullock relaxed his posture. He was no longer ready to sprint, instead appearing to desire the conversation. He needed to make his point. "Perhaps I've managed to end *your* show. That's somewhat of a win. But there are more shows out there just like yours. Shows that parade young girls out into a world they were never meant to be in, in situations they were never prepared for. And for what? So perverts and dreamers can on sit their asses at home, and somehow kid themselves into believing they have fulfilled lives by watching someone else's agonies and ecstasies." His face twisted into a mask of pure disgust. "We've become a world of do-nothings, feeding off the pain and pleasures of other people, like the worst kind of parasites. And people like you sell this shit as entertainment."

She had him talking. That was a plus. Even though it wasn't going the way she'd hoped, if there was communication she still had a chance to send and receive a message. All she had to do was change the angle of the attack, and perhaps she could reach this man.

"Mr. Bullock, in the short time I spent with Kristine I..."

"You don't get to do that." Bullock snarled and took a step toward her.

Brooke jumped back and brought her hands up. She fought back defensive tears.

"You don't get to talk about her as if you were friends, and you have wonderful memories together. She was nothing more to you than a ratings ticket, and you know it. If she hadn't died, you wouldn't even remember her name. But she was my daughter." His voice cracked slightly, and he was breathing harder.

Brooke felt she was getting to him. "Yes, Mr. Bullock. She was your daughter." She spoke slowly and calmly. She knew she was nearly in control now. "And look what you're doing to her memory."

She saw Bullock's face soften at the thought.

Brooke knew she was getting through. "Kristine had a life. She had friends. She had things she liked to do, places she liked to go, people she loved, and causes she believed in." She took a step forward and spoke softer. "But if you go through with all of this, all people will think of when they hear her name is this spectacle that happened after she was gone. Is that fair to her?"

Bullock said nothing.

She pressed her advantage. "What do you think she'd say right now if she saw all of this happening in her name? Do you think she would be proud? Would she be inspired? Or would she just think her dad lost his marbles?" Brooke cringed inside. That last part might have been too far.

Bullock's lip raised and his eyes thinned. He spoke in a harsh whisper. "Nice try." Then he slammed the door shut.

Brooke pounced on the closed door. "No, Mr. Bullock wait!" She pounded several times. "I'm sorry. I'm sorry."

The key turned in the lock and she heard Bullock storm off and scream.

"I'm sorry." Brooke turned her back to the door, slid down onto the floor, and pulled her knees in tight. She'd had him listening, but she pushed too hard, too fast. She knew she would never get another chance like that again. She needed to start preparing to die. She buried her head in her arms and shook while she cried.

CHAPTER THIRTY-ONE

Matthew slowly walked up to the set of double glass doors. He checked them over, top to bottom, to make sure it was clear before opening the one on the right and walking through.

He stepped across the lobby to the interior access door. He peered through the small window to see only a hallway wall painted the same color beige that they had seen on the videos. He dared not try the doorknob because he knew it would be wired, so he knocked lightly and waited. When nothing happened and nobody appeared, he knocked a little harder. There was a flash of movement in the window, and he was quickly staring into the barrel of an M007 9mm pistol.

Matthew stepped back and saw Bullock's eye peer around the side of the gun. When there was recognition, the sergeant appeared to sigh and shake his head. He lowered his weapon, held up a finger, and mouthed, "One sec."

Matthew nodded and looked back out at the wall of law enforcement vehicles at the edge of the parking lot.

The latch clicked, and the door opened slightly. Bullock pushed his face to the crack. "What do you need Vecoli?"

"I have something for you from your friends outside here."

Bullock slid his hand out the door.

"And they wanted me to check on the hostages."

"The hostages are fine," Bullock grumbled. "Just give me what you need to give me."

Matthew's personal mission was to get Brooke out of there. He wasn't going to just walk away. "Look, sir, you're the one who just sent out a hostage beaten to within an inch of his life. You'll have to excuse them if they don't take your word for it."

After a moment, the hand pulled back and the door opened slightly wider.

Matthew slipped in through the opening and Bullock closed it, locked it, pulled out his phone, and punched in a code. There was a small beep and a green light appeared on a black box that sat on a small metal drum.

"Let me guess...ammonium nitrate?"

"Damn right. There's enough in here to take out half the block." Bullock said.

"In that drum?" Vecoli asked. It didn't look big enough to do what Bullock was threatening.

"No. There's one of those at every doorway leading into this place, on every floor—even the roof entrances." He smiled at Matthew. "I don't want anybody to interrupt my mission. Now, what do you have for me?"

Matthew pulled out a small cell phone and handed it over.

"Sure. Expected." Bullock took the phone and slipped it into his pocket.

"I want to see Winthrop."

Bullock sneered, but nodded his head for Vecoli to follow.

Matthew walked down the hall of offices, to the door that led out into the main plant. The place smelled of stale air and machine oil. He was bothered that Brooke was being held in such circumstances. They walked past several doors, which had obviously housed plant maintenance and foremen-type offices. Bullock walked up to one and knocked on it, pulled out a large ring of keys and unlocked the door. He poked his head in. "Miss Winthrop, you've got a visitor."

Vecoli was surprised that Bullock referred to her as 'Miss Winthrop,' though he shouldn't have been. The man was career military, and respect was the number one asset of a military man. So, even if he had no respect for the woman he'd abducted and put on trial, he was required, by his own programming, to make sure he showed her respect.

Bullock stepped back and gestured for Vecoli to enter.

Matthew stepped forward, looked into the doorway, and almost gasped at the sight. Brooke was sitting on a cot in an old office, wearing dirty, lime green sweats. Her messy hair pulled back into a ponytail, she looked exhausted. The beautiful television host, always on top of the world, always looking perfect with boundless energy, was beaten from the inside. She looked up at him, a puzzled look on her weary face.

Matthew took a deep breath and held it for a moment. He fought his first instinct which was to turn and face the cold-hearted beast who would do this to a weak, defenseless woman. But he knew that would only make matters worse. And he was here for Brooke. He needed to make sure she was doing well. "Hi, there. May I come in?"

Her brows knitted and she nodded.

Matthew walked over to stand in front of her. Bullock closed the door behind him. "How are you?"

Brooke shook her head slightly. "How are you even here?"

"We'll get to that." He sat down on the cot and put his hand on her back. "Are you hurt?"

Brooke folded her hands in her lap and looked down at them. "No. But others are."

"Others? What others? You mean someone other than the guy that girl just dragged out?"

Brooke nodded. "Him, and Alanna."

"Alanna?" Vecoli was surprised Bullock would let any harm come to a girl. "Who's Allanna again? And what happened to her?"

"Alanna is Becca's assistant." A tear dripped off Brooke's cheek. She wiped away the moisture. "He broke her fingers to teach Becca a lesson."

"He what?" Vecoli couldn't believe what he was hearing. This was not the sergeant he had served in the Middle East. "How does it teach Becca anything to break somebody else's fingers?"

Brooke wiped away a few more tears. "Becca can be a handful. She lives kind of reckless. Like she's not afraid of anyone or anything. Bullock obviously can't beat her and then put her on camera, so he hurts someone she cares about. That can't be me, but Becca loves Alanna, too."

"How many fingers are we talking about here?"

Brooke turned her red eyes to Vecoli for a moment, then looked back down. "The first one was to send a message to Becca, to keep her doing shows. But then when Becca broke all of the cameras, he broke another finger for each camera." Brooke began to cry. "Everybody could hear it. Alanna screamed at the top of her lungs and just kept crying, 'Why? Why?'" Brooke laid her head on Matthew's shoulder and wept.

He took her in his arms, rubbed her back, and stroked her hair.

"I'm so sorry for this," He whispered. "I never meant for any of this to happen."

Brooke sputtered a few times and pulled away. "What does that mean?"

"Never mind," Vecoli said. "I'm getting you out of here right now." He took her hand and stood.

"What?" Brooke said. "How?"

"Never mind how. I'll take care of that. But we're walking out of here." He eased her up to her feet, walked her to the door, and opened it.

Bullock was leaning against the wall. He stood straight when the door opened, looked at Vecoli, then Brooke, and back. "What the hell is going on here, Vecoli?"

Matthew tightened his grip on Brooke's hand. "Sir, I'm leaving, and I'm taking her with me."

Bullock put his hands on his hips and sighed. "Look, kid. You know I can't let you do that. She's the reason I'm doing this."

"You will still have Dodge, and it will show a great deal of faith to everyone out there if you release one hostage. All I'm asking is that I get to choose the hostage."

Bullock's eyes grew fiery. "Do you think I give a shit about what people out there think? I'm only concerned about what's going on in here." He pointed at Matthew. "You've put yourself too deep in this to wuss out now."

Brooke looked up at Matthew. "What is he talking about?"

Matthew glanced over at her, shook his head, and turned back to Bullock. "It has nothing to do with wussing out, sir. But this is not what I signed up for. You never mentioned any of this when you came to me."

Brooke shuffled back a step. "Matthew. What's going on here?"

"Your little boyfriend is the one who gave me all the intel I needed to put this show together."

Matthew looked over at Brooke, her eyes widened. "Is that true?"

Matthew sighed. "Yes, and no." He was afraid that it would come out like this, and this is what he was hoping to avoid. "The sergeant asked me to get dirt on either you, Becca Dodge, the show itself, or Chris Haddock because he wanted to take the whole thing public. Wanted to do something so that what happened to his daughter didn't happen to anybody else. He never mentioned anything about kidnapping you, or this show, or trial, or whatever he is trying to call it."

"Don't play dumb, Vecoli, just because you've got a hard-on for the star," Bullock growled. "You were just as mad as I was about Kristine. At least you said you were. Or are you trying to back pedal on that now too?"

"I was mad," Vecoli said. "I *am* mad. But you can't blame Brooke or Becca for what happened to Kristine. It was just an unfortunate incident."

"An unfortunate incident is when a train jumps the tracks and mows someone down. That's unfortunate. Marrying someone off to a psychopath isn't an unfortunate incident. It's a criminal act. And you agreed with me at the start of all this."

"So, when you came into the office that day?" Brooke's voice quivered. "You were just trying to get information to use against us?"

"That's right, darling?" Bullock said.

"*No.*" Vecoli turned to Bullock. "Don't put words in my mouth, sir."

"You know what, Vecoli? It's time for you to leave." Bullock said.

"I'm not leaving without Brooke."

"Yes," Brooke said, pulling her hand loose from his grasp. "You are." She stepped back and slowly closed the door.

"Brooke, wait." Matthew stepped toward her, and Bullock grabbed his arm. Matthew shook off the older man's grasp, pointed his finger in Bullock's face. "Don't touch me, sir. I mean it."

"Vecoli, you're in this now. Whether you like it or not. You used government time and resources to get me the information that allowed this very situation. If I walk out there now and tell them everything you supplied me with, you'll be sent up the river, and you know it."

"Fine with me," Matthew said. "At least I'd know Brooke was

safe and away from your crazy ass." He reached for the doorknob. "Now, I'm going in there to get Brooke, and we're walking out of here."

Bullock took a step forward, but Matthew reached over, snatched Bullock's gun from his holster and pointed it at him. Bullock stopped and sneered. "You traitorous little coward. After everything I've done for you."

"You don't get to do that, Sergeant. You don't get to call me traitorous or a coward just because I don't follow you down a path of kidnapping and murder."

"Murder is what happened to Kristine. All I'm doing is seeking justice."

"You could have done that in a court of law. Filed charges. Sued them for wrongful death. You would have probably won."

Bullock scowled and shook his head. "And what? Make them pay a fine? You think that would have even made a dent in their lives? Some studio would have covered their legal costs, and they would have just moved on and not given another thought to the woman they let die."

"Either way, you made the wrong decision, sir." With his eyes still on Bullock, Matthew turned the knob and pushed open the door. "Come on, Brooke. We're leaving."

"No, we're not," Brooke said, and the door slammed. Matthew looked over, startled by the sound, and that was all Bullock needed. One hand chopped at the arm, the other grabbed the wrist and twisted, and in a blink, the gun was out of his hand. Bullock turned and threw the gun into the darkness of the plant. Long seconds later, they heard it clatter on the cement floor.

But Matthew was quick too, and when Bullock had turned back around, Matthew was standing there holding the knife he had pulled from a sheath in his pant leg.

"You've really become a disappointment," Bullock said.

"*I* have? Do you know how much I looked up to you? Do you have any idea how important you were to me? I probably wouldn't be alive today if not for you. And then you go and pull shit like this?" Matthew took a step forward. "This moment right here could be the greatest heartache of my life." He pointed the knife at Bullock. "You sir, *you* are the disappointment."

Bullock let out a primal scream and lunged at Vecoli, slamming him into the door jamb, and pinning the knife hand against the wall. The impact was bone shattering. But Marines, especially those who reported to Sergeant "Slam Dunk" Bullock, didn't cede to pain. They fought through it, and Vecoli's training was instinctual. He clenched his other fist and jabbed it quickly into Bullock's throat. There was a small gasp on the first punch, but the second punch caused the older man to gag and fall back. This was the opening Matthew needed to slash with the knife.

Bullock tried to dodge the blade but was stunned by the throat punch and couldn't move quickly enough. The knife cut through his shirt, then the skin and muscle of his left breast. Bullock stammered back and held his chest, a bloodstain blossoming on the front of his shirt. The sergeant looked up, his eyes no longer looking human. More like an injured wolf's, sensing a survival situation. The cold stare sent a chill through Vecoli, who had never seen his beloved sergeant look that way. He thought of the poor five souls in Kandahar whom Bullock slaughtered. Maybe they saw these eyes.

The door opened behind Matthew and Brooke screamed. "Stop this. Now!"

Matthew turned his head to tell Brooke to close the door, but … Whoompf! Bullock slammed into his mid-section like a five-star linebacker, knocking the wind out of him. The two men blasted through her doorway, careened off the edge of the desk, and crunched to the floor. Matthew was sure he felt his right shoulder dislocate with the impact on the desk. His injured shoulder hit the cement of the floor, and he yelped in agony.

Brooke's scream echoed in the room, along with Bullock's rage-filled howl.

Matthew felt a stone-hard fist collide with his face, heard the crack, felt the jitter through his bones as his nose broke. Then with another fist from the other direction, he felt his teeth cut through his lip, saw his blood spatter on Bullock's shirt. Matthew felt two more blows and was losing consciousness when he heard Brooke scream, Stop!" She grabbed for Bullock's arm.

Straining to keep his eyes open, he watched the scene unspool, seemingly in slow motion. Bullock reached back, grabbed Brooke, and lifted her over his head. His face twisted with rage, and he heaved her across the room. Brooke landed with a heavy thud on the cot.

Seeing her tossed like a salt sack shocked Vecoli out of his stupor. He reached up, jammed his fingers into the cut in Bullock's chest, and gripped down.

Bullock screamed, a high pitch sneaking into his normally low register. Vecoli had hurt him—good and bad news. His sergeant wasn't one to get hurt and melt away. He would hurt back harder. Much harder.

Rather than rip Vecoli's fingers out of his wound, Bullock jammed his fist down hard into Matthews's gut, forcing the last drop of air from his lungs. There was no oxygen, no energy to hold on. He was forced to release his grip.

With another howl, Bullock unloaded a storm of blows, on Vecoli's face, chest, stomach. Matthew tried to block them but flailed uselessly, then with one final shout, Bullock grabbed the knife off the floor and plunged it into Matthew's chest, between his heart and his left shoulder.

Matthew gasped at the fiery pain. If he'd had any excess air, he probably would have screamed. But there was nothing there. He looked up at Bullock, who hovered over him, a bleeding, raging, hulk of a man, rocking with the effort of catching his own breath.

Matthew turned his head and looked over at Brooke. She was leaning on her arm, her face was bright red, and wet from crying. She looked like she was screaming something to him, but for whatever reason, he couldn't hear what she was saying. He noticed the room was growing darker. It looked like someone had their hands on the controls of a dimmer switch and was slowly bringing it down. They must have also had their hands on the thermostat too because it was growing very cold.

He shivered in the darkness.

CHAPTER THIRTY-TWO

The knife stuck up out of his shoulder, and unbelievably he peered at her over the handle. She felt this was somehow her fault, and it was a look she would see in her nightmares. Then Matthew's eyes slowly closed. "You killed him!" Brooke screamed.

Wincing, Bullock leaned forward and placed two fingers aside Matthew's neck, then pulled back. "Nah, just passed out. But he's going to need help." Though in pain, Bullock was calm, as if Matthew had just nodded off watching television.

Brooke had never experienced violence on this scale and certainly never dreamed she'd be at the center of it all. She had no idea how Bullock could brush it off, as if his bludgeoned friend were a mere nuisance, like the wind blowing napkins off the picnic table. She dropped back down, buried her head in her pillow, and cried. There was a jingle of keys, and she felt the key ring plunk down on the bed next to her.

She raised her head to see them on her cot, splattered with blood. Bullock was sitting in the chair, breathing hard and cringing at the pain. "Go get Riser." He stopped to wince. "He needs to get Vecoli out of here to get medical attention."

219

Brooke looked down at the keys, picked them up with her thumb and forefingers, trying to avoid touching the blood.

"Go," Bullock said, more demanding this time.

Brooke jumped from the bed.

"Winthrop," Bullock called.

She stopped and looked at him.

He was breathing heavy, holding onto his chest. "Don't try to leave the building. I meant what I said. The whole place will blow."

The fact that he just said that made her want to cry again. Then she was mad at herself for feeling that way. Becca never had those feelings. How was Becca so strong?

She walked out the door, taking a moment to peer out into the darkest part of the plant. It was brighter now that the sun was shining. She scanned for the gun that Bullock had thrown, but she couldn't see it. She had no doubt it was a long way away. It would take too long to find it, and Bullock would be on her in seconds anyway.

She walked to the next door down and looked at the keys. They had gotten her fingers bloody now, too. She grimaced at the sight and wiped her hands on the wall, leaving fresh red streaks next to the dark streaks from years ago. Then she realized she had the power right in her hands. Bullock was hurt, she could unlock all the doors, let everyone out, overpower him, and escape.

She glanced back toward her room. Heard him wincing from the pain when he tried to move. He was a wounded animal now. Weren't they the most dangerous? And he had the code to the bombs at the doors. He would never tell them what it was. And in the end, Matthew would die. That was why she had the keys in the first place. Because Matthew was terribly hurt. Anything else she tried to do now would surely kill him, and she didn't want another death on her hands—couldn't live with that, no matter how she felt about Matthew at that point.

She fumbled with the bloody set of keys, looking for one that seemed right. They all looked similar, so she just picked out one and tried it. No luck. She slid it down the ring and tried the next one. Again, it didn't work. Three keys later the lock turned, and she opened the door.

Mike Riser was sitting on his bed, his eyes wide as saucers. "What the hell is going on?"

"Come on. We need you." Brooke waved for him to follow her.

Mike jumped from his bed and followed her back into her room. Looking at Vecoli, lying there unconscious, beaten and bloody, a knife sticking out of him, and blood splattered everywhere, he locked his fingers on top of his head, and took a deep breath. "Oh shit, oh shit, oh shit."

"You just hit the jackpot, Riser," Bullock said. "He's your ticket outta here. You get to go be with your girlfriend." It took Bullock two attempts to stand because the pain was so intense, but he managed. "You remember how I showed Brandt how to drag someone unconscious?"

Mike nodded, never taking his eyes off Vecoli.

"Go ahead and do that with him."

Mike walked around, bent down, and pointed to the knife. "Shouldn't we take that out first?"

Bullock shook his head. "You pull it and he could bleed out before you even reach the front door."

Mike nodded, reached under Vecoli's shoulders, lifted, and tried to turn him around, but the room was too small and the cot was in the way.

Brooke grabbed the end of her cot and lifted it all the way up, pushing it against the far wall. This gave Mike the room he needed to get Vecoli headed in the right direction.

A long, slimy streak of red blood trailed Vecoli's body out the door. Bullock groaned when he stood, then shambled along as Mike dragged Matthew around the corner.

Brooke followed, watching the convergence of blood trails on the cement floor—Vecoli's bright red mixed with the now dark streak of Andy's. When they reached the door to the office hallway, Brooke rushed up and opened it for them.

Mike slid Matthew around, positioned him in front of the doorway to the lobby, then looked up.

Slowly, Bullock lowered the arm that was holding his chest wound and reached it into his pocket to retrieve his phone. When he pulled it out, he lost his grip on it and it dropped from his hand clattering to the floor.

"Son-of-a-bitch," he whimpered.

Instinctively, Brooke reached down, picked up the phone, and handed it to him.

Bullock looked at her. There was a look in his eyes she had never seen before. It was calm, serene, almost grateful, and yet perhaps a little sad. He took the phone from her hand and whispered. "Thank you." Then he fired up an app and punched in a code. The green light on the little box turned off. "Go," he said to Mike, and then fell back against the wall.

Mike reached up, opened the door, and tried to block it with his feet while he dragged Matthew.

Recognizing the awkward struggle, Brooke grabbed the door and held it open for him—watched him cross the lobby and back out the glass doors to freedom and safety. She realized that she could run. Freedom was hers. All she had to do was make the move. Bullock would never catch her; he was much too hurt.

But the list of consequences flashed through her brain. Whenever things didn't go Bullock's way, somebody got hurt. Alanna was proof of that. She had four broken fingers now because Becca challenged him. If Brooke were to escape, she would be leaving four innocents behind to face his rage. She couldn't do that. Especially to Becca, her best friend in the world. If something were to happen to Becca because of her own cowardice, she would never be able to forgive herself. Sure, she would be alive, but she would never be able to sincerely enjoy another minute of her life, knowing she was responsible for her best friend's death. Like it or not, Brooke knew she and Becca were in this together. She watched Mike drag Matthew down the sidewalk toward the police cars, saw police and paramedics meet him, start assessing him. Then she closed the door on her own freedom, and turned to her captor.

Bullock tapped in the code and the green light flickered on once more with a beep.

"Come with me," Brooke said to Bullock, and for whatever reason, she couldn't understand, numb to her soul, she did what she felt needed to be done, without thought. She walked back into her room, picked up her towel, snagged the side of it on a sharp edge of the big metal desk, and tore it lengthwise into a long strip.

Bullock wandered in slowly.

"Turn around and take off your shirt," She ordered.

Bullock looked at her, almost disbelievingly, but followed her instructions. He turned, tried to lift his shirt, and grimaced.

Brooke grabbed the bottom of his shirt and hoisted it over his head, eliciting a long, pained sigh. She snagged a seam on the desk and ripped something close to a square from a clean portion of the back of it. She folded it over, reached around, and carefully placed it on the gash on his chest. "Hold this."

He reached up and held the fabric in place. She then took the strip of the towel, wrapped it around him to hold the makeshift gauze, and tied it in back to keep it firmly in place. "That should stop the bleeding."

Bullock turned, holding his chest. "Thank you."

She nodded. Said nothing.

He looked around the room, then looked her up and down. "We need to get you cleaned up, then move you to another room that's not so...messy."

She knew the word was supposed to be "bloody," but she let it go. She grabbed her bag and let him escort her to the bathroom where she washed the blood off her hands, splashed her face with water, and changed back into her pink sweats. The last thing she did was rinse all the blood off the ring of keys and put them in her pocket.

Bullock then escorted her to Lyssa Brandt's old room.

Brooke stepped in, turned, pulled the keys out of her pocket, and handed them over, knowing she had just given her jailer the keys to her cell.

Looking confused, Bullock took the keys and gazed at her. It was the first time, during this whole experience, that Brooke could recall him ever appearing unsure—as if there were a debate going on inside him. Was it possible he had a conscience? Were Brooke's actions tantamount to pulling the thorn out of the lion's paw? Only time would tell.

His expression stiffened with resolve once again, and he muttered, "Thank you." He slowly closed the door, and Brooke heard the familiar sound of the lock click.

CHAPTER THIRTY-THREE

With Captain Vargas having returned to Headquarters, Ostrowski and Shaneel were waiting outside the Mobile Command Center for some word from Vecoli. They both stood in the shade, leaning on the side of the van away from the building, staring out at the horribly crowded and hot mess that was the media pool. There were hundreds of cameras and reporters set up in a taped-off media section. The police had to close off the access road off of South Brea Canyon, so the video lines could be run across the street to the parking lot on the far side. There were upload trucks and production vans from every major news organization on the planet.

"We're just like them right now," Shaneel said.

"How do ya figure?"

"We're all just standing around waiting for someone else to do something."

Ostrowski chuckled. "Welcome to the glamorous life of police detective work."

They heard Hostetler's radio blare. "Doors are opening.

Someone's coming out."

Ostrowski watched all of the cameramen step up and look through their viewfinders. He followed Shaneel around to the backside of the van and stood by Lt. Hostetler, and the hostage negotiator, Jackson Smythe, while they watched a skinny-armed, red-headed kid drag a body out of the front doors of the old factory.

"That's got to be Riser," Shaneel said, "and he's dragging Vecoli. This can't be good."

Someone behind them called for medical aid. Four paramedics ran up with their kits on top of a gurney. They stopped and waited at the perimeter.

Riser had to pause halfway to the parking lot. He stood to breathe and stretch his back. He turned briefly to judge the distance he still had to go, and then grabbed Vecoli under the arms once more and breathing hard, reached the medical team with nothing to spare.

Two paramedics lowered the cot and placed it next to the curb. Then they carefully placed Vecoli's limp body on it and raised it up. The knife stuck prominently out of his chest.

Shaneel gasped. "Oh, my God." She looked up at Ostrowski. "So much for Bullock being his hero."

"That's the problem with heroes," Ostrowski said. "They have a habit of letting you down."

The phone rang inside the Mobile Command Center. Ostrowski, Johnson, and Hostetler crowded in to listen. Shaneel waved away Hostetler's offensive cigar smoke.

Jackson sat back in his chair. "He's calling us. That makes it easy." He flicked a switch and the ringing stopped. Heavy labored breathing could be heard over the speakers. "Hello Sgt. Bullock," Jackson said. "I'm Jackson Smythe. Thank you for contacting us."

"Cut the shit, Smythe," Duncan Bullock growled. "I didn't call to have a chat, I just wanted to let you know what the rules are. Every door in this place is rigged to blow. I also have an app on my phone that I can click at any time, so any attempt to storm through the windows, and the place will blow. You can be sure of that. I've given you three hostages now, so there will be no negotiations for more. Do not try to strong arm me. The detonators are currently using electrical power. If you cut the power to the building, you will trip the switch and blow up everything yourselves. Are we clear?"

Jackson looked over at Lt. Hostetler.

"Are we clear, Smythe?" Bullock demanded.

Jackson looked back. "Ahhh, we're clear, Duncan."

"Good. Bullock out." A click was heard and then silence.

Ostrowski and Shaneel stepped away.

The paramedics had already whisked Vecoli and Riser off to the ambulances.

"We should go question Riser," Shaneel said.

A black Cadillac sedan pulled up to the back of the barricade. "We can do that later. Besides, I doubt he'll be able to tell us anything more than Andrews already has." Ostrowski pointed at the Cadillac. "Anyway, our secret weapon just showed up."

Special Agent Ramirez got out of the driver's door, stepped back, and opened the back door. Slowly, Corrine Bullock stepped out and shielded her eyes from the sun, her face creased with stress and worry. She looked around at the large police presence and the hundreds of reporters and cameras.

Agent Cameron stepped out from the passenger seat on the other side. Agent Ramirez turned to them when they walked up. "We got her here as fast as we could."

Ostrowski shook his hand. "Well done. Thank you, Agent Ramirez."

Shaneel approached Corrine and put an arm around the poor woman's shoulder. "Hello, Mrs. Bullock. I'm Detective Johnson. Thank you for coming."

Corrine reached out and clutched Shaneel's other arm. When

she spoke, her voice was sheepish and quiet. "Where is my husband?"

Shaneel gestured toward Ostrowski. "Detective Ostrowski and I hope to take you to him in a moment. But first, we need to get things coordinated. Why don't you walk with us, and we can get you some coffee or whatever you'd like."

Ostrowski followed along and smiled. When she wasn't snarling at him, Shaneel was quite charming. He realized he'd been unfair to her. Just because she was a rookie and...not Sykes, he'd acted like she was a chain around his ankle—some sort of punishment. But seeing her here, where the real work had to be done, this young woman was dialed in, and could shift gears to handle a new situation at a moment's notice. He would have to tell her that sometime when she wasn't jumping down his throat about one thing or another.

Shaneel walked Mrs. Bullock over to a chair next to the Mobile Command Center and sat her down. "So, can I get you anything? Coffee? Water?"

Corrine nodded. "It's been a long flight. I could use some coffee, black if you don't mind."

"Not at all. Cooper, black coffee over here." An officer, some distance away nodded and headed toward the food truck.

Ostrowski leaned down and patted the woman on the shoulder. "Mrs. Bullock, give us a few minutes and see if we can't get your husband on the phone." He walked out of ear shot, over by Hostetler. Shaneel, Ramirez, and Cameron followed along. "Okay folks, we need to make this happen."

"I've tried to call the man back," Jackson said. "He ain't answering."

"He somehow needs to see her," Shaneel said, pushing forward. "He needs to look into her eyes, see the pain he's putting this woman through. Maybe it'll affect him enough to just shut down the bombs and walk out."

Agent Cameron spoke up. "I think it's your best shot at this point for a peaceful end to this stand-off. And we didn't bring her all this way to make a phone call. She could have done that from up north."

"Agreed," Ramirez said, with a nod.

Hostetler pulled the cigar from his mouth. "She does provide us with a tactical advantage."

"How so?" Ostrowski asked.

"If it appears that if Bullock won't back down, at least she will have him exposed. Our sharpshooters can..."

"Are you freaking kidding?" Shaneel whirled on him. "You're not going to blow this woman's husband's brains out right in front of her. She's been through more than enough. She'd be catatonic for the rest of her life."

Hostetler looked over to the FBI agents. "One woman's sanity for several lives and no property damage?"

"It's not happening, and that's final," Ostrowski said. Shaneel looked up at him and nodded appreciatively.

"I can solve this," Ramirez finally said. "If I think you are inclined to shoot this poor woman's husband's head off right in front of her, Agent Cameron and I will put her back in the car and head straight to the airport. You will have lost your possible ace-in-the-hole."

"Okay, you can argue about this as much as you want," Jackson said. He leaned in from his chair in the MCC. "But like I said, he isn't answering the phone. How am I supposed to let him know she's here? Telepathy?"

They all looked at each other for a moment and then Ostrowski finally answered. "Just send him a text every minute, and Detective Johnson and I will go ahead and walk her up. We'll stand in the lobby as long as it takes him to check his messages." He looked down at Shaneel, who nodded in agreement. He was continuing to be impressed with her. She was showing a certain amount of fierceness. Good and bad traits for a detective.

Jackson shrugged. "Okay, we'll try it. Do you want to bring

her in here and we can get a wire on her?"

"No." Ostrowski shook his head and waved it off. "Don't bother the poor woman with that. I'll wear the wire and stand close."

CHAPTER THIRTY-FOUR

Becca laid on her cot, hands behind her head, straining her ears to hear something more of the ruckus that had taken place in Brooke's room. She had heard Brooke's screams and frightful sounds of a tremendous struggle. At first, she thought Bullock was attacking Brooke, but then she heard the screams and shouts from two men. She wasn't sure if Ben or Mike had gotten out and attacked Bullock. But she felt that couldn't have happened. Neither of them had the balls to try something like that.

And now Brooke's room was eerily silent. She was hoping Brooke wasn't hurt in the fracas and was just lying in there, suffering. She had knocked on the wall and called out several times but received no answer.

Becca had spent the last several minutes staring at the ceiling and concentrating on deep breathing to help with the stress of not knowing what was going on.

Keys rattled outside her door, and she heard the lock click. Becca bolted upright when the door opened. "What's going on? How's Brooke?"

Bullock entered holding a Lean Cuisine meal and a bottle of

water. He dropped them on her desk along with a plastic spoon and a napkin, then turned to her. He was moving gingerly as if he were in some pain. "She's fine." He pointed to the food. "Eat." Then he turned to walk out.

Becca couldn't let him leave without taking the opportunity to get in a dig. "Things aren't working out as you planned, are they *Sarge*?"

He stopped and looked back. "Nope. I expected to be able to hold my grandchild one day. But you made sure that wouldn't happen, didn't you?"

Becca refused to take the bait. "I'm talking about the ruckus that happened with God knows who. And now it looks like you're walking around in a bit of pain. What happened?"

"A conversation with an old colleague didn't go well. But that's none of your concern. You worry about yourself." He headed out the door.

"So, you don't command as much authority as you thought you did, huh?" Becca was doing her best to rattle him. She wanted to kick him hard while he was down.

He turned and rested his arm against the door jam. "What do you know about commanding authority? You have to be the worst leader I've ever seen in all of my days."

She'd expected that. Wounded animals always strike back when provoked or feel threatened. But they're still animals. And this beast was more animal than anybody she'd ever seen. "That's rich, coming from a man who has to fight tooth and nail to follow through with his crazy-ass schemes. For your information, I'm the leader of the biggest show on network television."

"I'm not talking about what was handed to you because of daddy's legacy. I'm talking about real leadership."

Becca snarled. "I got *nothing* from my father. He committed suicide before I even graduated from high school, and don't you *dare* bring him up to me. I earned everything I got."

"And yet who do *you* fight for?"

"What?" She was the one getting frustrated and angry now. "I fought for the show. Just like a producer should."

"Wrong answer. That's what makes you a terrible leader."

"Bullshit," Becca said, standing up. "It's what makes me a great leader. And it's what made our show number one in the country."

Bullock continued with a calm easy tone, which pissed off Becca even more. "A real leader's answer would have been, she fights for the people on her team. Because with a solid team that believes you have their best interests in your heart, you can conquer the world. How many people on your team feel that you even care about them? How many wives or husbands or significant others of your team members can you name?"

Becca said nothing. She just stood there glaring at him.

"That's what I thought? How many times in the last week have you screamed at your team members to get them to do something? Or threatened them when they simply disagreed with you or tried to offer advice?"

Becca still said nothing. She thought about George in the last production meeting and how she'd threatened to throw him out if he contradicted her ever again.

Bullock nodded. "Again, that's what I thought. Don't get on your high horse about having the number one show. Your show *was* number one because you fed off of people's baser instincts. Everyone wants to feel better than somebody else, and you gave them that by throwing people out in front of them so they could tear them down. That's what happens. Once your show is over everyone starts talking, posting, blogging about this person and that. It becomes a gossip-fest that gives everyone not only a voice but a *right* to judge the idiots you let on your show that night. They don't know a thing about these poor people. They only know what you show, and they feel empowered to give their opinion on whether the individuals are worthy enough. It's harmful and pathetic, but it does bring in ratings."

Bullock pulled his arm down and leaned his shoulder against the door jamb as if this was a casual conversation. "Did you see any of the posts about Kristine?"

Becca didn't say anything because she always tried to avoid things like that.

"Of course, you didn't. That would mean caring about someone other than yourself. I'll tell you what they said. They said, 'She'd look good ten pounds lighter.' How would that make you feel if someone judged you like that?"

Becca wished she'd just kept her mouth shut now.

"They said they couldn't understand why a guy like Chris would pick her. She was overweight and had no personality to compensate for it. How do you think that made her feel?" When he didn't get a response, he continued. "It crushed her. She left for her honeymoon feeling she wasn't good enough for the man she just married. These people didn't know my daughter. They had no idea the type of bright light she was in the world. But because of what you and your team showed of her on the screen, they felt they had her pegged. And what's worse, they felt they had a right to judge her unworthy."

Bullock paused for a moment. Becca thought his eyes were becoming glassy. She felt he was going to lose it right here in front of her. She was now nervous about what she may have wrought.

A phone buzzed in Bullock's pocket. He grumbled and pulled it out to check the screen. "Shit. I have to go take of something. Conversation's over." He pointed to the Lean Cuisine. "Eat. You'll need your strength for tonight's recording." He stepped back, pulled the door closed, and locked it.

Becca stared down at the food on her desk. There was no way she could possibly eat it now.

Chapter Thirty-Five

After the slow walk up the sidewalk, due as much to the fact that Corrine Bullock was a slow walker as much as it was for caution, Ostrowski opened the lobby door for Mrs. Bullock and Shaneel. He followed them into the lobby-that-time-forgot, decorated in the late eighties, early nineties style. The walls were white except for the wood-paneled wall behind the massive desk/console where a greeter would have sat, but was easily big enough for five greeters. There were no more chairs left, but a few side tables were still sitting around. The paneled wall had a sign across it that read "Metalworks." Above it were holes in the wood, and although the entire wall was faded over time, you could still make out the outlines of the letters that had been removed: L-Y-N-F-I-E-L-D.

Ostrowski crossed the lobby and headed to the far door leading into the plant, and peered through the small window. Seeing nothing but a beige wall, he stepped back. "He's not here yet, but we'll wait."

Shaneel's eyes widened, and she pointed to the window. "Ummm, Ostrowski?"

Ostrowski turned back around to see the barrel of a Sig Sauer pointed at him. "Oh, I was mistaken. He *is* here." He stepped back and gestured to Corrine.

The gun came down and Bullock's scowling face appeared in the window. His harsh edges softened when he looked at his wife. He put up a finger and stepped back out of view.

Corrine Bullock took a few steps closer to the door.

They heard the distinct sounds of a key in a lock and the sharp click as it was turned. The door unlatched and opened cautiously. Bullock stuck his head out of the opening and spoke softly to his wife. "Corrine, why are you here?"

Corrine stepped up to him. "Because I wanted to have the chance to do this." She pulled back and slapped his face hard. The smack echoed through the empty lobby. "How dare you do this to me!" she screamed. "How dare you make this decision without me. I just lost my second and last child. I was devastated. But I've always known, in all of life's terrible storms...horrible circumstances, that I would always have you, and that you would *always* be my rock. I could make it through anything, even my worst nightmares with you and your strength beside me. And then you go and do this." Her anger was giving way to grief and she began to cry. "Now you've taken *everything* from me, I'm completely alone in the world, and for what? So you can go on some stupid vendetta against two women who *didn't* kill Kristine?" She paused and gasped for a breath. "I know there's nothing I could ever say that will stop you, but I wanted the chance to look you in the eye and let you know that you've taken away everything I had left. Not those poor girls, not that Haddock boy. It's *you*!" She sobbed, her hands covering her face.

Shaneel took a step toward her, but Ostrowski put a hand on her arm to get her to wait and let it play out.

Duncan Bullock stared sullenly at his shattered wife while she broke down in front of him. He didn't step out to try and console her, knowing that would make him a target for the snipers. And she would probably just push him away and slap him again anyway.

Corrine collected herself enough to speak again. "I just wanted to be able to tell you to your face that...I'm ashamed of you, Duncan." She took another deep breath. "You can go to hell for all I care." She turned away from him and broke down once more in irrepressible sorrow.

Shaneel stepped over and gently took her by the arm. The woman's wails filled the lobby, and she cried so hard she could barely walk. Shaneel carefully guided her back out the door and down the sidewalk toward the police barricade. When the glass door finally closed, the lobby was deathly quiet.

Ostrowski looked back at Duncan Bullock's face in the opening of the doorway—a face of pain and sorrow, watching the love of his life walk away with nothing left but contempt for him.

"Well," Ostrowski said. "*That* certainly didn't go as planned." He looked back out at Mrs. Bullock. "She sure is a pistol, I'll give her that."

"Good day, Detective," Bullock said and pulled his head back.

"Hey, wait a minute," Ostrowski said, taking a step forward. "How about a word with me?"

Bullock looked out and shook his head. "I have no interest in talking with cops."

"No. Not as a cop." He reached over and slid up the sleeve on his left arm to reveal a small tattoo of an eagle with a sword in its talons over the words, "Semper Fidelis."

"How about as a brother?"

Bullock looked at the tattoo, and Ostrowski saw his expression ease almost imperceptibly. "How long were you in?"

"Three years," Ostrowski said. "Went in on the G.I. bill."

"Ahhh. A non-committal."

"Hey, cut me some slack. I could have gotten the same G.I.

bill going straight Navy, but I took the hard road."

Bullock raised an eyebrow and nodded. "Yeah, I can give you that I guess."

"So how about it? I'm not going to try anything. I saw what you did to Special Agent Vecoli. I have no interest going to the hospital...or the morgue."

Bullock thought for a moment, then nodded. "Leave the sidearm out there."

Ostrowski pulled his gun out of its holster at his side, set it on a nearby table, and stepped through the door Bullock held open for him. Bullock pulled the door closed and locked it. Ostrowski looked down at the metal drum next to the doorway. "That looks serious."

"Oh, it is. I can assure you." Bullock leaned against the wall. "Shit." He sighed. "Remember when we were young and had the whole world figured out?"

"Hell yeah." Ostrowski leaned against the wall next to him. "It was one of the best weekends of my life."

Bullock managed a smile.

Ostrowski put his hands in his pockets and leaned his shoulder against the wall. "We've been studying you the past few days as you may have guessed."

"And what did you find out about me?"

"Well, we heard about your private who was killed by an IED."

Bullock's head drooped, and he fumbled with the gun in his hand.

"We also learned how you avenged that boy's death."

Bullock was still now.

"You can get real serious when you want to."

Bullock scoffed. "Is that what they're calling it? Serious? Yeah, I guess I can get *serious* when the situation calls for it." He looked over at Ostrowski. "You see any action, short-timer?"

"Hell, yeah." Ostrowski pulled his right sleeve up and showed a long thin scar on the outside of his arm. "Angry hooker took a knife to me. Gashed me right there."

Bullock laughed out loud.

"Sure, you laugh, but when you don't have all of the money, she's madder and faster than any wimp-ass terrorist."

Bullock laughed again.

Ostrowski let him. It wasn't something he'd probably done for a couple of weeks, and it had to be good for him. When the laughter subsided, Ostrowski continued. "Nah. I was a cold-war marine. There was no real action in those days. Just a lot of chest-puffing. I spent most of my time in Boeblingen."

Bullock nodded. "Panzer Kaserne Marine Corps Base."

"You know it?"

"Spent a year there myself. Stuck out in the middle of a god-forsaken forest with the towns around there still living life like the late 1800s."

"It was like a living time capsule."

Bullock chuckled.

Ostrowski was doing well. Time to get serious. "But enough about me, let's talk about you."

"You don't know everything about me already?"

"I don't know what you're doing here?"

Leaning his head back, Bullock thought on it a moment. "I'm taking care of things. Bringing them to light."

"Bringing what to light?"

"Bringing the reason my daughter died to light."

"And these women are the reason your daughter died?"

"Their show is the reason my daughter is no longer here."

"Do you really believe that?"

"Yes, I do," Bullock said. "When you get cancer from smoking, you don't just take care of the cancer and move forward. You stop

239

smoking, too. If you don't stop smoking, you'll get the cancer again." He looked over at Ostrowski. "If I don't take care of this now, some other poor innocent girl is going to get hurt or killed. And their show is the cancer I'm going to cure."

Ostrowski thought for a moment. "No. That would make their show the cigarettes."

"What?"

"Never mind," Ostrowski said, shaking his head. "But that's not what you're doing here."

"What are you talking about?"

Ostrowski shifted his weight, leaned back against the wall and crossed his legs. "When I was in Panzer Kaserne, we had this sergeant there, Sergeant Calhoun, the biggest dirtbag on the planet. Nobody liked the guy, not the enlisted or the officers."

"Sergeants aren't there to kiss your forehead and tuck you in," Bullock said. "They're there to make sure the place runs properly."

"I get that. But there is a general humane level to anything. And this guy acted as if he had it out for the whole world. There was one day, one of the enlisted said something. I don't even remember what the hell it was now, but it had nothing to do with Calhoun. But that jackass came in there, perhaps he didn't like the sound of laughter, but he busted through the door at that moment, told us all to shut our damn mouths and give him 500 sit-ups right then. So, we start doing that, and one of the guys rips a fart."

"Is there any point to this?" Bullock said.

Ostrowski waved his hand. "There's a great point. You just have to wait a little bit for it."

Bullock sighed.

"So, Sergeant Calhoun takes great offense to this poor man's bowel issues. And to be honest, it was a pretty offensive fart. The rest of us were holding our breaths, and it's pretty hard to hold your breath and do 500 sit-ups."

"The point?"

"Okay, right. The point. Calhoun was enraged by this, he lifted the guy up by his shirt, screamed in his face, told him how disrespectful it was to everybody else in the room. He made all of us stand by our bunks, backs out, and pull down our pants. Then he told this private that if he liked smelling shit so much, he could sniff each of our asses. He made the private crawl, on his hands and knees, to each man in that barracks, and take a big, long whiff of their ass."

Bullock pursed his lips and nodded. "Seems a little intense."

"Intense?" Ostrowski said. "It seems medieval."

"You said this had a point."

"The point is that Sergeant Calhoun was equally shitty to everybody. It didn't matter if you were his subordinate or his superior, he hated you and you knew it. He was an equal opportunity scumbag."

"Are you comparing me to Calhoun?"

"Hold on." Ostrowski held up a finger. "One night a bunch of us went into Boeblingen to get some food. After dinner, we were sitting around the table drinking beer, and flirting with the waitresses, because that was really all there was to do there, and in comes Calhoun, seventeen sheets to the wind. He was so drunk he could barely walk, but he managed to pull up a chair to our table and sit down. That cleared us out pretty quickly. We were all terrified of the man. For some reason, I stayed. I was the only one. I guess I'd drank just enough courage, but I sat right there, looked that son of a bitch in the eye, and asked him why he was such a son of a bitch." Ostrowski stood, uncrossed his legs, and leaned back again.

"He didn't get mad at me, didn't make me sniff people's asses, didn't scream, nothing. He just lit a cigarette, and talked to me clear as a bell. He sounded as if he hadn't even had a drink at that point. His story was stone-cold sober." Ostrowski rested his head back against the wall as he recalled the conversation.

"Calhoun had been through Nam. Had done something like three tours there. The reason was because there was a girl in one of the villages he was in love with. She meant everything to him. He never told me how they met, at least I don't remember if he did. I was drunk at the time too. But whenever he got leave, he would head to this village and see her. Take things to her. He'd spend every single second of free time he could with her. He knew he was going to marry her, bring her back to the U.S., leave the military and build a life with her here somewhere. But one day when he went to see her, the Vietcong had already been there. Apparently, someone told them that village was full of collaborators and that she had a relationship with an American. The Vietcong didn't take kindly to this news, and they considered the whole village traitors. When Calhoun had arrived, the entire population of the village was lying dead in a row. They had taken everybody and lined them up, shot them all, and left them like dogs in the street. All except for one. Calhoun found her hanging at the end of the road, naked. She had been beaten and raped, stabbed and hanged. The entire town had been murdered, all because he dared to love a woman."

"Damn," Bullock said. "That's tough."

"Yep. He never recovered from that either. He signed on for two more tours and went on a killing spree. Every single North Vietnamese he saw, he imagined was one of the men in that village that day who killed all of the people and raped the love of his life. By the time the war was over he was medaled several times, including the Silver Star. When we were done talking, he started crying. I'll never forget the sight." Ostrowski paused and sighed. "Then he got himself together and walked out of the bar. I found out the next morning that he went back to the barracks, grabbed his M1911, walked deep into the woods, and swallowed the barrel."

Bullock looked over at him. "And this is supposed to relate to me, how?"

"Calhoun was never happy, not one minute of his life, after

he lost his bride-to-be. He was angry. There was nothing he could do to protect her, and there was really nothing he could do to avenge her either, other than kill as many North Vietnamese as possible, which he apparently became proficient at before the end of the war. You've already lost a son from a disease you couldn't protect him from, and now you've lost your last remaining child. You have no way to avenge her, and no way to seek real justice for her because Costa Rica isn't giving up her killer. So, knowing you are never going to have another happy day as long as you live, you do what *you* consider to be the next best thing. You hold a bunch of innocent people hostage, trying to make them pay for something not even they could control."

"They created the show that took my daughter's life."

Ostrowski looked over and shook his head. "Come on. They had nothing to do with it, Bullock. You just don't have any other options to avenge your daughter, so this was your last hope."

Bullock stood straight, frowning.

Ostrowski held up his hands. "All I'm saying is it's just like the old adage, 'hurting people hurt people.' It's actually the sadness in your shattered heart, Bullock, that's holding these people hostage. You're suffering just like Calhoun suffered. Men are good at being sergeants, not because they take or give orders well, but because they take charge. They lead to protect their men. I don't believe Duncan Bullock is the kind of man that causes pain. But Sergeant 'Slam Dunk,' when he has someone to avenge, will make sure that vengeance will be served and served justly."

Ostrowski could see Bullock's eyes redden, and then get glassy. The hard man turned away from him, wiped at his eyes, and then stepped back. "Okay. Enough ladies talk. It's time for you to go."

Ostrowski stood away from the wall. "You're right. Tell you what, just give me the girl with the broken fingers and I'll head out."

"Like hell," Bullock said.

"Come on, Sergeant. Don't make me go back out there looking like a complete failure. Help out a fellow brother from the corps."

Bullock looked at the door leading to the lobby, sighed, then nodded. "Okay. She wasn't supposed to be here in the first place." He pulled his phone out of his pocket, opened an app, and typed in a code. Ostrowski watched as a green light lit up on a black box on top of the drum. The bomb was now armed.

"Wait here and don't touch anything. I'll be right back with her." Bullock walked down the hall and exited into the plant area through a large metal door. As soon as it slammed shut Ostrowski turned to see a hallway made of beige, metal walls. This was obviously the main office wing for the plant. He took a few steps down the hall and peeked into a couple of windows, thinking perhaps some of the kidnapped individuals were held in there, but it appeared as though all the lights were out so he couldn't see through the tiny thin windows anyway.

Distant screams pulled his attention back to the door Bullock had just gone through. Ostrowski turned and headed in that direction when the door was slammed open. Bullock stepped through and held the door. He narrowed his eyes at Ostrowski. "I told you to stay put."

"Sorry," Ostrowski said with a shrug. "Cop instincts take over when I hear women screaming."

Bullock nodded, then looked back through the door and waved his hand in. "Let's go. Your ride's waiting."

Two girls walked through. One had messy red hair, and dirty sweats, the other had short brown hair, leggings, and a t-shirt dress. Her hand was wrapped in a towel, and she was crying. Both girls looked tired and hungry. They stepped into the hall and stared at him fearfully.

"I'm Detective Brett Ostrowski of the L.A. Police Department. I'm going to escort you out of here."

Both girls looked at Bullock, who waved them forward. They then walked quickly over to Ostrowski. Bullock pulled his phone out of his pocket and tapped in a code.

When Ostrowski saw the green light go off on the box, he looked up at Bullock. The sergeant nodded. Ostrowski opened the door and both girls rushed out. He looked back at Bullock.

"Thanks for the show of good faith. This will go a long way," Ostrowski said. He took one step out the door and looked back. "I enjoyed our talk, Sergeant. I want you to consider ending this. It's time."

"I'll end it," Bullock said. "The way it needs to end." He pointed a thumb at the parking lot. "But you let them know out there, I have one button on my phone. I push it, the whole place goes. And they're all pretty close with what I've got wired up in here."

With a nod, Ostrowski walked out, letting the door close behind him. He headed out the lobby doors and strolled casually back to the police line.

Chapter Thirty-Six

The door unlocked to Brooke's room. Bullock stood back and let it swing open. He had a gun in his right hand. "Come on, princess. It's time for the last show."

Brooke saw the gun and froze. This was supposed to be the second to the last show. This was where Becca and she were supposed to simulate the escape room episode. Something must have happened to make him drop that part of it. Suddenly there was no oxygen. She sat on the edge of her bed, gasping for breath.

Bullock waved her out of the room with his gun hand. "Come on. Let's go."

Brooke stood, but her legs were shaking. Each step was tremulous torture. She struggled to control her feet, and she slammed her shoulder into the door jamb on her way out. She reached up, and rubbed it, and very nearly dropped to her knees in tears.

"After you," Bullock said, impatiently.

Brooke managed to make it to the hallway door. He opened it for her and gestured her through. She walked out, passed by the lobby, and saw several police cars and vans sitting in the parking lot outside the building. She realized that was why the escape room was dropped. Bullock was running out of time. He had to end it quickly.

"Pay no attention to them," Bullock said. He rushed past her and opened the door to the makeshift studio.

Ben and Becca were already in there waiting. But there was no sign of Fiona. Tears streamed down Brooke's face when she saw Becca. She rushed over to her best friend, her safe haven. The two embraced as if this were the last hug of their lives.

Bullock pulled several tissues from a box on the desk by Ben. He handed them to Brooke. "Here, clean yourself up and get it together. I don't want you looking like this on camera."

Brooke took the tissues and was surprised when Becca took some too. Her friend was tearing up as well.

Bullock seemed agitated, and he casually waved his handgun around as he paced the room.

Brooke wiped at her eyes and blew her nose, but her blood ran like ice water. She couldn't take her eyes off the gun. She stared at it with frightened fascination. She felt like she should be dropping to her knees right now and begging for her life. But there was a numbness overcoming her. Something akin to resolve.

Bullock looked at Ben. "We only have one camera for this, so set it on a wide shot. Once we're rolling you can wait outside. I'm sure you don't' want to be in here for this. I'll let you out of the building once this segment is finished."

Ben hesitated, briefly glanced in Becca and Brooke's direction, then nodded.

Without looking at either woman, Bullock walked over and took his seat, gun clenched in his hand, placed politely on his lap. He cleared his throat, sat up straight, and looked up at Ben. "Let me know when you're rolling."

Ben reached down and clicked something on the keyboard. He looked at the screen, then gave the thumbs-up sign.

"Okay, you can go," Bullock said.

Ben paused, looked at Brooke, looked at Becca, then put his head down, walked out of the room, and closed the door quietly.

Brooke wanted to scream at him, call him a traitor and a coward, ask him why he wasn't doing anything to help them, why he was just going to walk away and let them die. But there was that numbness again, keeping her from doing anything but to sit there and patiently await her fate. Besides, that was more Becca's style anyway, and she wasn't doing or saying anything either. Perhaps the numbness was settling in on her, too. That simple acceptance.

Bullock looked at the camera and smiled. "Hi, and welcome. As you and everyone else in the world know, the Los Angeles Police Department, Los Angeles County Sheriff's Department, and the Federal Bureau of Investigation are right outside this building. So, I've decided this will be our last show. On *I Do or I Don't*, the fourth segment was always the escape room. I'm skipping that segment and moving right on to the conversation. The fifth segment is when they have previous show contestants on to discuss the current episode with them. So, I've decided to just bring on Becca Dodge and Brooke Winthrop to have a discussion."

He turned to the two women. "Miss Dodge, Miss Winthrop," he said with a courteous nod. "I have said all along that this has been a trial of sorts, using the rules of your own show. And in each segment, I have tried my best, and if I'm being honest, I think quite successfully, to demonstrate that the lack of controls in *I Do or I Don't* have directly led to the death of my daughter."

He paused for either her or Becca to speak. Brooke couldn't say anything, even if she wanted to. She glanced over to see Becca hunched in her chair, arms crossed over her stomach, looking past Bullock at something beyond him and the wall. Brooke thought Becca was mentally and emotionally shut down.

"Nothing?" Bullock shrugged, raising both of his hands,

palms up. You have nothing to say for yourselves? Nothing in defense of your show?"

If Becca wasn't going to speak, Brooke knew she must. She grasped the handles of the old office chair to get her hands to stop shaking and opened her mouth. But she couldn't breathe. The back of her throat clenched, and her lungs wouldn't let her take a breath. All that came out was a high-pitched squeak that sounded like the door to the kitchen cupboard that held the plates in the house she lived in when she was a kid in Pennsylvania. She wondered why her mind would think of that at a moment like this.

"Were you going to say something, Miss Winthrop?" Bullock leaned in and cupped a hand behind his ear.

She closed her mouth, slumped in her chair, gripped the chair tighter, and fought the urge to break down in tears.

"Could it be because you know I have been right all along?" Bullock sat back, looking as serious as she'd ever seen him. His harsh, raspy voice had an irritated edge to it. "I can only assume you aren't speaking because you believe I've proved my point as well." He turned to look at the camera. "These two individuals were so caught up in the production of a ….," He used finger quotes. "'*reality*' show, that they forgot to think about what was real."

He slowly turned back, and Brooke felt her whole spine shiver. Bullock's lip was curled, his eyes were cold, and his brows pinched together. "You were so caught up in the business end of everything, you lost track of the human aspect of it all. Not even the military does that. But you did. Your industry does. Everything is for ratings. Nothing is real. But let me explain something to you. Nothing is more real to a father than the love of his daughter. The moment he first looks into her eyes when she is born, he makes an unspoken promise. That he will do what it takes to care for her, to love her, to keep her safe from everyone and everything. Three days later he fails—when he accidentally pokes her in the eye with the baby bottle at four in the morning because he's so damn tired he can't see straight. But he never gives up that promise. Never stops trying. When the girl is three, and she skins her knee on the sidewalk, the father picks her up and gets her ice cream to make it better. When she's five and sick, her father is the strong and soft place to land. She crawls up on his chest and falls asleep. The father is so afraid to move because he doesn't want to wake her. So he lies there and lets the most precious thing in his world get her rest. When she's seven and she can't keep up with the boys anymore because she can't ride a bike, it's the father who takes her to the playground and teaches her, runs alongside her to make sure she doesn't fall, and then helps her to become fast, so not only can she keep up with the boys, they can't even catch her if they wanted to. Why does he do all this? Because she is his light. The relationship between a father and daughter is special. He should have the chance to meet the man his daughter is going to marry. Have a chance to size him up—to look that man in the eye and make sure he is up to the task of replacing her father as the man in her life. You two *stole* that chance from fathers. You stole that right from *me*. And not only was the man you set her up with not up to the task, but he was also the villain who took her life."

It took all the self-control possible for Brooke to hold back her tears. She gulped in her fear and her sorrow, and tried to see things from this man's perspective. She leaned forward and words finally made their way out. "Mr. Bullock, we're so very sorry." She reached for the man's arm, but he flinched and pulled away as if there was acid on her fingertips. He did not want to be touched. He did not want to form any closeness with these women whatsoever. Closeness would mean some sort of connection and he couldn't have a connection with someone he intended to kill.

Brooke shook her head and sat back. Accepting her fate, she no longer tried to be strong. Tears leaked from her eyes. "We're so sorry," is all she could mutter before she dropped her face in her hands.

"You're so full of shit," Becca said. "You haven't the slightest clue about what you're talking about."

Brooke couldn't believe her ears. 'Tearless and Fearless had stormed back into the room. For what it was worth Becca Dodge was going to go down swinging. Brooke clutched the arms of her chair tighter. Bullock probably wasn't going to take Becca's crap, would probably just put a bullet in their heads to shut her up.

"No?" Bullock said. He gestured to the camera. "Then why don't you enlighten us all Miss Dodge."

Becca leaned forward in her chair and snarled at him. "I don't want to hear about this special connection between a father and daughter because that's all made-up, fairy-tale bullshit. My father committed suicide. He overdosed on sleeping pills because he wasn't man enough to put a bullet in his head. And do you know why?" Becca jumped up from her chair. Bullock instinctively slid his chair back a little.

"Because the piece of shit pimped out his *own* daughter."

Brooke heard herself gasp. Becca looked down at Bullock like she had just fired the shot that took down a boar. Her face was red like she'd just sprinted a mile, her fists were clenched, and her nostrils flared.

Bullock was totally disarmed. His eyes were wide, and his mouth hung open slightly. To Brooke, it seemed this was the first time he was not in control, and he appeared totally unprepared for what could be coming next."

"Yeah, that's right," Becca said. "One night when my folks had them over for dinner, the head of the network—Derek McGregor—took a shine to me, an innocent 15-year-old girl. He later told my dad he had a thing for me, so my father with his *special connection* to his daughter, would take me to McGregor's office on occasional afternoons. Yeah, he'd wait in the lobby while McGregor worked out his silly fixations. How's that for protecting the most precious thing in a father's life? Well, he didn't protect me, but I did help Mr. Billy Dodge to become the number two man at the network. All it took was letting his daughter get raped by a perverted old fucker, who controlled his destiny. What do you think of fathers now, *asshole*?" She took a step toward Bullock, but he didn't back up this time.

"My father didn't stop to think that perhaps he should turn in the creep. Didn't think about going to another network. Didn't think about anything but getting ahead. And the sacrifice of my safety, my self-respect, and my *entire life* wasn't too steep a price to pay. How's *that* for a father's love?" Becca screamed.

Brooke gaped at her in horrific awe. She watched her friend release her deepest darkest secret. Becca always came across so tough, so strong, so put together, so in control of everything and everyone. But all the time she was fighting against this secret, this horror, never able to live without fighting, because the shame and shock of it all would have certainly consumed her. But now, facing her own mortality, she had nothing left to hold back. If she was going down, she was going to take McGregor down with her. She was no longer tearless and fearless. Both emotions were taking over completely. Becca's eyes and nose were running so hard now, a small stream dripped off her chin.

"My mother knew it was happening, too. But she didn't fight for me either. She just left. Said it was all too hard, so she went somewhere that was easier, and left me to my fate. I never heard from her again!" she cried. "And you know the worst part? Billy Dodge ended up having a conscience after all. It was the conscience that finally got him. But he still had no backbone. All he did was leave a note next to my bed that I found in the morning. It said, 'I'm sorry.' I found his body that day and all he could say was 'I'm sorry.' He was such a fucking coward he couldn't even stick around and listen to what I had to say. Never once gave a shit about *my* feelings! Just an 'I'm sorry,' and he's gone." She took another step toward Bullock, but the man didn't back away. "So, how's that for a father's love, huh, asshole?" She balled up her fist and sent it crashing against his face.

His head flung sideways, but he showed no emotion. He looked back at her, slowly stood, and placed the gun on the chair behind him. Then he dropped his arms to his side and remained motionless.

"That's what *I* think about your fatherly love." She swung again, connecting hard, knocking his face back. "Well, that's what I think about it," she screamed.

Bullock made no move to defend himself. Did nothing to stop her.

"I think it's all a bunch of shit!" Becca screamed and let fly a torrent of swings and jabs with both fists, unloading a lifetime of pent-up emotion and pain on Duncan Bullock. His head snapped from side to side, with each blow. He exhaled sharply with each punch he took in the gut, but he accepted everything. Never ducked, dodged, or backed away, and his arms remained firmly at his sides.

After what seemed like several minutes of the onslaught, Becca stumbled back and tried to catch her breath. Bullock stood there looking at her, emotionless as if he were one of the kick-boxing dummies in a gym. Though he now had blood running from his nose and his lips, and his face was red and becoming puffy.

Breathing so hard she looked like she was going to hyperventilate, Becca collapsed back in the chair, buried her face in her hands, and cried. It was a harsh, aching, painful wail that lived up to the years it had been buried.

Brooke stared at her, speechless.

Bullock picked up his gun and lowered himself back to his seat. He watched Becca, listened to her tortured cries. Then he turned his beaten and bloody face to the camera and spoke quietly. "You were correct, Detective Ostrowski. Hurting people *do* hurt people." He looked back at Becca, still sobbing into her arm, then turned back into the camera. "And that's *never* right. This show is over."

Bullock stood, walked to the computer, hit the space bar to stop the recording and walked out of the room, locking the door behind him.

Brooke reached for her friend, and Becca buried her head in Brooke's chest and shook while she wept.

Minutes later, Bullock opened the door and waved at Brooke to come with him.

Brooke patted Becca on the shoulder. "Come on, honey. We need to go."

Becca held on tight. "No, I don't want to go." She sounded like a three-year-old, not wanting her mom to move.

Brooke looked up at Bullock. He was patient, stoic, perhaps the slightest bit remorseful. She rubbed Becca's back. "It's okay, sweetie. It's over now. It's going to be fine." She grabbed Becca's shoulders and gently lifted her sobbing friend upright. Both girls stood, and Brooke kept one arm tightly around Becca as they made their way out of the room, Becca, buried her head in Brooke's shoulder—refusing to look up at Bullock when they passed.

Bullock escorted them down to Brooke's new room. Inside, both girls' cots were sitting side-by-side against the wall. Brooke looked back at Bullock, who had still not even wiped at his bloody face. His eyes were sad, like a basset hound's—his harsh smoldering anger now faded completely. She mouthed, "Thank you." He looked away, then pulled the door closed and locked it.

Brooke walked Becca over to the cots and laid her down, then crawled in and wrapped her arms around her tortured friend. She held her for over an hour until Becca's tears finally ebbed, and they could fall asleep.

Chapter Thirty-Seven

"But I want *you* here to tuck me in."

Ostrowski smiled at the adorable tiny voice on the phone. Though Shaneel didn't have the speaker on, they were sitting close enough he could still hear everything.

"No, young man. Momma's still working, and I don't know when I'm going to be home. You need to go to bed so Daddy's tucking you in tonight. And you just have to help me out and let him do it. Okay?"

"Oookaaay."

Ostrowski almost laughed out loud at the boy's very unhidden disappointment.

"Thank you, sir. Momma loves you very much. Now put Daddy on."

A second later a much deeper voice said, "Thank you, babe. And I'm proud of you."

Shaneel smiled and looked at the sky. The last rays of the day were fading from orange to purple on the horizon. "Aww, thank you, baby. I love you."

"I love you too. Stay safe."

"I will. Bye." She pulled down the phone, cradled it in her hands a moment, and smiled.

Ostrowski sipped at his coffee and looked at the beautiful sunset. "Listen, Detective," he said. "I know I've been a disappointment to you, and I'm sorry. The truth is, from what I can tell, you're already a very good detective. You know protocols and you've shown you can handle yourself in any situation. If I have *anything* to teach you, it's this." He looked over at her. "Don't let this job take over your life. Because it'll want to do that every single day. It will be a constant battle you'll have to fight. Don't let it win. Learn something from my three failed marriages. It's why I now never take anything seriously—a habit that has driven you crazy, I know. But please *never* forget, it's your loving husband and that beautiful, bright son of yours that's important. Not the dirtbags on the street. Don't let them take anything from you, or your time with your family. Do whatever it takes to keep them at arm's length. If that means acting like a complete goofball every chance you get, then do it. Do you understand?"

Shaneel looked up at him, pondered his words a moment, then smiled and gave him a nod.

Ostrowski looked away. "And I'm proud to be your partner." He quickly took another sip of his coffee.

A moment later she spoke.

"Just so you know, I was at the MCC when you were talking to Bullock. I heard every word you said to him, and I just want to say that as crazy as you have been driving me, and as disappointed as I've acted about all of your bullshit, *that* conversation made every minute leading up to this point worth it. It helps me understand what you're saying to me. So, thank you. And I'm proud to be your partner, too."

Ostrowski looked back at her and smiled. Then he took a deep breath and said, "Okay. Best cop TV shows. Let's go."

"What?"

I Do or I Don't

"Obviously you can't have this conversation without starting with *Dragnet*." He added an arrogant nod. "It goes without saying that it was a groundbreaking series."

"*Dragnet*? Seriously?"

Ostrowski shrugged. "What? Two L.A. police detectives. How could anything be better? It's just like us. I'm Detective Joe Friday and you're Detective Bill Gannon."

Shaneel shook her head and chuckled. "I don't think so."

They spent the next few minutes talking about the best episodes of the best cop shows in the history of television and they were laughing—something he never thought he'd do with his new partner. But now that he was over the fact she wasn't Sykes, he could accept her for who she is. And that person turned out to be someone he actually liked.

"You can't keep throwing out all these pre-1960s shows that nobody's ever heard of," she complained to him.

Ostrowski laughed, "Detective, you've been saying you want to learn from me, then get out your notebook and start taking notes." He sipped from his coffee. "First of all, *Hill Street Blues* is not pre-60s, it is from the 1980s. And second of all, you would be well-advised to go to the store as soon as you're off duty and buy the entire series on DVD. For it is definitely the best cop series in the history of television."

Shaneel rolled her eyes. "I'm a *Law and Order* girl. Besides, I can't stand black and white."

Ostrowski laughed out loud and was about to refute when a taxi pulled up. The door opened and a tall, dark-haired man in his thirties stepped out, wearing a blue skin-tight Under Armor shirt. "Oh shit," he said.

"Who's that?"

All of the cameraman in the media barricade immediately jumped up to their cameras and spun them around to face the newcomer. Some had to reposition their tripods to get the shot.

Ostrowski sat down his coffee on the ground and stood.

"That's none other than Jake May." He wound his way through the mass of squad cars over to the former Browns quarterback. "Just when I think the circus couldn't get any bigger, another monkey shows up." He held out his hand. "Detective Ostrowski."

The big man grabbed his hand and held it firmly. "Hi, I'm Jake May."

"I know who you are," Ostrowski slapped the top of the cab. "And I want you to hop in here and leave. This situation is complicated enough without you here to make it completely untenable."

Jake held up his hands. "Look, I know what you've probably heard, and I understand your reaction. But the honest to God truth is that I still love Brooke with all my heart. I'm worried sick about her, and I just want to be as close to her as possible right now. I want to be there for her when this is all over."

Ostrowski shook his head. "Ain't gonna happen, superstar. Even if you were still married, I'd be throwing you out. We can't have emotional people running around here making extra problems for us. We have to stay frosty about the situation. Understand?"

Jake opened his mouth to protest, but an officer called out from the Mobile Command Center. "Ostrowski! Phone!"

Ostrowski turned to see Jackson Smythe hanging out the back. "Take a message."

Smythe held up the phone. "It's *Bullock*."

Ostrowski pointed to Jake. "Go. Now." Then he jogged over to the MCC and took the phone from Smythe. "Hello?"

"Detective Ostrowski?"

"Sergeant. It's good to hear your voice. How are things going in there?"

"It's about to end. But I need your help with something."

"Name it."

"Meet me in the lobby. Just you. Alone."

"You got it. I'll see you in a sec."

"And no riflemen. I don't want anybody thinking they can be a hero. Not now when the girls are going to be released in the morning."

"That's terrific news, Bullock. Give me a few minutes, and I'll get everyone to stand down."

The phone clicked, and the call ended.

"What's up?" Shaneel asked.

"It sounds like things are coming to an end. But he's got some demands." Ostrowski handed the phone up to Smythe and turned to Lt. Hostetler. "I need your men to stand down."

Hostetler took the cigar out of his mouth. "Is he coming out?"

"He said he's getting ready to end it, but he needs me to come into the lobby. Wants me to take care of something for him. But he wants all sharpshooters to stand down."

Hostetler spit on the ground and chuckled. "I bet he does." He shook his head. "No dice."

"Look. We're coming to the end of this. He's willing to stand down if you stand down." Ostrowski grabbed him by the arm. "Are you telling me that you're intentionally going to lengthen this stand-off or even escalate the violence because of your own stubbornness?"

"Look, he's been running this whole show, literally, by putting bombs on tripwires and holding us at bay. He can't keep running everything."

"So, your answer is yes, then?" Johnson asked.

Both Hostetler and Ostrowski looked at her surprised. "So, if things get out of hand," Johnson said, "and people get shot and hurt, and the news asks me, what happened, I want to make it clear that you're okay with me saying that it looked like it might have had a peaceful ending but Lt. Hostetler wasn't having any of that. Is that okay?" She took a step closer and looked him in the eye. "I just want to make sure we get our stories straight,

Lieutenant."

Hostetler looked at her, and then up at Ostrowski. He pointed at Johnson with his cigar. "Obviously a protege of yours."

Ostrowski chuckled. "One of the rising stars of the LAPD."

"Yeah, I'll say." Hostetler grabbed his radio. "This is Hostetler. I want all units to stand down until further notice. I repeat, all units are to stand down. At ease, gentlemen."

A second later a call came back, "And women."

Hostetler looked over at Johnson. "Satisfied?"

"Thank you, Lieutenant."

Hostetler jammed his cigar back in his mouth, growled something incoherent, and walked away.

Ostrowski wiped fake tears from his eyes. "They grow up so fast, and make you so proud."

Shaneel giggled. "Get the hell up there." She gave him an easy shove toward the building.

He walked up the sidewalk and opened the door to the lobby. When he did, the door on the other side opened up. A man, medium build, with mussy brown hair stepped out, his eyes wide and lost. Ostrowski could only assume it was Ben Hufnagel, the cameraman and the last hostage, other than Winthrop and Dodge. He held the door open and Hufnagel ambled past him in a daze, down the sidewalk, and into the waiting mass of police and paramedics.

When Ostrowski looked back, Bullock was standing halfway out the door to the office area. He looked as though he had been through another tough fight. His face was puffy, and blood ran from his nose and his lip.

"What the hell happened to you?"

"I cut myself shaving."

"I can get you fresh blades."

Bullock waved him in. "Not right now. Come here, I need something else from you."

Ostrowski strode across the lobby and pointed a thumb toward the parking lot. "That looked good, letting Hufnagel go like that. Dodge and Winthrop coming out now, too?" Ostrowski held out his hand.

"Not yet," Bullock said, shaking his hand. "First thing in the morning. But the world is going to be a very different place for these girls then. Just trust me on that. And they're going to need some help."

"Different? How?" Ostrowski didn't like the ominousness of that statement.

Bullock handed him a stack of money, and two notes. "All you need to do is take care of these for me. One note is for my wife, and the other is something I need you to get for Dodge and Winthrop. Use that money to do it. Anything left over, give to my wife. Can I count on you to do that?"

Ostrowski looked at the money and the notes then raised a hand. "Look, Bullock, I just told them..."

"I know," Bullock said. "So, take these, do what I need, and I'll make sure you're not a liar."

Ostrowski sighed and took the papers from Bullock. "So, what hap..."

"Thanks," Bullock said. He slammed the door and locked it.

Ostrowski walked out, opened the note, and read it in the yellow exterior lights of the building. Shaneel was standing there waiting for him when he reached the edge of the parking lot. "What's going on?"

Ostrowski smiled. "Saddle up, Detective." He jammed the money and the note in his pockets. "We're on a very important mission."

Chapter Thirty-Eight

Brooke's eyes blinked open, and she found herself still lying in the same position on the cot, cradling her fragile friend in her arms. She had been so emotionally exhausted that once she was asleep, she slept hard. She didn't know what Bullock had planned for them next, but it appeared, after Becca's horrifying revelation, he was going to let them live. She wiped sand from her eyes, and then straightened a few strands of Becca's short and very mussed hair.

"Good morning," Becca said.

Brooke leaned over her. "You're awake? Why didn't you say something?"

"I didn't want to bother you."

"What are you doing?"

"Just lying here thinking about what I've done."

Brooke laid back down and rubbed Becca's shoulder. "Becca, *all* this time? Why didn't you say something?"

"Why would I? What is it that you think you could have done?"

"I don't know. How about, just being there for my best friend?"

"It became my secret weapon," Becca said. "I was creating an empire off of one man's faults."

"What are you saying?"

Becca rubbed an itch on her nose with the back of her hand. "It was the key to everything. It was how I got the studio, the crew, the time slot, shit, the whole damned show."

Brooke slid her hand out from under Becca's head and sat up. "Are you saying, you blackmailed Derek McGregor into giving in to your every wish?"

Becca slowly pushed herself up, turned around, and sat with her back against the wall.

"Let's just say I convinced him that it would be in his best interest to give us a little extra help."

Brooke gasped. "Becca, that's extortion."

Becca shrugged. "Is extortion any worse than rape?"

"Two wrongs, Becca."

Becca shook her head. "There are no two wrongs here, Brooke. I did what great artists do—I used my pain to create. In this instance, that pain happened to give me a little extra leverage."

"And when did you make this decision?"

"The night we were lying in our bunks in the dorm, back at U-Penn and we first had the idea for the show. We pinky swore that night that we wouldn't rest until we had our crazy idea of a show on the air." Becca smiled. "I knew that very night, it was going to happen. I decided right then that McGregor and I were going to have a chat. And from that little talk, our show would become a reality."

Brooke shook her head. "So, it was all fake? All of our success wasn't even real?"

"What are you talking about?" Becca took Brooke's hand. "All I did was get our show on the air. I didn't make people watch it. *You* did that. *You* were real. The show's success was because you were genuine. I didn't have to be genuine; I was behind the scenes. But people tuned in every Tuesday because you were there to greet them. That's not false. And that had nothing to do with me." Becca raised her hands and let them drop to the cot. "But now I've gone and ruined everything with my own damned mouth yesterday."

"If not for your mouth, I don't think we would even be here. I'm sure he was ready to kill us, Becca. If you hadn't said what you did, he would have probably shot us right there." Brooke took her hand again. "You saved our lives."

"Yeah, but what lives do we have left now?"

A knock came at the door, then keys jingled, and the lock clicked.

"Since when does he knock first?" Becca said.

The door opened slightly, and Bullock peered in. He sported two black eyes, a puffy and scabby lip, and scratches here and there across his face, that had scabbed over.

"Ah, you're awake. I have something for you." He opened the door the rest of the way and scooted a large cardboard box into the room.

Brooke heard scratches and whimpers coming from the box. "What do you have?"

Bullock sat a laptop down on the desk, opened the lid, and powered it up. Then he pulled the chair over and sat down next to the box. "You've both had a rough time. But none worse than Miss Dodge." He looked at Becca and his tone changed. Became softer. "I'm sorry you didn't have a father to stand up for you, to fight for you. You deserved that."

A yelp came from the box, along with more vigorous scratching.

"I want you both to leave here today, but I wanted to equip you for the world you're heading out into." Bullock slipped open the flaps of the box, reached in, and pulled out two, tiny, fuzzy puppies—one black and white, the other brown and white. "And nothing will equip you better than these guys." He handed them over to the two stunned women.

Brooke held hers close. The little puppy squirmed in her hand, whimpered, and licked at her face. She looked over at Becca, who held her puppy in both hands, away from her, not really knowing what to do with it. It wiggled and pawed frantically at the air.

"When I went on deployment, I would leave Kristine there alone with her mother. But I wanted her to feel like I still loved her as well, so I got her and Danny each a puppy. I'll never forget how their faces lit up when they saw them for the first time."

Brooke's puppy licked at her face and her mouth. She looked up and giggled.

Bullock chuckled and looked over at Becca, who was still holding her puppy away from her like it had mud on it, and she didn't want to get dirty. "You have incredible strength, Miss Dodge." Bullock rubbed his face. "And I'm not just talking about your right hook. I'm talking about your very soul. But there's a hardness there, too. A hardness that comes from never feeling safe. And never having been given the love that you deserve." He pointed to the puppy. "This little guy will help with that. Nobody will love you more deeply, and more unconditionally than him. He will show you what love truly is and be by your side through everything you have coming up. But you have to give him the chance."

Brooke reached over, gently touched Becca's hand, and guided the puppy to her face. It pawed at her neck, licked her cheek, and whimpered excitedly. Becca closed her eyes and giggled.

Bullock chuckled, turned, and logged into his laptop. A screen appeared showing the GINfo website, and the headline, "Network CEO Steps Down Amid Mounting Allegations." There was a picture of McGregor, Becca, and two other women below them.

"Oh, God," Becca said, and dropped her head into her hand. "What have I done?"

"You've stood up to a bully," Bullock said. "He's a piece of shit. A predator. The worst kind of human. And you've saved a lot of young women from a similar fate." He stood. "But I know I'm the last person you want to sit around and shoot the shit with, so it's time you two were on your way."

"You're letting us go?" Brooke said.

Bullock nodded. "Only if you want to."

Brooke jumped up from the cot. "Yes! Come on, Becca."

Becca was still staring at the screen. "I'm not so sure I do."

Brooke waved at her to come. Letting her puppy down, she hooked Becca under the armpit and dragged her friend from the cot.

Bullock stepped aside and let the two girls pass.

When she stepped out of the room, the lights in the plant were on for the first time. Brooke could see that in the center were all the drums of explosives that had been previously wired to the doors. They were clustered in a group with a chair next to them.

"What is that?" Brooke asked.

"Don't worry about that," Bullock said. "Take your puppies and go. They're all you need to be concerned about now."

Brooke would have left without another thought if not for the chair sitting next to the group of explosives. She walked toward the canisters. "Why is there a chair here?"

"Brooke," Becca said, sounding tired. "Let's go."

Brooke stepped over to the cluster and saw they were all wired together and connected to one black box that sat on top of the center one. She looked over to the folding chair next to it, and a chill ran through her. She kicked at the chair and sent it tumbling over. Then she turned back to Bullock. "Okay, lead the way. We'll follow you out."

Bullock put his hands on his hips, let his gaze drop to the

floor. "You already know I'm not coming. So just go already. Good luck to you both."

"Oh, no," Brooke said, shaking her head vigorously. "We're not going to let you sit in here and blow yourself up."

"We're not?" Becca said.

Brooke gasped. "No, we're not." She walked up to Bullock and looked him in the eye. "There's been too much pain through all of this. You killing yourself has no meaning. No point."

Bullock did not look up at her. "I find it hard to believe you're even saying this to me after what I've done to you."

Brooke held the puppy up to him. "Look what you gave us? You did that to make amends. To take care of us." She pulled the puppy back and cuddled it. "Now you can teach us how to raise it."

"Brooke, come on," Becca said. "He knows what he's doing."

Brooke looked over at Becca. "How can you say that? Don't you know he's been hurting, just like you've been hurting?"

"I didn't kidnap and torture a bunch of people. He did."

Brooke stepped back from her friend, surprised and hurt at what she just said.

"Don't give her that look," Bullock said. "She's no-nonsense. Everything she says is the truth, and whether you want to believe it or not makes no difference." Bullock pointed to the door. "There's nothing left for me out there anymore. After what I've done, they'll lock me away for the rest of my life anyway. I have no interest in living like that."

Brooke snarled at him. "You have a wife out there. She needs you. You can live for her."

"I will never spend another minute with her," Bullock said. "What is she supposed to look forward to—a July Fourth picnic in the pokey?"

"So, you're just going to leave her broken and alone?"

"She'll never be alone. Corrine has so many friends they will

270

be fighting over who will take care of her next. And she won't have to worry about money. I set up a Go Fund Me page for her yesterday, and as of 30 minutes ago it had 23,000 dollars in it. As soon as I'm gone, it will make her a millionaire."

Brooke looked over at Becca, and back at Bullock. She wiped the tears from her eyes.

"You see. This is the best thing I could ever do for her. My wife will be much better off without me." He pointed to the door again. "So, go. Please."

"Come on Brooke." Becca took a few steps toward the door.

Brooke stood her ground, not wanting to just let this man end it like this.

"Okay. Enough of this Pollyanna bullshit." Bullock pulled his phone out of his pocket, typed in a code, and the black box on the containers beeped.

Brooke looked over and saw that a timer had blinked on, and green numbers were counting down, from 00:04:59. "What the hell are you doing?" she yelled at him.

"I'm through screwing around," Bullock said. "I don't want to talk about this anymore. You need to either leave now, or pull up a chair, and we can have a little four-and-a-half-minute chat."

"Oh, my God, Brooke. Let's go!" Becca screamed.

Brooke's face twisted with rage. "You selfish bastard! Why do you always have to have it your way? Are you that much of a coward that you can't face the consequences for what you've done?"

"Is that what you're worried about?" Bullock stepped toward her. "Me facing the music?"

Brooke did not back down. She stepped forward as well. "It's not just facing the music. It's not *dying*. This whole tragedy has brought nothing but pain and anguish, and you want to increase that by killing yourself to end it."

Becca backed up more. "Brooke. Shut the hell up and let's get out of here!"

"My staying alive will only muddy the waters, and give the bottom feeders called the news something to chew on for months. In the meantime, all the good that you and Miss Dodge could be doing would be buried and lost behind the stories of me." He pointed to the door. "Now get the hell out of here and go change the world."

Brooke looked at him, then at the clock again. 00:03:42 "Screw it," She said. She reached down, grabbed the chair, set it back up, sat down, and cuddled her puppy.

Becca looked at the ceiling and let out a loud cry of exasperation. "Girl, I've said before that you were going to be the death of me." She nuzzled her puppy, walked over, patted Brooke on the shoulder to scoot over, and sat on the other half of the chair.

Bullock looked at the two, shaking his head and frowning. "Dammit. All you've wanted to do since you got in here is leave, and now you sit next to the damn bomb. Makes a whole lotta sense."

"We want to leave," Brooke said. "We just want to leave with you."

Bullock threw up his hands. "Fine. You win. But we need to get out quickly. I can't shut that thing down. So, let's go."

"What?" Becca jumped up. "You can't just turn it off with your phone?"

"Nope." Bullock shook his head and spit blood off to the side. "Hadn't planned to, so I didn't program that part in."

Becca snapped back to Brooke. "Get off your ass now, and let's get out of here!"

Brooke jumped up and Bullock ran with the women to the main door to the lobby. He exited first and then helped them through. Then he pushed them to the outer door. Brooke was out in the sunshine before she realized that Bullock wasn't with her anymore. She spun around to see him closing the door to the plant. "Bullock!" she screamed. She ran back across the lobby and pounded on the door. "Bullock. You son of a bitch!"

Bullock looked back at her through the window. His face stoic and resolved. "I'm sorry, Miss Brooke Winthrop for everything. You have about one minute to get yourself and everyone out there clear. There's a lot of explosives behind me and this place is going to go big."

Brooke stared at him, crying so hard she couldn't move.

Bullock's eyes grew wide, and he screamed at her. "RUN!"

That's what it took to awaken the flight response in her. Brooke shot across the lobby, and out the glass doors. Police and paramedics were coming up the walk to meet her, but she waved them back with her free hand. "No. Get back *now*! It's going to explode!"

They stopped and she ran past them. "Everybody down!" She screamed and wound her way around cop cars. Police officers were scurrying and crouching as she went. Copters overhead careened away, trying to put some distance between them and the concussive force of the bomb.

Then Brooke felt the heat, a split second later she heard the explosion, and right on top of that was the shock wave. It knocked her off her feet and sent her skidding across the pavement, hitting her head, tearing the skin from her shoulder, and sending her puppy rolling another ten feet, yelping all the way.

"Brooke. Oh my God!"

She was dazed, understood there was danger, but only wanted to lie there. Had no strength to move. She felt herself grabbed under her armpits and dragged. It hurt like hell. Her eyes didn't seem to work right. Everything was foggy.

"I'm here, babe. You're going to be okay."

She felt her puppy licking her face.

Then came the bangs, thuds, and crunches as pieces of the building fell around her. She heard men howling, women screaming, cries of "Officer down!" She heard another voice yell. "May, get her to cover!"

She opened her eyes and tried to focus. The world was still spinning but she could make out a bald man with a tie and rolled up sleeves, rushing over in her direction. A large chunk of debris dropped from the sky and hit him. He fell hard.

The world spun away. Brooke couldn't keep her eyes open. She felt her body dragged across the pavement again. Her puppy licked at her face. She heard more thuds and thumps around her.

Then all went dark and silent.

CHAPTER THIRTY-NINE

Screams and shouts echoed through her ears. Several panicked cries of "officer down," and the distant chorus of sirens and fire truck horns, growing louder as they drew closer.

Her puppy licked at her face and Becca pushed it away and opened her eyes to see the sky filled with a red, smoky haze. Her head was pounding. It had just bounced off the asphalt. She sat up to see a young cop sitting next to her, holding his head. Blood was running down past his ear, and he was out of it. Becca felt her own head all over and kept checking her hand.

No blood.

The cop had just crouched down next to her, in between two police cars, when Bullock's bomb blew. They were still knocked off their feet, and even though her head felt like it had been split open, it appeared that only his had been.

The puppy yelped and put two feet on her lap. His head hung low, and his big brown eyes looked up at her. His tiny tail, which should have been wagging, hung down between his legs. It was terrified of all the mayhem and needed to feel safe.

Becca sighed and shook her head. She lifted the puppy up and looked it in the eyes.

"What was he thinking giving you to me? I'm not four years old. What am I supposed to do with you?" Becca had never had a dog before, or any pet for that matter. She couldn't understand what all the fuss was about.

She closed her eyes and tried to shake away the pain in her head but quickly realized that was a bad idea. It only made it worse. She'd seen enough football to know she should probably be checked for a concussion. And then another thought hit her. "Brooke?" she called. She looked both ways but couldn't see much while she was still sitting between two police cars.

Becca climbed to her feet and steadied herself on the police cruiser. Red and black smoke spewed into the sky from the hot fire blazing at the plant. It smelled like burnt shit and made her nauseous. People were running in every direction, sirens blared as firetrucks and ambulances roared down the street and into the parking lot, red lights flashing brilliantly in the haze of the smoke.

"Brooke?" Becca called out to her friend, searching the mess in every direction. She doubted anyone could hear her in all the commotion, so she took several steps, carrying her puppy at her side like a furry football.

She had only walked about ten yards or so when she spotted her best friend's legs lying in the parking lot around the edge of another police car. "Brooke!" she ran around the car and stopped, hardly able to believe her eyes. Brooke was unconscious and Jake May, of all people, was holding her head in his lap.

Could this even be real? Was this some sort of hallucination from her head injury? Becca's jaw clenched, and her eyes narrowed. Brooke had gone through enough. She didn't have to finally escape the villainy of one man, only to be cast back into the danger of a former.

Becca was determined this was not going to happen to the only person she had really ever considered family. She turned and stormed back to the police officer who was still sitting in a daze, reached down, unsnapped his holster, and grabbed his gun. He reached to stop her, but she was too quick.

"Stop," he called to her, but she turned and hurried off.

Coming back around the police car, Becca raised the gun and pointed it at Jake. "Get the hell away from her, you piece of shit!"

Jake looked up, saw Becca, and then the gun.

"Whoa!" He leaned back slowly and raised his hands. "Becca, wait. I'm trying to help her."

"The only way you can help her is by leaving her alone and *never* seeing her ever again. Now get the hell out of here."

"Becca," Jake's voice quivered. He was clearly afraid of her. Good. "You have to know....I love..."

"Don't say you love her!" Becca screamed. She took another few steps toward Jake. He flinched. "You would have fought your own demons if you loved her. You would have never hit her if you loved her. You would have never left a mark on her beautiful face if you loved her." Jake's raised hands were visibly shaking now. "She's been through so much, and for you to be here now is just cruel," Becca snarled at him. Jake wasn't just the man who hurt her friend. Right now, he represented everything wrong in Becca's world. He was the embodiment of the sins of Duncan Bullock, Derek McGregor, and even herself for blowing up the entire world that she had so carefully and skillfully crafted out of her torturous past. Becca knew her life, as it had been, was now over. But she could still do some good for Brooke. She could make sure this piece of crap never hurt her sister again.

Gritting her teeth, Becca raised the gun higher and pointed it at Jake's face.

Jake wept and he slowly shook his head, "Becca, please. No. I'm trying to help her. I swear."

Becca watched Jake, the football superstar, quaking in fear and breaking down. She discovered a deep dark part of her heart actually enjoying it. It was somehow a good thing that she had the power to make him afraid of her. She paused for a moment to try to tap into this new feeling. Or was it new?

Then her view of Jake was obscured by a set of dark slacks. She raised the gun up to the head of this new individual. He was obviously a police detective. He wore black pants, a white shirt, and a tie with his sleeves rolled up. His bald head was bleeding and nearly half his face was covered in blood. He looked uneasy standing there. He rocked slightly, and it was obviously an effort to remain standing, but he was calm.

"Hey, Miss Dodge. I could use a beer. How about you?"

In all the craziness happening around them, this detective acted as if it was Sunday afternoon.

"Why don't you hand me the gun and we'll get some lawn chairs and a couple Corona Lights with lime. Doesn't that sound better than shooting someone and ruining your life completely?"

It did sound good. Becca thought a beer would actually taste great right now. But her life was already over. Her show was over. She would probably never be a producer again, which was all that she'd ever wanted to be. She went from the biggest and the best to now being nothing. It was over. And now another man stood in her way.

"Of course, you'd say that." She pointed the gun at the detective's bald bloody head. "A man. Keeping me from helping Brooke."

"But I'm not." A young black woman stepped in front of the detective. "*I'm* a woman."

She was shorter and Becca had to drop the barrel of the gun to see her. "But it was the wise man behind me who told me not to let the bad guys steal your life."

She crossed her arms.

"You see, Miss Dodge, one thing I do know is that no matter how bad my life may seem, at least it's *my* life. And as long as I don't let others steal any part of me, I can recover from anything." She smiled. This woman was warm and helpful. "Because the moment you let them take that from you, you become one of them. Nobody looks at you like the victim anymore. You're just another bad guy."

Becca nearly laughed. "I *am* the victim here. There's nothing wrong with making the bad guys pay."

"No there isn't. As long as you do it the right way. But if you do it *like* the bad guys, you become indistinguishable from them." The woman spread her arms. "Look around you. Do all of these officers think you're the victim right now?"

Becca looked away from the woman for the first time. She had been so focused, she didn't see all of the police officers gathering around her. There were at least a dozen or so, and they all had their guns drawn and pointed at her. As if *she* was the bad guy.

The bald detective dropped to his knees and fell over unconscious.

The black woman looked down at him and then back to Becca.

"He is *very* important to me." She held out her hand. "Please give me the gun, so everyone can start healing. Let's stop the pain right now."

Reality hit Becca straight between the eyes. Looking down the barrels of several police guns, she realized her fall was now complete. This had to be the bottom.

The puppy squirmed and whimpered at her left hip. She had forgotten she was even holding it. She felt startled looking into the puppy's bright eyes. She read concern there. Like the puppy was worried about her and wanted to take care of her. She pulled the puppy up and it proceeded to lick her neck and the side of her face. It didn't think she was a bad guy. Was it possible Bullock had been right in giving it to her? Maybe her puppy was the only thing she needed in her life right now. If this was truly rock bottom, at least she had her puppy as her companion while she climbed back out of the pit. She began to cry. "I'm sorry," was what she tried to say, but it came out as an awkward squeal. She let the gun hang from her forefinger with the trigger guard.

When the woman grabbed it from her, Becca dropped to her knees, clutched the puppy close, and cried.

The police around her holstered their weapons and took a step toward Becca.

"Whoa," said the woman. "No cuffs. She's been through enough. Take her to an ambulance, not a cruiser." She pointed toward Jake. "I want May arrested. Interference with public duties." Then she dropped to her knees next to her fallen friend. "Officer down!"

CHAPTER FORTY

"I did nothing wrong."

That voice. Brooke recognized that voice. Her chest tightened.

"*She* had the gun. Why am *I* being arrested?"

How could she possibly be hearing that voice at this moment?

"I was trying to help."

Though it felt like a jackhammer had spent an hour pounding her head, Brooke managed to flutter her eyes open. Thick plumes of dark smoke billowed into the sky and sounds of the catastrophe were all around her. Sirens, helicopters, the spraying of fire-hoses, and voices: curses, shouts, orders, desperate cries, "Officer down. Oh God, stay with me, Ostrowski."

But one voice cut through all the noise, like a meat cleaver through a side of beef, and sent shivers to her soul.

"Hey, wait. Her eyes are open. Please, just let me help her."

She turned her head in the direction of that voice and saw that it was indeed her ex-husband, Jake. Her stomach did a somersault.

"Brooke, tell them I'm just here to help you."

Jake was restrained by two police officers and appeared to have his hands cuffed behind him. They held him in place until she responded. Another officer was holding her puppy, keeping the little guy safe.

She took a breath and spoke, quieter than she had expected. "Jake, why are you here?"

"Because Brooke," Jake sounded exasperated, "I love you, and I wanted to make sure you were okay."

Brooke was lying there on hot pavement, near a blazing factory. But hearing Jake say those three little words made her shiver with chills. They didn't give her a warm feeling. They felt like someone was holding a plastic bag over her face. She struggled to breathe, thinking about how to respond.

"We need a gurney over here!"

Brooke looked in the direction of the voice. A black woman was holding the bloody head of the white bald man who Brooke had seen get hit with debris. The woman's hands were bloody and so were her clothes, but she didn't seem to care. All she cared about was the man who was bleeding. "I got you, Ostrowski. Just hold on."

Placing her head back down gently on the pavement, Brooke's mind raced with the events of the past few days. She had gone out with Matthew, and that had been thrilling. Until she discovered that he had conspired against her and Becca. Then he turned out to be just a piece of crap too. She had spent the rest of the time in constant fear for her life, afraid of what Bullock was going to do next. Wondering if the next day would be her last. If the next jingle of keys and turn of the lock were going to be the last sounds she ever heard.

Now she was out of that situation. It was over. She was free. She should feel relieved. But she couldn't because Jake May was there telling her he loved her.

Then her attitude changed. It surprised her.

She grew angry.

She'd been through too much to take this shit now. Brooke had faced her own mortality and realized she didn't need to spare Jake's feelings any longer. She ground her teeth, set her jaw, and looked into the sky. Her voice was stronger now.

"Jake, I don't know what would make you think it's good to see you, especially right now. But you're wrong."

"But...Brooke, I..."

Brooke sat up and leaned on one arm. "Don't say you love me." The world spun after such a quick motion, and she had to close her eyes and collect herself for a moment while her head settled.

"Babe," Jake started.

Brooke felt nauseous.

"I am so sorry for how things ended. But I do love you. I know the trust has to be rebuilt between us, but I'm willing to do the work," he pleaded.

"Trust?" Brooke would have stood to look him in the eye, but she knew she didn't have the strength. "Jake trust *can* be rebuilt. But this goes way beyond trust. You made me feel unsafe. You terrified someone you were supposed to love. And I will never, *ever* feel safe around you again."

Jake nodded. "I know you're talking about the black eye, and I'm sorry."

Brooke screamed. "You broke my damn eye socket, and I nearly went blind in that eye."

"Get him out of here," one of the officers said. Two officers pulled Jake up and walked him away from her.

"No. Give me one second." Brooke said.

They turned Jake back. He looked at her, stunned as if he'd just been shot.

Brooke narrowed her eyes and looked up at the man whose very existence caused her pain.

"Jake, let me make this as plain as I possibly can. I don't love you. You killed that. I don't ever want to see you again. I don't want to speak to you. Don't call me anymore. I won't answer. In fact, these are the last words that will ever pass between us. Is that clear?"

Jake looked back at her with sad, remorseful eyes.

Seeing him sad infuriated her even more. She looked up at the officers.

"Okay, now get him out of here." She waved him away as if he were a fly on her sandwich.

The officers turned Jake around and escorted him out of her life forever.

Brooke's arm began to shake and give out. She lowered her pounding head back down to the pavement just as two paramedics arrived. As they carefully lifted her onto the cot, Brooke finally realized she was free. She did have courage. She finally broke away from the last uncomfortable entanglement.

Yes, her life was a complete mess. But it was her life alone now. And she would fix it...on her own.

Chapter Forty-One

The first sounds that reached his ears were the digital, steady beeps of medical equipment. When Ostrowski opened his eyes, he saw clean, gridded ceiling tiles.

It felt like there was something in his nose, so he raised a hand to investigate, and saw an IV running from the back of his hand.

"Thank God!" someone said.

He looked over at the voice to his right.

Shaneel Johnson jumped from a chair and stepped over to the side of the bed. "You had me scared outta my head." She put a hand on his shoulder. "How do you feel?"

Ostrowski did a mental check. The only thing that was really bothering him was a dull headache. "Fine, I think." He looked back up at her. "Unless you know something I don't."

She shook her head. "It's just that there was so much blood coming out your head, I didn't know if you were ever going to wake up."

Ostrowski remembered getting hit, trying to get to Winthrop. Then he remembered stepping in front of Dodge's gun.

"You made some pretty stupid decisions out there yesterday," Shaneel said. "You would have had my ass if I'd done what you did. And now you'll probably get another medal."

"Yesterday?" He looked at Shaneel. She was still wearing the same, wrinkled, and filthy clothes she had on at the plant. "You've been here all night?"

She nodded. "Yes. I couldn't walk away knowing my partner was hurt."

"Thank you." Ostrowski reached up and patted her arm. "Sykes would have probably left a sticky note on my chest that said, 'Call me when you wake up.'"

Shaneel laughed. "Then it's a good thing he's retired."

Ostrowski sighed and looked up at her.

"Uh oh." She pulled her hand back. "What?"

"I think it's time I did the same."

She shook her head and was going to protest, but Ostrowski held up his hand.

"Hear me out." He looked over at the clock on the wall and tried to collect his thoughts. "I looked down the barrel of the gun that Becca Dodge was holding, and it was the first time I really wondered what I was doing. I got into this business because I wanted to stop the bad guys. But for the first time, in my entire career, I didn't know who the bad guy was. Was Bullock the bad guy? Or was he just a father filled with so much grief that he did the only thing that made sense to him? And if he wasn't the bad guy, it had to be Dodge and Winthrop. But all they did was put on a show to entertain millions. You could argue that Becca Dodge was bad because she was pointing a gun at Jake May. But all she was trying to do was protect her best friend in the whole world. So does that mean May is the bad guy? If it weren't for him, Brooke Winthrop would have never jumped ship at GInfo and this whole mess would have never happened in the first place. But that doesn't make any sense." He looked up at Shaneel. "And I'm too old to figure all this shit out. It's all just too depressing to me.

So, it's time for me to call it."

Shaneel's eyes grew moist. "But I still need to learn from you."

Ostrowski shook his head. "You don't. You got this. I've never seen someone more well suited for this work in all my days. The truth is, I probably would have learned more from you, and that's depressing to me too." He smiled up at her and she chuckled. "Now you get home to that fine husband of yours and your beautiful son, and you let them know, every day, that they're the only reason you get out of bed in the morning. Is that clear?"

Shaneel nodded.

"Go hit the showers kid. You're a mess."

Shaneel smiled, walked over and picked up her notebook and badge from the windowsill. With her back still turned, she wiped at her eyes. Then she spun. "Okay, before I go, I want you to be straight with me."

"What about?"

"That whole story that you told Bullock about your mean, angry Sergeant. Was that real, or was that just to plant a seed in his head about killing himself?"

Ostrowski, smiled. "You're good."

Putting her hands on her hips, Shaneel said. "So none of that was real?"

"Plenty of it was," Ostrowski said. "Just not the part about killing himself. Oh, and the sniffing the asses thing. I just thought that was funny."

"Why make up anything?"

"The man was in a corner with only one way out, and that was to follow through with the crazy plan he started with. All I did was make another door for him. Another option. And hope he took it so those girls could live. But I just thought he would take a bullet. I never expected him to take a whole city block too."

Shaneel shook her head. "You're certifiable, Ostrowski." She stared at him a minute more, before taking a deep breath. "All right, Detective, I'm headed home. Call me if you need anything."

Ostrowski saluted, and she hurried out of the room.

He rested his head back on the pillow and thought about the future. He would have to call Sykes and see what old detectives are supposed to do once they cross over to the pasture.

Chapter Forty-Two
Three Months Later

Brooke pulled into the circle drive of Becca's Hollywood Hills home. Though it was the smallest house on the block, it was easily the prettiest. Roses, pansies, and petunias were in full bloom out in front. Becca still had a lawn service and gardener coming to the house. Appearances were always the most important thing to her friend. If you looked up Becca Dodge quotes online, the first one that always came up was, "Always show the world you have your shit together, even though you may have no idea what the hell is going on around you."

Brooke and Becca were put through a lot after the stand-off and explosion in the City of Industry. They had both been into the police station several times giving statements. And the media had been relentless, trying to get on-air interviews and waiting for them whenever they emerged from anywhere, clicking pictures of the two and trying their best to get sound bites. The attention finally slowed when a terrorist bombed the U.S. embassy in Poland.

But now Brooke hadn't heard from her friend in over a month, and she was growing concerned. She rang the doorbell and could see faint movement in the frosted glass next to the door. A latch clicked and the door opened.

Becca's weary face appeared. "Hey," she said upon recognition. She swung the door open and stepped back.

"Hi there." Brooke looked Becca up and down. Her friend's hair was greasy and unkempt. She wore L.A. Rams pajama bottoms and a green sleeveless t-shirt. When she stepped into the house, she saw two pizza boxes on the coffee table; one still had three pieces in it, now old and crusty. Beer and Diet Coke cans were sitting about. And in the corner of the living room were stacks of cardboard boxes filled with office supplies and decorations from Becca's old office at the studio. Brooke felt she'd arrived just in time. She knew the signs of depression, and her friend was sunk deep.

Becca closed the door, picked up the remote, and turned off a Gilligan's Island rerun.

"Can I get you anything?"

"Becca, what's going on?"

Becca rubbed her eyes and stretched. "Nothing. Just relaxing. What's going on with you?"

"I haven't heard anything from my best friend in weeks," Brooke said. "She doesn't return calls or texts. And when I finally make it out this way to see her, I find…," looking around the room, "…this."

Becca shrugged, loped over to the couch, and plopped down into it. "I'm just relaxing while I figure out my next move."

Brooke sat in a chair next to her and set her satchel on the floor. "And what have you come up with?"

Becca shook her head. "Nothing yet. I'm still thinking about how bad the last one turned out." She picked up a Diet Coke can and took a sip.

"Becca, you can't keep dwelling on this. It's not doing you

any good."

Becca swallowed and put down her soda can. "I don't know what else to do. How do you handle it when your life's ambition turns out to be the worst thing in the world? It gets people killed and destroys the lives of others?"

"Hello, girlfriend." Brooke waved. "I know. I was right there with you."

Becca's dog walked into the room and stopped at Becca's feet. Becca tapped on the couch next to her. "It's okay, Dunk. Come on up." The dog jumped up next to Becca, placed its paws on her leg, and laid down.

"You named him Dunk?"

"Yes." Becca scratched her dog's ears and petted his head. "Because he turned out to be right about everything, especially me."

Brooke sat back in her chair. "How do you figure?"

Becca took a breath and blew it out slowly. "Well, he showed that somehow we screwed up on our casting process. We can't deny that. And it cost his daughter her life. But he was also right about me. Because of what happened to me, I had an ax to grind. I was treating people like shit. I had ready-made excuses for it all." She looked up at Brooke, and her eyes were red. "He may have been crazy and desperate at the end. But in a weird, twisted, and sick way he was better for me than my own father." She picked up Dunk and cradled him in her arms. "And he gave me a dog. Not even my own dad got me a dog. So, I named it Dunk. After him."

Brooke thought about it for a minute. She had to admit, Becca was making sense.

Becca looked up at her. "And he helped *you* find your fierceness which was good, too."

"What are you talking about?"

"Oh, please." Becca tilted her head. "The way you handled Jake that day? I'm almost ashamed I tried to help you out."

"Oh, that." Brooke sighed and looked away. "Yeah, that was bad, wasn't it?"

"Bad? What are you talking about? It was great."

Brooke shook her head. "No. It wasn't. I was just feeling something after finally being free and the explosion and everything. But Jake really does still love me."

"*Love* you? He *hit* you."

"No, he didn't. His addiction hit me. And Jake *isn't* his addiction. Jake is separate from that. He's a good man who found himself on the wrong road in life—one that's very unforgiving."

Becca's mouth dropped open. "Are you saying you're going back to him?"

"No." Brooke looked down. "All I'm saying is that he didn't deserve what I did to him at that moment. Especially in public like that."

Becca nodded and looked back down at Dunk.

After a moment of silence, Brooke took a deep breath. "So, what's next?"

Becca shrugged. "I've got no clue. For the first time in my life, I'm without a plan of any kind."

Brooke picked up her satchel. "Well, I've been making plans. I was hoping to get your opinion on them if you have the time."

"Time is about all I've got left," Becca said.

Brooke pulled out a folded piece of paper and opened it up. "I've gotten funding to build a special place right here in L.A. County." She turned the paper to show an artist's rendition of a building. "What do you think of the 'Kristine Bullock Women's Home.'"

"What?" Becca said. "What the hell is that?"

"It's a place where women can go to be safe from domestic violence." Brooke smiled and looked at the drawing. "And they can also stay in-house and deal with the PTSD associated with domestic and sexual assault."

292

Becca's red eyes grew wide. "Where did you get the money for that?"

"Believe it or not, the network. When they called me to let me know they were paying off the rest of the cast members who didn't get their shows produced, I approached them about this idea. I told them it would be a grand gesture to help them mend their destroyed image. They bit at it." Brooke folded up the paper. "Under one condition."

"What's that?"

Brooke smiled. "That you and I are there at the groundbreaking and ribbon-cutting ceremonies."

Becca shook her head. "No way. I'm not interested. This is your thing."

"There's more," Brooke said, holding up a finger. "We are going to be working with the residents in the building."

"What?" Becca was agitated. "There's absolutely no way."

Brooke reached over and touched her friend's knee. "Becca, listen. You just said that Bullock was right about you. And the truth is, we're both broken. But right now, we can be examples for the women of the world. That it's okay to ask for help. We need to get our own help and then use our experience to help others. We have the opportunity to do some real good here."

"And then what?" Becca snapped. "This is what we're doing with the rest of our lives?"

"Oh no. There's one more thing." Brooke slid out a blue folder with what looked like a ream of paper inside."

"And what's that, now?"

"That is the contract to our new show, which goes into effect as soon as the Bullock Home opens."

"Show? What kind of show?"

"A magazine show that features women, and even some men, who have pulled themselves out of violent and destructive relationships and turned their lives around." Brooke smiled. "We have a chance to make an impact here, Becca. But the show will need the best producer in Hollywood."

Tears trickled down Becca's cheeks. "You set all this up *without* me?"

Brooke nodded. "I set it up *for* us. What do you say?"

Becca looked down at the big blue folder, and slowly a small smile formed, for what Brooke thought, was probably the first time in three months. Becca nodded. "It looks like the Queen Bs are back."

I Do or I Don't

Edwards

Thanks for reading!

If you would, please take a moment and leave an honest review. Reviews are extremely helpful to authors. It would be greatly appreciated. Thank you very much!

For more information on upcoming books please stop by my web page, rob-edwards.net and sign-up for updates. I will be sending out a newsletter every few months which includes tidbits about previous books. For instance, the letter that Bullock wrote to his wife can be found in the "Goodies" section of the website, which you will be able to access as a newsletter subscriber.

You can also connect with me on Facebook at @robedwardsstoryteller, on Instagram at robedwardsstoryteller, or on Twitter at @robedwards5000.

Edwards

Acknowledgments

If you break this story down to its most basic thought, you realize it's all about a father's love for his daughter. That is why I have dedicated this book to mine. We have two strong, smart, charming, and wonderful daughters who are just as much alike as they are different. I know that makes no sense until you meet them. They are taking on the world and finding their place in it, and We couldn't be more proud of them.

Let it be known that we also have two amazing sons, and perhaps I will also dedicate a book to them one day. But as Martina McBride proudly sings, "This one's for the girls!"

I also dedicated the book (as with every book) to my wife, Dayna, for whom, without her support and encouragement, these stories simply wouldn't be told. She is the strongest person I know and I am continually in awe of her resilience and light spirit.

I absolutely must thank my incredible beta-readers. I take to heart all of your notes, and these stories are better because of your input.

I would also like to thank the remarkable editing and spot-on recommendations from Anne Stanton, and all the folks at Mission Point Press. Thank you all for your work and continued support of writing in Michigan. You help make the high-five state a great place for writers!

Made in the USA
Middletown, DE
30 April 2022